KT-561-571

# AROUND ANOTHER CORNER

## Grace Thompson

Severn House

This first world edition published in Great Britain 2006 by
SEVERN HOUSE PUBLISHERS LTD of
9–15 High Street, Sutton, Surrey SM1 1DF.
This first world edition published in the USA 2006 by
SEVERN HOUSE PUBLISHERS INC of
595 Madison Avenue, New York, N.Y. 10022.

Copyright © 2006 by Grace Thompson.

All rights reserved.
The moral right of the author has been asserted.

British Library Cataloguing in Publication Data

Thompson, Grace
    Around another corner
    1.    Fatherless families - Fiction
    2.    New business enterprises - Finance - Fiction
    I.    Title
    823.9'14 [F]

    ISBN-10: 0-7278-6348-7

*The author wishes to express her thanks to:*
Margaret Partington of Elegant Hats in Datchet, and
Nigel Rayment, Milliner in Luton.
*Their assistance was greatly appreciated in the research for this story.*

Except where actual historical events and characters are being
described for the storyline of this novel, all situations in this
publication are fictitious and any resemblance to living persons
is purely coincidental.

Typeset by Palimpsest Book Production Ltd.,
Polmont, Stirlingshire, Scotland.
Printed and bound in Great Britain by
MPG Books Ltd., Bodmin, Cornwall.

# One

Ancret's bedroom was more like that of a student than a twenty-four-year-old woman. On the walls, the posters she had designed showed hats in various stages of completion, examples of her work throughout her training. Half-finished hats filled shelves and designs overflowed on to the papers that cascaded from her desk. Completed hats covered many of the shelves too, fashioned out of everything from felt to straws and silk to paper as well as the popular sinamay and abaca, made from the fibres of the banana tree.

Then there were her dresses, long and full-skirted and mostly in shades of blue and green, scattered chaotically across chairs and hanging outside the over-full wardrobe, revealing the occupant's artistic and creative mind which quickly left one idea to embrace another. A glance would suggest a mind that rarely finished a project before starting another, but Ancret was fastidious about her work, giving lie to the implications of her room.

Standing in the middle of the clutter was the incongruously neat figure of Jonathan, hair carefully combed, wearing a formal suit and even a tie, having dressed from his naked state after leaving her bed.

'I have to go to the workshop,' she said, watching as he pulled the covers back over the crumpled sheets.

'Ancret, surely you can spare me a few hours on a Sunday afternoon? Can't we make the most of your mother's absence? She rarely gives us the chance for a few private moments. Her life is spent trying to stop us spending time alone.'

Ancret gave him one of her wide, generous smiles. 'She doesn't trust us. I wonder why?'

'Come on, you're twenty-four and I'm thirty. She can't treat us like precocious fourteen-year-olds. She expects you to fill your life with nothing but hats. It's ridiculous working as hard as you do. I need some of your time, can't you see that?'

'I've promised three hats for a christening and I have some work still to do on them.'

'I want to talk to you.'

'Then walk with me.'

'I mean really talk. We rarely get the chance. And, with your mother out for the afternoon, I thought – Ancret, darling, I want to know whether we have a future. I love you, you must know that. I want us to be together all the time, not when you can fit me in between your mother's presence and your clients' needs.'

Something inside her froze. Surely he wasn't going to propose again? Even if she were deeply in love with him – something she regularly doubted – the edge of resentment in his tone would have told her that marriage to Jonathan wouldn't work. Some aspects of his personality gave her doubt. His almost obsessional fear of having a child, for one thing – something he refused to explain. And for another, his continuing obedience to his own mother. Surely, at the age of thirty, he should have untied those apron strings? Anyway, she couldn't envisage a life in which she put her work second to a demanding man, even if those demands were loving and gentle. Besides, how could she marry before she knew who she was? And with her mother's refusal to talk about her family, that was a riddle that might remain forever unsolved.

'Coffee?' she offered.

'Sure you have time?' Again the petulant tone made her edgy.

'Not really. It's a concession to your mood.'

'What mood? I want to be with you, how can you call that a mood?'

Ancret didn't reply. She fiddled with a few hoods, waiting until he had remade the bed to his satisfaction. 'Stay a while,' he pleaded, sitting on the edge of the bed. 'I need to know whether you feel the same as me.'

'I have work to do and that will come first for a long time. You must understand how I feel? You started a business from

2

nothing and built it by your own efforts. You must see that after all the years of training, success is important to me?'

'Time passes, Ancret. Ambition is fine, I applaud it, but don't put the rest of your life on hold. One day you'll want marriage, and to build a home of your own, and you might find out it's too late.' The pouting, spoilt only child that he had always been was so visible it was almost funny. Ignoring him, increasingly irritated by the hint of petulance in his voice, she went barefoot down the stairs and into the kitchen. With the coffee dripping steadily through the filter she went into the living room. There, sitting in a chair, silent but with an expression that spoke volumes, was her mother.

'Mummy? I didn't hear you come back. I'm making coffee, would you like one?'

'What's he doing here? Hiding around the corner, watching for me to leave, was he?' She walked to the bottom of the stairs and called up, 'Jonathan, you can come out now. No need to hide like a child caught stealing sweets.'

Rather sheepishly at first, Jonathan came down the stairs, then, seeing the mischievous half-smile on Ancret's face as she stood there with the tray of coffee and cups, his mood changed to anger.

'I wasn't hiding and I'm insulted by you suggesting that I was. Ancret and I have been talking. Nothing secret, we've been discussing our future. Isn't that right, Ancret?'

'Yes, but we've reached no conclusions, have we?' Ancret replied firmly. She pointedly took away the third cup which she had just added to the tray and said, 'You'd better go, Jonathan. I'll be working most of the afternoon and evening. I'll see you early next week and perhaps we'll talk then.'

'No. I won't be dismissed like an unwanted salesman! This time I'm determined, Ancret. I'm staying here until we get this sorted.' The trill of his mobile phone sounded in the momentary silence of his defiance and he answered it, muttered a few words into it, then said, 'I have to go. Mother is out near Roach Park and needs a lift home.'

Ancret gritted her teeth but said nothing. His impressive determination had lasted only until his mother needed him; then she was of secondary importance. Her mother, Loraine, raised an eloquent eyebrow, amusement in her dark eyes. As

3

Ancret returned from seeing Jonathan out, she was startled by her mother shouting, 'Fool!'

'Me or Jonathan, Mummy?' she asked calmly. Loraine was standing near the fireplace, her hand resting on the old willow basket that always stood on the table beside her chair, something she always reached out to touch when she was upset.

'Fools both of you,' she said. 'Him for thinking he's good enough to interest you and you for *giving* yourself to someone as useless as him.'

'Giving?' Ancret smiled. 'There was some taking too, Mummy.'

'Don't be crude.'

'Sorry.'

'It's too soon to think of marriage. After getting this far, with the beginnings of a reputation for making beautiful hats, you can't give it all up for love. Or whatever passes for love these days!'

'That's what I've been telling Jonathan. But he reminded me that I'm twenty-four and I might wait too long for the other important things.'

'Things like a child? A home away from me?'

'Well, yes. Those things will happen.' She said nothing about Jonathan never wanting a child. It wasn't something she was easy with and therefore she was unable to discuss it. 'I will want a place of my own. But not at the other side of the world, Mummy. I could never be far away from you.' She kissed her mother's cheek and went out, a glittering shawl thrown carelessly across her shoulders, her feet in toe-post sandals.

She wore a dreamy expression, her eyes dark and almost sleepy and certainly unaware of the many glances of admiration she attracted that Sunday afternoon – tall and fashionably slim, walking with a slow, languid grace. Her hair was long, falling about her shoulders in loose waves, shiny and touched with a hint of red in its blackness. Her turquoise-green dress fell loosely from her hips and the effect was of undulating movement like waves on the sea, or wind across a corn field. She was aware of the excitement engendered by the crowds in the thriving city of Cardiff, loving it, proud of being a part of it. She was on her own, but never lonely.

She walked through the busy city streets, where families and groups of young people were taking advantage of the freedom of the late Sunday afternoon. She frequently slowed her progress to watch people passing and today she divided them mentally into groups. There were the very young girls with their black leather coats and short skirts puffing cigarettes; as they looked into blank windows admiring their reflection, she guessed they saw sophistication, whereas the rest of the world saw skinny legs, wobble walks and self-conscious defiance. Then there were the girls who silently roared their frustrations by wearing outfits that suggested pure aggression; torn and dirty jeans, ill-fitting tops often with crude slogans blazoned across the front, ugly shoes, haircuts designed for men, skin piercings shouting a warning like war paint. Most were somewhere between the two extremes, but today they all made her feel sad. Where would they find room in their lives for beauty? She tried to imagine them wearing one of her luxurious and elegant hats, and was even sadder when she failed.

Moments, the shop where she and her mother worked for Helena Mortimer, wore an air of abandonment in the way of a closed shop on a Sunday afternoon. Locking the door behind her she went through the salon and the fitting room, out to the workshop beyond. As always, once she began working, all her thoughts were concentrated on creating the perfect hat, and Jonathan's and her mother's disapproval were banished from her mind. This one was a straw made from yellow parisisal; it had begun with a crown that was little more than a saucer with two dozen quills, dyed, stiffened and curled out and up like the golden rays of a sun.

Her hands were small and slender, the fingers long and amazingly nimble; a scar at the side of her left hand, made when an extra digit had been removed at birth, the only imperfection.

When the hat was completed she placed it on the model head standing in front of a triple mirror so she could see it from all angles, and she smiled in satisfaction. It was a dream of a hat, a happy hat, promising the wearer a wonderful day.

It was six thirty when she locked the door of the shop and began to walk home.

She turned heads and attracted admiring glances wherever she went.

The evening was mild, the rays of the April sun blinding her with their final fling. Cardiff was a vibrant city, she thought as she moved gently through the crowds, so much going on that the streets were rarely quiet. Even on this early Sunday evening, people were out and heading for restaurants that offered a wonderful variety of dishes. Some places were dark, cool and atmospheric, others wide open to the warm evening sun, tables and music spilling out on to the pavements. So early in the evening there were cinema-goers, discussing animatedly the film they would see, wending their way through the lively crowds, and church-goers, more formally dressed, some with bibles or hymn books clasped in their hands. Later the composition of the crowd would change and young people, dressed to kill, would be heading for the nightclubs and bars.

The lively mood of the city, the shouts and the laughter delighted her and she was in no hurry to get home. As she passed a church the sound of singing slowed her steps even more. She didn't attend the services, but there was something stirring about the well-known hymns. As she stepped off the pavement, intending to go closer, where a seat offered her a place to enjoy the sound, a car drew up. The horn sounded, startling her, discordant in the melody of the church and the street.

'Ancret, let me give you a lift,' Jonathan called, snapping her almost painfully out of her mood. With a sense of disappointment that would have been impossible to explain, she reluctantly left the busy street with its stimulating atmosphere, her sense of belonging to the crowd, of sharing its hunt for where the action was, falling away in a cloud of dismay. Not for the first time, Jonathan's appearance was unwelcome, an intrusion into her mood of contented joy. Nevertheless, she smiled as she slid into the passenger seat. 'I was happily daydreaming,' she said.

'Of us, I hope?'

'Of the future,' she answered ambiguously.

Jonathan said very little as they travelled the short distance to her home. When they went in, his arm was firmly around her and he didn't release her until Loraine had been made aware of his proprietorial action.

'I want your daughter to move in with me,' he said. Ancret turned to him with a startled expression. 'One day we'll marry.' This was unexpected.

'And how does my daughter feel about this?' Loraine asked, without looking at Ancret.

'Something is holding her back and I think you know what that is.'

'Her career?'

'I can cope with her career. I understand more and more how she feels about her work. Sharing her life with me needn't interrupt that. In fact, as an estate agent I'll be able to help her, set her up in premises where she can build on her successes.'

'And—?'

'And the other thing holding her back is something you can help her with. Ancret needs to know something about her childhood. It seems ridiculous that she doesn't even know who her father – your husband – was. Why the secrecy? Was he a murderer? A wife beater? Did he abandon you? You must realize how your reticence to talk has fired Ancret's imagination?'

Loraine had stood up and was glaring at Jonathan. She took two short steps towards him, threatening, her eyes bright with anger. His final words faltered. 'She needs to know,' he muttered, backing away.

'Don't upset yourself, Mummy.' Ancret went to her mother and put an arm around her shoulders, pulling her away from the confrontation.

Putting her daughter gently aside, Loraine answered calmly. 'We have no family. There is no one belonging to us anywhere in this world. And there are no secrets that would cause her any concerns. Isn't that enough for you?'

'For me, yes. But for Ancret, no. I want you to tell her, then she'll be free from the demons created by her uninformed imaginings.'

'There's nothing to tell.'

7

'Please, talk about her father, and your childhood, and her father's. She needs to know.'

Ancret watched her mother's face as she turned away from Jonathan's determined stand. Loraine's distress was clear to see. She wanted to push him from the room, tell her mother to forget it, that she wasn't curious, it was all in Jonathan's head. She became aware that – as on so many occasions before – she too was trembling, with anticipation that was gradually turning to dread. She wanted to cry out, *Don't tell me, I don't want to know.* But she held back the fear that knowing everything would destroy her. Surely it was better to know, better to bring it out and deal with it? She moved away from her mother and took a step closer to Jonathan, glad that if her mother's defensive barrier was finally breached she would have him there to help her. She was glad not to be alone. She felt his arm tighten around her and was aware of her need of his strength.

'Loraine?' he coaxed.

'They're all dead.' She spoke sharply, almost shouting. 'My family are all dead. There, are you satisfied? My mother of TB, my two sisters of TB and my father falling in front of a car. There, is that enough for you?' Loraine turned away. Ancret pulled herself from Jonathan's arms and went to hug her but Loraine pushed her away, anger and grief in the fierceness of her refusal to accept comfort.

Jonathan returned to the office. The estate agency was busy and he sometimes went in on a Sunday to do work; it was easier without the interruption of clients walking in and telephone calls. He and his friend Jeff Talbot had started the business about five years previously; as their names, Power and Talbot, had seemed to lack something, they invented the name Pen-Marr. Caroline, Jonathan's mother, immediately began calling herself Mrs Pen-Marr, delighting in the hyphenated title which she announced with reverence to new acquaintances. They had recently moved house, so it had been a good time for a change of name as she introduced herself to neighbours and the local shopkeepers. Her existing friends were told that she was reverting to her maiden name now she was a widow, a claim that was readily accepted –

although with a degree of amusement by the more malicious.

When Jeff died suddenly, Jonathan had inherited his partner's share of the business. They had both signed an agreement in preparation for such a sad event, though the plan had been to rescind it after a few years when the firm was established. But Jeff's unexpected death had occurred during the early struggle for survival.

Jonathan worked contentedly for a couple of hours, like Ancret putting aside all other considerations and concentrating on his task. But after a while his mind wandered and he tried to think of ways to persuade Ancret to leave her mother and share his flat. Marriage was a strong consideration, although Mother was against it, he mused. Perhaps he could begin making enquiries about Ancret's family without telling Loraine. Once the truth was known, both Ancret and his mother might be content to allow their relationship to grow.

Would the registry of births, deaths and marriages help him find out something of her family? And should he do so without her knowledge and agreement? It suddenly seemed too complicated. Better if he could persuade her to forget it, and keep on asking, wearing her down until she agreed.

The phone rang, startling him. He picked it up, expecting it to be Ancret as she had been filling his thoughts. But it was his mother.

'Jonathan, dear, dinner will be ready in twenty minutes. Don't be late, will you?'

'Thank you, Mother. I'll be there.' Packing away his dreams and his papers, he locked the office and drove obediently home.

Moments was increasingly busy coping with the spate of spring weddings, as the month of May drew near. Helena Mortimer had started the business as a quality gown shop with Loraine as her assistant, but had gradually made a name for bridal dresses and outfits for wedding guests. She also kept a good stock of accessories for special occasions. When she left college, Ancret had joined them, her hats being a natural addition to the shop's offerings.

Although Saturday was one of the busiest days of the

week, Ancret had been given the day off from dealing with customers to finish work on the hat she was making for the mother of a society bride. A Saturday girl, Angela Grey, had been employed to take her place in the salon. Loraine would be there between eleven and five and Helena knew they would all be kept extremely busy.

On her way to her workroom, Ancret stopped at a café in Morgan Arcade and bought coffee and a sandwich. She could have eaten at home, but had been unable to resist the opportunity to sit and watch people passing, imagining the hats she would design for some of those who paused to look in the shop windows. On many days she stared into the faces wondering if one of these strangers was an unknown relative: her father, an aunt, a cousin. Besides, she might meet Jonathan if he could escape from his mother for a moment or two.

They had become closer since the most recent, distressing attempt to persuade her mother to answer his questions, although even now they usually met away from Loraine's unwelcoming presence. But instead of Jonathan, it was her mother who arrived at the café.

'I thought I'd find you here,' she said, pushing her way through the doorway with numerous plastic bags. 'I thought I'd do some shopping in the market before going to the salon.' Ancret helped her with her shopping and pulled out a chair for her facing away from the door, then ordered more coffee. The café was a long room, divided almost into two with the doorway in the middle; when Jonathan came a few minutes later he smiled and went into the second room. Ancret could see him from where she sat but he was out of her mother's sight.

Sharing a glance of which Loraine was unaware was as exciting as if she had been a teenager with a forbidden book; titillating and adding to the excitement of their next meeting. She blew a kiss as she and Loraine went out, and walked with her mother through Howells department store, leaving her there before making her slow, swaying way towards Sloan Street.

A man stepped out of the doorway of a pizza restaurant and stood in front of her.

'Darling,' he said. They hugged, oblivious to the people pushing past them, people who ignored the kiss that followed. Breathlessly, Ancret's first words were not of love, but 'Where is she?'

'My mother or yours?' Jonathan laughed, a relaxed laugh that she loved to hear, his head thrown back, his eyes intriguing slits as he managed still to look at her. 'Do you often wonder at the stupidity of this?' he asked as he held her close.

'Frequently. And one day we'll look back and wonder why our mothers demand such obedience of us.'

'And at our own complicity.'

'Mummy was so upset and I can't put her through that again. Best we keep away from her, just for a while, until she's recovered and—'

'And until we promise never to ask about your family again. Can you do that? Forget about your hidden past? I can, easily. I love you and I have no great need to know where you came from, who you are, or why you are who you are. But I can see how much harder it is for you.'

'You must agree it's odd? I have so few clues to tell me where I belonged. She still wears her wedding and engagement rings but she refuses to talk about my father.'

'I'd better go. Saturday mornings are for my mother. I have to carry her shopping and taxi her around like a manservant.'

'Do you mind?'

'I find it amusing. You see, I know where we came from and there's nothing grand in my past, no valuable jewellery or antique furniture or china. My father was a partner in a factory making double-glazed windows and doors and he made his money from hard graft. Mother's always hinted at a grand, mysterious past and now she's a widow, and we've moved to a new area, and the name of the business has miraculously become our own, she pretends even more. From Mrs Power, she's become Mrs Pen-Marr. It's a harmless enough deception.'

They quickly made plans to meet later and go to the cinema, then parted, holding hands until the last possible moment, oblivious of others. A few more paces and Ancret stepped through the door of the dress shop.

11

To her surprise, Jonathan's mother was there. She turned when Ancret entered. Forcing a smile she said, 'Good afternoon, er – Ancret. I understood this was your day off?'

So that's why she came today, Ancret thought with a quiet chuckle. 'It is,' she assured her. 'But as usual I've come in to work at my hats.'

'I simply can't stop her working,' Helena said.

'Nice,' Caroline Pen-Marr replied in mock politeness, before turning away to where the Saturday girl, Angela, was holding out a full-skirted pink dress that Ancret knew would be unsuitable for her rather heavy build and robust colouring. Away from Mrs Pen-Marr's view she pulled a face of amused horror at the choice. Angela would have a battle to persuade her away from that unfortunate colour, judging by the three similar dresses already on display. Ancret beckoned the assistant and whispered, 'Try and wean her away from pink if you can. Tell her the green is absolutely this season's latest. She'll look much nicer in the colour and the style.' She watched as Mrs Pen-Marr was offered the green, subtly fitted dress, her head shaking at first but becoming still as she listened to the girl's sales patter.

Waving elegantly to Helena, who was showing a second customer a 'Mother of the Bride' outfit in lavender, she went through to the workshop at the back, glowing at the thought of the recent encounter with Jonathan while his mother was just a few metres away from them. There were times when she believed they had a future together. If she could only find out who she was, perhaps she would be more willing to try.

Loraine arrived soon afterwards and mouthed to Ancret that 'Mrs Hyphen-hyphen' was in the salon.

'I know,' Ancret whispered in reply. 'Has Angela talked her out of the pink?'

'With difficulty,' her mother said grimly.

Although she was Helena's assistant, most of Ancret's time was spent in the apparent chaos of the workroom. There were several benches on which were spread hat blocks, heaters and the many other tools of her trade. A hairdryer, used to dry stiffener, hung on a hook, there were pliers and tape measures, a hot glue gun, boxes containing ribbons and other materials for decorations, wire of varying thicknesses and pliability, and several pressing irons. A separate table held the sewing implements and a heavy-duty machine filled a corner. Ancret was not a tidy worker and she began every session by rearranging the muddle to give herself room to work.

Today was an exception. On a separate table was a silk hat, covered with tissue paper against dust, needing only its final decoration. The loosely arranged flowers, made from feathers dyed to match the client's dress exactly, and to which she had added two bare quills, were ready to be sewn on to the front.

Helena took advantage of a quiet moment in the shop and came in to leave Ancret a cup of coffee, but she smiled at the concentration on Ancret's face and knew the coffee would grow cold, forgotten almost as soon as she had been thanked for it. When she worked on her hats, Ancret drifted into another universe.

When Ancret left several hours later, after her mother had gone home, the hat was finished and had been placed in the salon to await its owner.

'Did you finish the hat, Ancret?' her mother called as she went into the house, not far from the city centre, where she had lived for as long as she could remember.

'Not only have I finished the hat for Mrs Greener, I've made the brim and crown for another. This time in turquoise.'

'Who is this one for?'

'No one special. It's for Helena's window display, one of three designs to complement the dresses she's showing. But I'm sure they'll find a buyer. I'll make them irresistible, Mummy.'

'Darling child, you always do.'

'Child? Mummy, I'm twenty-four.'

'When d'you think you'll stop being my child?'

'When I marry?'

'That won't be for a long, long time. You haven't met the man good enough to win you yet.'

'I saw Jonathan today,' she said, testing the water.

'How nice for him. Was the dragon with him?'

Ancret laughed. 'She was in the shop, as you know, trying on short, pink dresses.'

'And her barely five feet tall. She's lacking in both taste and the sense to ask for advice. What a combination. Thank goodness you don't take Jonathan seriously. Imagine having that for a mother-in-law!'

Ancret smiled. 'I asked Angela to coax her away from the pink and choose a green instead. I don't know how successful she was.'

'I know. It was kind of you to try, dear, but she seems set on making an exhibition of herself.'

'I think she does it on purpose,' Ancret said thoughtfully. 'To make herself stand out, be noticed. She is a beauty consultant, remember. Her flamboyant style is her trademark. I wish she would just tone everything down just a little, though. But she knows what she wants and refuses to listen to any suggestions. She has been very successful,' she reminded Loraine. 'She's always in demand to give talks and workshops – you have to admire her.'

'She'll never be as successful as you will be, my daughter, as long as you stay clear of commitments with people born to fail, like Jonathan Pen-Marr – or whatever his name is!'

'He was trying to help me, Mummy. He wasn't intending to hurt you. He knows how much I long to know something about my family.'

'Forget it, my daughter.' Ancret was intrigued by the way her mother sometimes called her 'my daughter'. There was a hint of an accent or other foreign influence, but nothing she could define.

'Please, Mummy. Why won't you talk to me?'

'Open a newspaper and there's enough heartbreak and horror there without you listening to my stories of unhappiness and loss.'

'Was it so terrible?'

Her mother's lips tightened but she didn't reply. Ancret pleaded again but Loraine shook her head of dark hair, so like that of her daughter. 'Fill your mind with happy thoughts and they will reflect in your work. You are creating hats for people to wear at moments of celebration. Stitch them and mould them with joy in your heart, my daughter.'

'I do, Mummy. I forget everything else when I'm working.'

14

'Keep away from Jonathan, he isn't what he seems. He shows you only a part of what he is.'

'Mummy, that's rubbish. It's just you trying to discourage me from spending time with him.'

'Despite his words to the contrary, he'll want to own you. Even in the twenty-first century there are still such men. He'll expect you to forget your career and build your life around his. He won't want you to have a life of your own. He isn't the one for you.' She stared hard at Ancret with her dark, intelligent eyes. 'We both know that, don't we?'

Ancret didn't reply but in her heart she knew her mother was right. Marriage to Jonathan would make every step forward in her career a fierce battle for survival.

She had arranged to meet him that evening. Stating her intention of going to the cinema, she threw one of her favoured long shawls around her shoulders and phoned for a taxi. Unusually, they were meeting at the office where Jonathan and Jeff Talbot had begun their business, dealing with clients at the lower end of the market. He and Jeff had quickly realized their mistake and the rather run-down premises in an equally run-down part of the city had long been abandoned in favour of an office in a better location.

The shop premises had smelled strongly of fish when they had taken it over. The premises had been chosen only because they were cheap but he had decided not to sell, believing that the city's upturn would increase property values and make the area a more favourable investment. So far that had not happened, but he still retained ownership. He wondered whether this sentimental attitude to an earlier stage of his life could be likened to Loraine's fascination with her old willow basket. She would never talk about it, but there had to be a reason why she kept it although it was almost falling to pieces.

The abandoned office was now used only as a store room for clutter. He had spent most of that day emptying filing cabinets of unwanted papers, and had asked Ancret to meet him there. When the taxi dropped her off, the driver offered to wait until she had knocked the door and been invited inside.

'It's all right,' she said as she thanked him. 'I'm helping the owner refurbish the place. I'm a designer,' she added as explanation.

'I thought you were something special, miss.' The driver grinned in the darkness. 'You look very special and I hope your friend appreciates it.' He nodded towards the side door, which had opened, spilling a rectangle of light on to the pavement. Silhouetted in the brightness was Jonathan. The driver handed her a card on which he had written his phone number. 'In case you need me again later,' he said.

She thanked him and hurried inside.

'The taxi driver thinks I'm a prostitute!' she gasped. 'Jonathan, I'm never coming here again, d'you understand? Never!'

He tried to look suitably solemn but failed, and soon they were both laughing at the unfortunate misapprehension.

They had found a variety of places to meet, including both their homes when their mothers were out of town, but this abandoned office was the worst. She refused to be kissed, and stood still wearing her shawl and clutching her handbag as though it were a lifeline.

'It's a bit too early for the cinema. What would you like to do? Anything you say, darling.'

'To a restaurant, for a civilized meal with wine, sitting where everyone can see us and feel jealous at our obvious happiness.'

'We'll forget the cinema. You look too beautiful to be hidden.'

They drove out to the pretty Victorian town of Penarth with its charming buildings and restored pier, and walked in sight and sound of the sea for a while before driving on. They finally stopped to eat in Cowbridge and when they returned to Cardiff it was almost twelve thirty. Jonathan hadn't been able to risk a drink. Being without a car would be fatal for his business, but he had plied Ancret with her favourite white wine and saw her relax and become more loving. He hoped the wine would drive away her inhibitions and reveal her true feelings.

Jonathan found a parking place around the corner from her home and walked Ancret to her door. She stepped slowly inside, dreamily content and slightly drunk – to be greeted by her mother, wearing nightdress, chiffon headscarf and a frown.

16

'Don't ask, Mummy,' Ancret said firmly. 'I've been out to eat with Jonathan. It was a wonderful evening.'

'You'd better set your alarm. You hate to oversleep,' was Loraine's comment before she went up the stairs, leaving Ancret standing in the hall. 'And tell him to bring you home properly, not leave you in the street like a prostitute!' She couldn't understand why Ancret found the remark so amusing.

'Why don't we go away, right away, spend a few days in Crete?' Jonathan suggested a few days later. 'It's lovely in the spring with carpets of wild flowers and friendly people and wonderful food. We could just laze on the beaches or do some sightseeing, and you'd get inspiration for even more wonderful hats. What d'you think?'

'Jonathan, I'm tempted.'

'Then tell Helena you need a week or ten days off. I'll get someone to help Lucinda and Lottie run the office and we'll go.'

'I'll have to check with Mummy first. She might have something planned.'

'Can't you just tell her?' he asked with a sigh.

'Could you?' she retaliated quickly.

'I've already spoken to Mother and she's going to stay with Uncle Richard for a while,' he admitted, shamefaced.

'Promise me one thing, you won't talk about my moving in, or marriage? I'm not ready for that strong a commitment yet. And if you want to be free to find someone who is, well, I'll understand.'

'What are you saying? You want to end it?'

'I don't want to keep you hanging on a piece of string, expecting me to marry you, when I can't see that far ahead. I love you, but I'm not able to give you all my life.'

'You don't have to. I understand about your work. But we could be together, work together. Just the two of us. You could continue to design and make hats, for as long as you want to. We could work something out, live somewhere convenient to both our businesses.'

'I'd no longer be free to concentrate on what I was doing. One part of my mind would be always on us. No, Jonathan. I don't want all that.'

'And you won't come to Crete?'

'I'd love to go to Crete.'

'Then I'll go to the travel agents and—'

'But not yet. We're coming to the busiest period of the year. It's always quiet in January and February but now we're getting more clients every week.'

'I see. You're reminding me – in case I've forgotten – that your work comes first.'

'It always will,' she said softly. 'You have to understand that, darling.'

'A weekend then. A couple of nights in the Cotswolds? Surely you can manage that? Who can possibly be that indispensable?'

'Soon,' she promised.

'But not now.'

'Not now.'

Her mind kept returning to his suggestion as she sat drinking her coffee during a mid-morning lull. When she mentioned it to Helena, her comments surprised her.

'Go, Ancret. It doesn't have to be a weekend, does it? The early part of the week is usually quiet. And I can ask our Saturday girl to be a Tuesday and Wednesday girl, can't I? Your mother won't refuse to work some extra hours if I need her, she's very reliable. Go on, say yes.'

'Perhaps Jonathan can't manage a weekday?'

'That can't be a problem if he was suggesting a longer holiday in Crete, can it? Besides, if he can't then the fault is his and not yours. That must make a change.'

Jonathan agreed, and they booked a hotel on the Gower peninsula for Saturday through to Tuesday at the end of the month. Both mothers were told and, ignoring their disapproval, the pair began to look forward to their short break.

On Saturday, as Jonathan was carrying her suitcase to his car, the phone rang. Sensing trouble, he tried to get Ancret out of the house before Loraine answered. He opened the car door and she was actually stepping inside when Loraine called. 'Stop, Ancret! It's Helena. Her husband's had a heart attack and is in hospital. She needs you to run the shop, she's in a terrible state.'

Jonathan couldn't see Loraine; she had run back inside. But he just knew she was smiling.

18

# Two

Jonathan was about to cancel the hotel booking when he hesitated. Better to give it to someone else rather than face the battle of claiming back his money. With no notice, it was unlikely he would get more than a token amount. He didn't go in to see whether Ancret needed a lift to the hospital to see Helena. Instead he drove home.

'Mother?' he called as he entered the flat they shared. 'Would you like a weekend on Gower with a friend?'

Caroline Pen-Marr rang someone, hastily packed a couple of cases and, within minutes, Jonathan was watching with amusement as she got into a taxi already occupied by another woman of a similar age. Only then did he phone to find out what Ancret's plans were. He hadn't needed to wait and ask if she would cancel their short holiday; he knew that, as always, work and others would come first. Although in this instance he was determined to sound sympathetic.

'Darling? What's happening?'

'Oh, Jonathan, what a disaster. Helena doesn't know where to turn. I have to stay and man the shop for a few days, at least until the doctors can assess the outcome of the heart attack.'

'I understand.'

'You do? I thought you'd be furious.'

'Furious? Me? Come on. Surely not when someone is so ill? Besides, it isn't the first time we've had our plans changed and I suspect it won't be the last.'

'Will there be a refund?'

'Unlikely. My mother and her friend are going in our stead.'

'I'm sorry. If Mummy hadn't caught us as we were leaving, we'd have been on our way unaware of the problem.'

'Such a pity.'

'Well, hardly. Helena has enough to cope with, hasn't she? At least I can relieve her of any worries about the business. It was a disappointment, but it was fortunate really.'

'Yes, well, we'll have to try again – one day.'

'Once we have the prognosis on Helena's husband, and we know what's happening, we'll make it a priority. I really was disappointed.'

'Me too. Just bad luck, for us as well as Helena's husband.'

'Thanks for being so understanding.'

'I'll be in touch later.'

The reasonable tone was a screen for his irritation. Irrationally he blamed Loraine. He slammed down the phone and glared at it as though it too was responsible for the cancellation. He had no appointments for the few days they'd intended being away and he was at a loss to know how to fill the time. He went into the office and glanced at the new properties that had come in since he was last there. One caught his eye and he stared at it for a long time.

Ancret didn't stay at the hospital. After a quick exchange of sympathetic words, and having scribbled down a list of things to do, she listened to a report on the doctors' various pronouncements, then left to go to the shop. It was midday by the time she had familiarized herself with the following week's arrangements and had made several telephone calls to make sure the deliveries would be made at a convenient time. At five o'clock, after being reassured that Angela would be able to come and help for longer than planned, she returned home.

She telephoned Jonathan at home, at the office and on his mobile, but there was no reply. Guilt made her wonder if he had gone away as planned and the story about his mother and a friend was untrue. 'Has Jonathan phoned?' she asked her mother.

'No, and I doubt that he will. Even he must understand that you have to help Helena at such a time.'

'Of course he does, Mummy, but we were looking forward to the few days away.'

'At present, Helena needs your help more than you need a few days with Jonathan.'

The telephone rang and Ancret picked it up, expecting to hear Jonathan's voice. It was Helena.

'It's too early to be certain,' she said, her voice quivering with emotion, 'but the damage is serious. He might not work again and that means I won't either.'

'Oh Helena, I'm so sorry. But what d'you mean?'

'I'll be selling the business. Whatever happens, he'll need me to look after him for months, maybe years, and he's more important than the shop.'

'Of course,' Ancret said slowly, giving herself time to recover from the shock of Helena's statement, her mind racing over the implications. 'When you're ready, we'll talk about it. Perhaps I can run it for you, make Angela a full-time assistant maybe?'

'I can't think of anything right now, my head's in a whirl. I just want to concentrate on getting Jeremy well again.' The words became indistinct as emotion overcame her.

Ancret said, 'Go now, Helena. We'll talk about it later, when you have a better idea of what's happening. Jeremy must come first, I can see that, but don't make any hasty decisions. For the moment I'll make sure everything is running smoothly.'

Putting the phone down, she stared at her mother. 'Mummy, we might be out of a job. Helena's talking about selling Moments, and the new owners won't necessarily want a fashion shop. The premises could end up as a café, or an estate agency or just another house, and the lovely dresses and my beautiful hats will be no more.'

'We could buy it,' Loraine said.

Ancret turned to stare at her. 'How? The property is bound to be expensive. With the business as well, it'll be worth more than this house. So what would we use for money?'

'Wait until Helena has made her decision and then, when you and she discuss what is to happen, I want to be with you. And we'll go from there, all right? Just remember that if we do manage to buy it you'll be committed to its success. No thoughts of marriage for a year or so.'

Ancret nodded, but she held out little hope. Loraine probably had no idea how expensive property had become. Cardiff was an up and coming city, a fact reflected in property prices.

She had just been thrown over a cliff and there didn't seem to be a lifeline.

Caroline Pen-Marr and her friend Dorothy Piper-Davies – one of the reasons Caroline had been unable to resist giving herself a hyphenated name – sat in the lounge of the hotel just yards from the beach of Oxwich on Gower and drank a last gin and tonic. They had enjoyed a few days of cosseting in the charming converted vicarage, with good food, comfortable accommodation and delightful walks. In their mood of contentment and friendliness, Caroline began to explain her unease at the prospect of Jonathan marrying Ancret.

'You see, she's a dedicated businesswoman. They can be very ruthless, as you know. Far worse than men.'

'That's good, surely?' Dorothy replied curiously. 'You can't object to success.'

'Jonathan won't come home to a warm, organized home and a decent meal.'

'So what?' her outspoken friend asked. 'Since when has Jonathan expected all that? He certainly didn't have it from you, did he? You were out of the house more than you were in and your husband, bless him, had to shift for himself most evenings.'

'Don't be unkind, Dorothy. I cared for him well.'

'Rot. He hardly ever saw you!'

'All right, I admit I could have looked after him better. But it's different when it's your son, isn't it? We want better for our sons.'

'But not our daughters? You'd accept slavery for a daughter? Rot! Be honest, my dear, you'd be jealous of any girl who earned Jonathan's love. Tell me,' she added after an uncomfortable silence, 'What's she like, this Ancret? A hat designer you say. Any good, is she?'

'Her hats are . . .' Caroline hesitated, unable to praise the girl she was trying so hard to dislike. 'They're imaginative, unusual,' she said in a tone that hinted at the disapproval of someone trying to be kind. 'Very expensive. You pay a lot of money, and the less hat there is, the higher the price.'

'She sounds worth a visit,' Dorothy said.

\*    \*    \*

22

That evening Ancret was very late getting to bed. With the shop management to deal with, she knew there would be less time to make her hats, so she made several hoods in preparation, and with Loraine's help sewed brims to four straws she planned to make for their window display. She marvelled at her mother's neat and almost invisible stitching. Loraine was very talented and she silently, foolishly, thanked her mother for the genes that had been passed on to her. As she sewed she wondered sadly what she had inherited from her unknown father.

When she finally climbed the stairs to bed she heard noises coming from her mother's room and guessed she was having a dream. Loraine dreamed regularly and noisily, but this was a particularly distressing sound. As she went into the room she realized her mother was crying.

In the light thrown through the doorway she saw her mother rocking and crying, patting a bundle of her bedding that she clutched to her breast as though she were nursing a child.

'Don't worry, my daughter,' she was wailing. 'There, there, Mummy will do her best. Mummy will do her best.'

Ancret tiptoed in and sat on the bed beside her mother's writhing form. She didn't wake her, having long ago learned it was best to allow the dream to finish in its own time. In the past, wakening her had left Loraine trembling and shaken, the unfinished terror just out of sight, waiting for her to return to sleep. On those occasions Loraine had sat up for the rest of the night, drinking tea and waiting for the dawn.

'But we can't go!' Loraine wailed in the high-pitched voice of her dream persona. 'You can't do this to us. Where can we go if you won't help us?'

Ancret listened. The words were almost the same every time her mother had this dream, but none of them made any sense. Gradually the cries lessened and Loraine became calmer. Ancret waited until her mother's frightened eyes opened, the pupils wide, looking around as though working out where she was, and only then did she speak. 'Mummy? Are you all right? Shall I get you a drink?'

'How long have you been there?' Her voice was low, different from that in the dream. 'What have I been saying?'

'Nothing important. I think you were having the dream

again, where you were so afraid for me. Was it the same one, Mummy?'

'What did I say?' Loraine demanded. 'It was probably nonsense. Just a dream. Something I've seen on television, no doubt.'

'No, it was the dream you've had many times before. You were crying and nursing a baby, and you seemed so distressed. I – I couldn't make out any words,' Ancret told her.

'Too many cups of coffee, no doubt,' Loraine said with a trembly smile.

'So what's happening?' Jonathan asked when he called at the shop a few days later as Ancret and Loraine were about to close.

'I might be looking for new premises and a job. Helena is thinking of selling Moments,' she told him. 'I don't know what we'll do. Both working here means we're really stuck. It's a calamity.'

'Perhaps a new owner will buy the business, take you on, and you can continue as before?'

'Unlikely. As unlikely as Mummy's suggestion that we buy it.'

'Buy it? But would you be able to raise the finance?'

Ancret shrugged. 'Mummy won't discuss the whys and hows, but she said she wants to be included in the discussions when Helena has made her decision.'

'I might be able to help, put in a percentage of the cost – be a sleeping partner.' He smiled at the innuendo and she hugged him.

'Would you do that for me?'

'I'll do what I can, I promise.'

As Ancret smiled in delighted relief, he went on, 'Look – come with me, there's something I want to show you.'

'When, now?'

'Now!'

He waited with obvious excitement while she dealt with the till and the banking, and locked the doors. Then, refusing to discuss their destination, he drove out through the city and on to the narrow country roads of the Vale of Glamorgan.

The evening was warm and still and Ancret felt herself

24

relaxing. Knowing that for the present she could do nothing, she closed her eyes and allowed her anxieties to drift away. When the car stopped she reluctantly opened her eyes, aware of how tired she felt.

'Where are we?' They were parked in a layby and there seemed to be no building in sight, just green hedges with their skirts of wild parsley and banks of celandines and a few clumps of primroses. Beautiful wild flowers past which cars drove, their occupants often unaware of what lay just feet from them.

He opened her door and the pungent scent of wild garlic filled her nostrils, clean and fresh. He offered his hand to help her out. 'What will dinner be?' she asked with a smile. 'A picnic? Or do we manage with grass and fresh leaves?' She reached over and picked some of the newly sprouting leaves of the hawthorn. 'We used to eat these and call it the bread and cheese tree,' she said, popping the fresh green titbit into her mouth.

'Work first, food after,' Jonathan said. Still holding her hand, he guided her to a driveway leading to a house that from its elongated shape, appeared to have begun life as a trio of cottages. 'This property came on the market yesterday and after I'd had a brief look around, I though you might like to see it.'

She stifled laughter at the name proudly painted on a house sign: 'Toad Hall'.

'Very twee,' she remarked disparagingly.

'Apparently this is a place where toads get killed crossing the road on their way to lay their spawn each spring and the owners of this house have to agree to man the crossing to save as many as they can.'

The explanation sobered her. She knew how many of the poor creatures were lost as their instinct took them on their traditional route to water to spawn. 'Quite a task,' she said. 'It's wonderful that people are prepared to do what they can.'

'Oh, they have help. The local wildlife enthusiasts have a rota.'

Ancret was beginning to feel hungry and she was wondering why Jonathan had brought her to such an out-of-the-way place. If it was simply business, then surely he had

25

time during the day to deal with this? She was a city girl. Toads and their problems were far from her normal preoccupations.

The place was empty and, despite misgivings about the jokey name and the isolated situation and the talk of toads, she was impressed. The long, narrow building was elegantly furnished in a mock-historical style: original features surrendering to the need for comfort and efficiency. In the stone fireplace a fire was built and ready to light. Late sunlight filtered through the windows until Jonathan switched on the very modern electric lighting and spoiled the mood somewhat. But seconds later, she found the clearer view entrancing.

'It's lovely,' she gasped, touching the comfortable burgundy couch and the heavy curtains that framed the lattice windows. They wandered through a dining room with a table large enough for eight, and a dream kitchen with a utility room beyond. Upstairs there were two bathrooms and four bedrooms. As she opened each door and looked inside she gasped with delight. She couldn't imagine a place more perfect. City girl or not, this house was calling to her, welcoming her into its warmth and timelessness. After a while, as she looked again and again at the treasures it held, Ancret became aware that, while she was looking around her, Jonathan was not. He was watching her. 'What is it?' she demanded. 'Have I got jam on my face?'

'I'm wondering what you think of it, whether your obvious delight is because you can imagine living here. I love it and I feel it's waiting for us and no one else, just you and me. You do feel the same, don't you?'

'It's a beautiful place. It has charm and I can easily imagine it being my home.' She knew the mood of the place was beguiling her and she shrugged away the enchantment. It was wrong, she mustn't be tempted into making what could be a huge mistake. 'Already I can feel it wrapping itself around me, coaxing me to stay. But sadly, this isn't the time. With Helena considering selling the business and the threat of my being made redundant in a few weeks, I need to concentrate on my career. If, by some enormous stroke of luck, Mummy and I can buy Moments, I wouldn't have time for anything else.'

'Why put yourself through all that stress? If you want beautiful things I can give them to you.'

'I do want beautiful things, but the most beautiful would be success. An achievement that's all my own. I'm not very hopeful, but if Mummy can come up with a way of buying Moments, that's what I want to do. I want to build a name for the finest hats for the most joyous occasions. I want my name to be the first people think of when they want a hat for their most special moments. Hats by Ancret. What's wrong with wanting that?'

'Ancret.' He put his arms around her. The quiet, harmonious house seemed to hold its breath, waiting for her to look at him. When she lifted her head and did so, he said, 'Don't buy Moments. Marry me instead. This house is ours, we can both feel that. I knew the moment I saw the photographs, and you knew the moment you walked through the door. Marry me and live here where I know we'd be content.'

'There you go again! Why does marrying you have to be an alternative?' she repeated. 'Why can't we have both? Lots of couples marry and work out a way to continue careers, sharing everything except their work, so why can't we? It isn't as though you want children,' she couldn't resist adding.

He moved away from her and stood looking out of the window at the cottage-style garden. 'I had a miserable childhood. I'd hate to have a child and put it through the kind of life I had. A busy, working father, a mother I hardly ever saw. No. I want a marriage with just the two of us. Me putting you first and you putting me first.'

'Most of us can complain about a miserable childhood. It's something that no one can help. Every parent does what they think is right but there's no such thing as a perfect parent, and childhood is a difficult time for most of us.'

'My mother worked all through mine. I never had a place in her busy schedule.'

'Mummy worked too, but for her there was no choice. There was no father to support us. There was just the two of us.'

'I was one of one. My mother was rarely there, and my father worked every hour he could stay awake to provide the money she demanded. I was cared for by a series of nannies. They were all kind enough, well paid, so they made sure I didn't complain, but I always knew I was second to their own children. I was a hanger-on who no one really wanted, but I was tolerated because of the money I represented.'

'I'm sorry, Jonathan, but—'

'School holidays were a succession of different child minders,' he went on as though she hadn't spoken. 'Neighbours, friends – some not so friendly – where I sat watching as they enjoyed things I wasn't allowed to share. I remember waiting outside school, wondering who would arrive to collect me, and it was rarely my mother. Fashion shows, talks on make-up and beauty, anything but spending time with me. I came a long way down her list of commitments.'

'I'm sorry, darling. I know how it feels to have no one willing to put you first. Mummy had to work long hours in a dress shop, selling and altering clothes she hated to people who treated her like a servant. Although she was always there when I came out of school and she never missed a school play or concert. We both hated sports day and she always wrote a note excusing me from taking part.' She smiled at the memory. 'She managed better than most and I love her for it.'

'There was no need for my mother to be an absentee parent. My father earned enough to keep us well provided for.'

'There you go again! She wanted to work and why shouldn't she?'

'Because she neglected her duties when there was an alternative. Your mother had no choice, being a single parent. So can't you understand why I want something different? A wife who doesn't work? Someone who will put us, as a couple, first?'

'Darling, this is the twenty-first century!'

'Yes, and people have more choices today. The frantically busy mother juggling several things at once and doing none of them properly, that's one choice. There are others. For us life could be perfect. Can't you imagine, darling, just the two of us?'

'I sympathize and I understand how you feel, but I can't give up on my dreams to repair your broken childhood. People do make choices, and your lonely childhood doesn't come into the mix while I make mine.'

They closed the house up and walked slowly down the now dark drive.

'You do love the house though?' he asked, as she stopped to look back at Toad Hall with its persuasive beauty.

'If I were looking for a home I'd look no further. I couldn't find one I loved more. It's the timing that's wrong.'

'That's a pity, there might not be another we both love as much as that one.'

'Excuse me,' a voice demanded, startling them with its suddenness. 'Can I ask what you're doing here?'

'Who are you?' Jonathan demanded as he recovered from the shock.

'My name is Edmund Preese and I live a short distance away. And you are—?'

'My name is Jonathan Power, but I'm better known as Pen-Marr. I own the estate agency selling this property.'

'That hardly explains why you're here at this time of day, does it? There's no sign of a car. I thought you must be squatters or even vagrants. We do get some trouble around here.'

'It was a viewing. They have to be fitted in whenever the possible purchaser can manage.'

The newcomer was staring at Ancret as though waiting for an introduction, but Jonathan was not going to oblige. She stepped forward and offered her hand. 'I'm Ancret,' she said. He stepped closer than was really necessary and held her hand in his as though she had given him a gift. His smile touched her with a mild excitement, so she turned away and returned to stand beside Jonathan, who reached into a pocket and handed the man one of his business cards. 'Phone me tomorrow if you have a query,' he said, before hurrying Ancret towards the car.

Ancret turned back to where the man stood watching them go. 'I wonder what *he's* doing there at this time. It's too late in the season for rescuing toads.' The sound of her laughter on the air floated back to the man silently watching them.

Outside Toad Hall, Edmund Preese stood listening as their car drove away, the vision of Ancret still clear, etched on his memory. Her flowing movements were as though she had floated out of the woodland, like a fairy-tale character bringing the promise of happiness. He smiled at his fanciful thoughts, but knew that after that brief glimpse of her in the darkness he would hold the image of her beautiful face in his mind for ever.

He stared at the business card with the aid of a torch. Jonathan Pen-Marr Estate Agency; it seemed genuine enough. He wondered whether the fascinating young woman was Pen-Marr's wife. He fervently hoped not.

Loraine went to see Helena the same evening. She carried a bunch of flowers and a basket of fruit and at once asked for the latest news about Helena's husband.

'Thank you, Loraine, you're very kind. Jeremy is making some progress but it seems unlikely he'll be really well for a long time.'

Refraining from asking what her plans were, Loraine said instead, 'Ancret will look after the business for as long as you want, and Angela and I can work extra hours as we're needed, so that's one worry off your mind. You can relax and concentrate on caring for him.'

'I'm afraid I will have to sell. I know how upset Ancret will be, she's so good at helping people choose their clothes, besides using the workroom for her hats. The shop is her address, the place where people make contact. It's sad it should happen now, when she's beginning to become well known. People recommend her, their praise brings new people all the time, and that's the best way to build a business, satisfied clients spreading the word. Without Moments as a base she'll have to start all over again.'

'Unless we can buy it. The shop, the business and the name,' Loraine said quietly.

'That would be the perfect solution. If only—'

'Will you give me a little time, hold back on advertising it for a little while? Two or three weeks? Give me a chance to raise the money?'

'I haven't had a valuation yet.'

'When you do, will you tell me, privately, and give me a couple of weeks? Ancret has been an asset to the business, a part of its success. You owe her that, surely?'

'I'll arrange a valuation next week, before Jeremy comes home, and after that I'll give you a month.'

'Thank you. And,' she added, 'will you say nothing to Ancret? I don't want to build her hopes if it leads to disappointment.'

'It's just between ourselves. I'll tell her I haven't decided yet.'

'Thank you,' Loraine said again as she stood to leave.

Meanwhile, Jonathan went back to the office and made an offer on Toad Hall by email. It was time he sold the old building that had been his first office, and with what he raised and what he could scrape together he would have enough for a substantial deposit. It would be an easy property to rent, within commuting distance of Cardiff, just until he could persuade Ancret to marry him or move in with him.

The news at the hospital was not good. As she headed for the taxi rank with Ancret, Helena was crying.

'Don't give up hope, Helena. Jeremy isn't very old and he's always been fit. In a few weeks things will have improved, I'm sure of it.' She didn't say anything more.

After twenty minutes waiting, they were finally nearing the head of the queue when a voice said, 'Excuse me, but aren't you the young lady I met at Toad Hall last night?'

Ancret turned and stared at the tall, slim man in front of her, flustered as recognition came. 'How did you recognize me?' she asked. 'It was dark.'

'You dress so elegantly and with a style so much your own, I couldn't mistake you for anyone else.'

'Is that what's called a back-handed compliment?' she asked

'I think you're beautiful.'

Embarrassed by his words and the way he was staring at her, she began to explain about Helena and the absence of Jonathan and his car.

'I'm Edmund Preese, I would be pleased to give you a lift.'

Ancret laughed. 'You don't even know where we're going.'

'It's sure to be on my way.' He gestured widely with an arm, to where his car was parked. 'Nothing grand, it's the eight-seater Transit, I'm afraid.'

Slightly bemused, they followed him and got in.

'My parents and I run a guest house where we organize walks for naturalists. Varying subjects, depending on the time of year,' he explained as they drove away from the hospital. 'One of our guests fell out of a tree where he was photographing a bird and ended up in there,' he said, gesturing with a thumb to the lights of the hospital disappearing behind them.

Helena didn't add anything to explain the reason for their being there. She didn't want to talk to a stranger about Jeremy's illness. He dropped Helena off first. When he reached Ancret's home he handed her a card and said, 'Get in touch if you ever want a stress-free day out.'

'Mummy,' she called as soon as the door closed behind her, 'You'll never guess what happened.'

When Ancret went home the following evening after working late at the shop, she called to her mother as usual and was surprised to realize she was not at home. She began preparing a meal, something simple, a stir-fry which she would cook when her mother arrived. At nine o'clock she was still waiting.

At ten, while she was watching the news on television, a phone call startled her. Foolishly she began to imagine disaster; an accident, a mugging, a sudden illness. It was none of those things.

'Ancret, I'm sorry to be so late. I've been trying to get through but my phone isn't behaving. I've borrowed one and I just want to say I'll be home in an hour and I've eaten so don't worry.'

Ancret stared at the phone as though it could add an explanation. Then she dialled Jonathan's number.

'Mummy's not home.' She spoke anxiously. 'I've had a brief phone call to tell me she'll be home in an hour, but no explanation of where she is.'

'What a pity she didn't give us notice, I could have been

there to console you.' She could imagine the smile from the tone of his voice. 'Darling, what a wasted opportunity.'

'There's a stir-fry going to waste too,' she said, refusing to join in his mood.

They arranged to meet the following evening and she rang off, to sit and watch the clock hands that moved with exasperating slowness and wonder where Loraine could be.

She didn't learn much when her mother did return.

'Don't ask, darling. I had an idea but it didn't work out.'

'What idea? Where have you been?'

'I'm tired. We'll talk about it later. I'm off to bed. Sorry not to have phoned earlier.'

Ancret watched as her mother removed her coat and hat – her smartest coat and one of her own individual hats. Dressed in her best, but for what? She smiled, wondering whether her mother, at sixty-five, had found a male friend.

The following morning her mother was up and dressed before she came down to breakfast. 'Sorry I have to go out again, daughter. I'll see you this evening.'

'Will you be late?' Ancret called as her mother swept out of the door.

'It's possible, but I'll phone you.'

'Well, really!' Ancret gasped as the door closed and she watched her mother hurrying down the pavement to where a taxi stood waiting.

When Ancret reached the shop she was surprised and pleased to see Helena there.

'Helena! Thank goodness, I have so many questions.' She tapped a notebook on the counter near the till. 'I've dealt with all I can but there are a few things I need help with, payments and things. I didn't want to worry you, but one or two are urgent.'

The mornings were usually quiet. They spent a couple of hours going over the routine of the book-keeping in detail. Once or twice Ancret protested at the information offered. 'It's all right, Helena, I don't need to know your business, only how to deal with things as they crop up. Your costs and profits are nothing to do with me, I'm simply holding on to everything for you.'

'It won't hurt you to know,' Helena said casually, avoiding

any comment on Loraine's visit and request. 'If you're in charge you need to know how everything is managed.'

'Don't hold out a hope of us buying the business,' Ancret said sadly. 'Mummy hasn't mentioned it since. She must have done a few sums and realized the impossibility of it. There's little chance, unless the premium bonds surprise us with a convenient win! Jonathan offered to help, but I doubt he'd have enough to make the difference between what Mummy and I can raise and the value of this place.'

'Oh, you never know,' Helena said airily. 'Your mother's a very determined woman.'

Loraine's bank manager was sympathetic but unable to help. After a very few minutes he rose slightly from his chair in a gesture of dismissal. She had the impression he was already thinking about his next appointment.

She went next to discuss selling part of the value of her house, but was told she was not old enough. A couple could sell a share of their home when they were sixty-five but a woman on her own needed to be seventy years old. What could she do? It seemed hopeless. The amount was just too much.

She'd have to sell their home. Living above the salon would not be ideal, especially with Ancret's ability to fill every inch of space with her clutter. She knew her most sensible decision would be to put the property in the hands of Jonathan's firm, but this was not a time to be sensible. She approached three agencies and chose the one that gave the highest valuation.

Ancret was both surprised and pleased when she saw the 'For Sale' board outside their house. To know her mother supported her was a wonderful feeling, as she explained to Jonathan.

'I wish she'd asked me to arrange the sale,' he said, unable to hide his disappointment.

Two days later the house that had been their home for as long as Ancret could remember, was sold. Within three weeks everything was under way. Although they had achieved their asking price, the sale would not quite raise what was needed. With little hope and a lot of trepidation, Loraine decided to try just one more prospect before contracts were exchanged and there was no going back. Ancret was anxious. Where would the extra money come from? She didn't know what Loraine was planning – her mother was being very secretive – but she knew that her mother's skills of persuasion were to be seriously tested.

'Why should I?' the man said after inviting her in with ill grace. 'What have you ever done to deserve my help?'

'Ancret is young, talented and if she loses this chance, all she has, all she is, all she could be, will be wasted.'

She talked persuasively for a while. The man listened and shook his head almost continuously, his lips tight, his sad eyes staring out of the window up on to the hill beyond the garden.

Loraine's voice became harsher. 'She's your daughter, and if I tell the newspapers the full sorry story, they'll be here in their hordes to get the story.'

'You'd resort to blackmail?'

'Only if I have to. I've remained silent all these years, haven't I?'

'It will have to be done properly, with insurance for the agreed sum, and interest decided by a solicitor. Everything clear and legal, and—' he glared at her until she raised her eyes to stare back, both locked in defiance – 'and, this will be a private matter.'

'Absolutely private,' Loraine agreed, her dark eyes cold, hiding her excitement.

'Are – the rest of the family well?' she asked tentatively.

'None of your damned business!' he retorted. 'Now please get out of here.'

They agreed to meet at the solicitor's office the following day, and Loraine went home feeling as though she had been seriously kicked. Every bone in her body ached with the tension of the past hour.

Two days later, at the end of May, only hours before the deadline she had been given, she went to see Helena and informed her of both the sale of her own house and the raising of the money to buy the business.

\*     \*     \*

35

'Jonathan, Mummy did it! Our house is sold and she's bought Moments! Isn't it wonderful?'

Hiding his disappointment, Jonathan was glad to be hearing the news via the telephone. Hearing it face to face would have made it harder to pretend. 'Darling, that's amazing. She's a remarkable woman. I still think it's a pity she didn't ask me to sell your house though. I might have sold it for a higher price.'

Ancret heard the tightness in his voice, guessed he was disappointed and trying to hide it. She waited, unsure how to go on.

'Did you get the price you wanted? I could at least have valued it for you, even if you chose to use a rival firm.' The petulance was as clear as if she were staring at him. She took a deep breath and resisted the temptation to slam down the phone.

'Come with me to the shop and help me decide on the changes I might make. I think the glass cabinets that have been there since the sixties will have to go. We'll extend the window a little instead. I've arranged to talk to a builder tomorrow. And, well, I wondered, were you serious about putting money in for a share of the business?'

Jonathan's heart leapt. He had promised, but it had been an empty promise. He'd doubted whether the attempt to buy would succeed and now all his money was spoken for if he managed to buy Toad Hall. So far he hadn't heard whether his offer had been accepted, but he was hopeful. After all, he knew the people he was dealing with. Although another agent had to deal with the business side of things, as he couldn't buy a property though his own agency, he was certain to be fully informed of other offers.

'The trouble is, darling, I did mean it then, but since then something has come up and, well, I don't think I can.'

'But you promised!'

'I know, but to be truthful I didn't expect your mother to bring it off and I've committed the money elsewhere.'

'Exactly where?'

'Toad Hall.'

'Oh, I see. Your fantasy of me being the little woman

without a thought beyond the next meal, and you coming back every evening to the doting wife.'

'Oh, stop it, Ancret. You know that isn't what I want.'

'Isn't it? Anyway, the fact is that you're unable to offer the help you promised me.'

'Come on, Ancret, you must see how unlikely it seemed that you'd be able to raise the money.'

Without allowing further explanation she clicked the phone off and stared into space. This was the most exciting moment of her life, and Jonathan had ruined it.

Jonathan got into his car and drove to Ancret's house. The 'For Sale' notice on its front wall was emblazoned with 'Sold Subject To Contract'. He knocked and shouted, and used his mobile to call Ancret's number, but there was no answer.

Inside, Loraine was staring at the legal agreement showing the loan she had agreed without Ancret's knowledge. She hoped the man with whom she had made the agreement would remain unknown to her daughter. Nothing but grief would come of their meeting.

# Three

In the untidy, over-filled room, Ancret sat on a bolt of lacy material that had faded to the point where it was useless, fit only for the rubbish bin. Useless would describe much of the contents of these rooms above Moments, she thought looking around her. There were cardboard boxes, many holding nothing more exciting than other cardboard boxes; and, from the state of the dresses and hats she could see falling out of other containers, the room needed several trips to a rubbish tip.

Her mobile phone tinkled its announcement of a caller. She glanced at it, saw the caller was Jonathan and shut it off. Half-heartedly she began to gather up some of the rubbish, and filled one of the boxes. She pressed everything down to make best use of the space. When she lifted it to put it in a corner the bottom collapsed and the contents fell to the floor.

She sat there, tiredness making her giggle, and wondered if she would ever manage to make the bland rooms into a place where she and her mother could live. Her lack of enthusiasm was due to Jonathan having let her down. He had offered to help and the money he had promised would have been sufficient to get the rooms cleared and decorated. Instead he had bought a house, hoping to persuade her to marry him and live in it. So now, along with everything else, she had to face the fact that getting these rooms into a liveable state was down to her too. She folded the broken box, kicked the contents about to make her feel better, then found another, stronger one and began again.

Jonathan managed his estate agency with a staff of two. When he went to the office the following morning, Lottie, his late partner's niece, was already there, talking enthusiastically to someone on the telephone. At eighteen, she was a very useful member of the team, good with callers and highly skilled at turning a prospect into a sale. Lucinda was always the last to arrive as she had two children who needed to be trans-ported to school or into the care of her parents.

'Anything happening, Lottie?' he asked as he hung up his coat.

'That was someone asking to see the Harefield Road house. I told her there were several people waiting but if she was quick I could fit her in before any of them, and she's coming at nine thirty.'

Jonathan laughed. 'I don't know how we managed before you came to us, Lottie.'

'Just remember you can't manage without me,' she replied, blowing a kiss from the tips of her fingers. She answered another call and talked confidentially as though to a friend, but Jonathan knew it was a client. She almost whispered about what a good buy the flat in Park View Court was, sounding as though she were conveying a secret.

'Another one in the bag,' Jonathan said. He chuckled as Lottie raised a hand showing fingers tightly crossed.

After the call Lottie went into the area that served as a kitchen and made Jonathan a coffee. As she placed it on his desk, she said, 'Pity Ancret didn't give us her house to sell, wasn't it? I think we could have got about five thousand more, don't you?'

'Possibly. But she had her reasons.'

'I thought it was disloyal, myself.'

'I think she considered it wiser to keep business and pleasure separate.'

Lottie's quiet 'Mmm' made it clear she didn't agree.

Jonathan was considering a further comment, but Lucinda arrived at that moment and he was relieved. He didn't want Lottie talking disparagingly about Ancret – something she did on a regular basis – but neither did he want to lose her.

'Jonathan,' Lucinda said as she dashed in and threw her bags down on her desk. 'I've been told of a property that the owner wants to sell but it's a long way from our locality. If we can manage it, the owner wants us to handle it, out of friendship to me.'

'That's kind of her,' Jonathan said, taking the paper on which Lucinda had written the details.

'Kindness? That's loyalty, that is,' Lottie couldn't help saying.

Jonathan looked at her over the top of the paper. She mouthed 'Sorry', but grinned unrepentantly.

The property was in a small village not far from Brecon and after a glance at his diary, Jonathan decided to go that day. A phone call confirmed the appointment and he looked at Lottie. 'You can come with me if you like. You might enjoy the run and the experience of valuation will add to your knowledge. Although you'll have to tell your parents we'll be late back.' There was a hold-up while Lottie and Lucinda dealt with an offer made on another property, a rather difficult one in an unpopular area of the city. When the offer was accepted, Lottie hugged Lucinda. 'Didn't we do well? Isn't Jonathan lucky to have us?'

'Cream cakes with your coffee tomorrow morning,' Jonathan promised with a smile.

It was mid-afternoon before they were on their way. When they were out of the city, Jonathan explained a little about Ancret's move. Lottie said, 'You do a lot for Ancret. I hope she appreciates it.'

'Stop it, Lottie!' he said with a laugh. 'You sound like a jealous child.'

'I am. Jealous, that is, not a child.'

'Is there something you need help with? I'm your employer and I want you to stay with us for a long time, so if something needs sorting and you think I can help, you only have to ask.' He ignored the odd admission of jealousy. He had noticed her looking at him with a quizzical expression several times and wondered with dread if she were developing a crush on him. He was twelve years older, but that was no barrier to a romantically inclined young woman, as he knew from past experience.

'Thank you,' Lottie said, turning away and staring out of the window at the hills beyond hills, displaying greens of every hue, dotted with sheep and divided by ancient stone walls and the ever-present water that burst out of the ground, pouring down in streams and waterfalls.

It was quite late when they arrived at their destination and the sun was already dropping behind a wooded skyline, leaving a purple haze in its wake. The house was large and well kept, with grounds formally arranged in terraces and gardens and well-filled herbaceous borders. A large lake was fed by a stream wending its way through a small woodland. The whole property was breathtakingly beautiful.

The caretaker met them and offered food and drinks before they set about their task. The five bedrooms were measured and photographs taken. When they left they were both certain that two buyers on their books would be interested in viewing the house.

'It's good when there are two people interested,' Lottie said. 'I'll enjoy telling each of them how the other feels.'

'You really like this work, don't you?' Jonathan said.

'I love it and I love working for you. But now,' she added when he didn't respond, 'now I'm starving and I hope you'll feed me before we go back.'

'That's a good idea,' he said, glancing at his watch before turning towards a pub he knew where they would get a decent meal.

He phoned Ancret as they waited for their food and felt uncomfortably aware of Lottie's stare. He went outside still talking, and out of Lottie's hearing said, 'Darling, I think Lottie is developing a crush on me. Isn't that flattering? A thirty plus like me?'

'I know. So sack her,' Ancret replied. When he laughed, she could imagine the way he threw his head back and his eyes narrowed so intriguingly. She had said it lightly, but she nevertheless felt a shaft of jealousy and ended the call.

They stayed in the pub for a couple of hours and when they emerged it was dark. He led Lottie to where they had parked the car and it wasn't there.

Ancret lay in bed, touching the almost invisible scar on her left hand, as she often did in stressful moments, and wondered why her emotions were so muddled. She wasn't even sure she wanted to marry Jonathan. But then, she didn't want to marry anyone; not until she had achieved her goal of a successful business, and certainly not before she knew the truth about who she was and where she came from. Yet the thought of him being with Lottie was making her uneasy.

She knew she was being unfair to Jonathan, aware that one day he might give up on her and walk away. She would find that hard to bear. He was the only significant person in her life apart from her mother. She wasn't giving him enough to expect his loyalty, she thought, sadly.

Ancret didn't have time to phone Jonathan the following morning. She and Angela had a busy day ahead of them in the absence of Loraine, who was meeting the solicitor and the estate agent. There were fittings arranged for a wedding dress that had undergone alterations. Ancret had two hats to decorate for a new and prestigious customer whom she wanted to please. The dress was tried on and considered a perfect fit, thanks to Angela. The hats needed a few changes, and Ancret carried them out while her client waited. Several customers came to choose dresses for special occasions and it was one o'clock before she could take a break. Then Jonathan wasn't in the office and it was a jubilant Lottie who answered the telephone.

'Jonathan is at home. He was so tired after yesterday and being out half the night,' Lottie said.

'What d'you mean?'

'Well, we had to stay the night because of the car being stolen and – oh, he's here now and I expect he'll tell you what happened himself.' Ancret heard the bell ring on the office door as, presumably, Jonathan entered, but the girl's voice and the implications of an overnight stay were something she had to swallow before listening to Jonathan's explanations. She replaced the receiver.

The phone rang immediately but she ignored it. Locking the shop door, she went upstairs to take out her frustrations on the piles of junk still to be cleared. She had no reason to think Jonathan would do anything stupid, especially with one of his employees, but why hadn't he told her himself?

By the time Jonathan arrived and started banging on the shop door, she had calmed herself and even managed to smile a greeting as she let him in.

'I hope that stupid girl didn't give the wrong impression,'

he said as he marched in. 'Never again will I take her with me! I thought she would enjoy a little treat, an afternoon out of the office and the experience of valuing a rare and beautiful property, but never again.'

'Sack her,' Ancret repeated, stepping forward and offering her face for a kiss.

They went out and bought sandwiches, eating them in the upstairs rooms while Jonathan gave her a humorous account of the previous day's events. Ancret listened and then said, 'And what will you do about Lottie?'

'Nothing. I know how she behaves and the warning will be heeded, but really she's an asset to the firm and more than justifies her wages. You aren't worried that she'll steal me from you, are you?' he said jokingly.

'I'm not in a position to complain when I refuse to make a commitment,' she said sadly. 'And until I know who I am, and get this place on its feet, I'm unable to do so.'

'Marry me, Ancret. Everything else can be sorted out between us.'

'I'll try again to persuade Mummy to talk.'

'Tell her we're getting married, book our wedding, then you'd be in a stronger position. She'll have to tell you what you want to know.'

'It has to be the other way round. I want to know before anything is settled.'

'Thousands of people manage without knowing who they are, where they came from. Children are without parents for many reasons and they cope. Why can't you accept it like others have to?'

'That's the same as suffering the agony of toothache and being told that thousands of people are in the same situation. It doesn't make the pain go away.'

When he returned to the office Jonathan told Lottie she could have the afternoon off, insisting even though she protested that she would prefer to work. When she had gone he told Lucinda what had happened and the way Lottie had implied to Ancret something more than the simple inconvenience it had been. 'Ancret and I laughed over it, but it worried me, and I wonder whether I should let her go. She'll have no trouble getting a job. She's very good and I'd give her a reference stating that clearly.'

'She is an asset, but no one is indispensable. But before you let her go, why don't you talk to her and explain that she's just an employee and nothing more?'

'That would be difficult. How could I say what I feel? She'd probably laugh at the suggestion that I'm attractive to her. I'd sound so vain.'

'Then sack her. Ancret is right, it's usually the simple solution that's the best.'

Lucinda stayed until the office closed its doors the next day, and waited at her desk while Jonathan explained to Lottie that he was cutting down on staff and was 'letting her go'. To his alarm she burst into tears and ran from the room.

Lottie didn't go home. She went to see Jonathan's mother, and when Caroline opened the door her face was red with crying.

'My dear girl, what has happened?' She stood back to allow Lottie to enter and bustled her into a living room that was gaily decorated in tones of red, orange, every shade of pink and splashes of sunshine yellow. Bright cushions and rugs vied with each other for prominence, there were dozens of pictures, displays of live and artificial flowers and brightly coloured feathers in vases. Net curtaining hung in generous drapes and folds, layer on top of layer framing the windows and small tables. Caroline sat her down and packed cushions around her. 'Tea, dear? Or coffee?'

'Oh, Mrs Pen-Marr, Jonathan's sacked me.'

An hour later the tears had subsided and Lottie had left the brightly decorated room, Caroline's promise to sort this out ringing in her ears. Caroline was sitting tight-mouthed waiting for her son.

Jonathan walked in, hesitating when he saw the expression of anger that pursed his mother's lips. 'Someone upset you?' he asked as he removed his coat.

'Yes, dear. You have. I've had poor little Lottie here sobbing her heart out, telling me you spent the night with her then told her she was sacked.'

Jonathan gave a sigh. This was no longer a joke. Explaining

to his mother was difficult. There was nothing between him and Lottie, and they had only 'spent the night' in the sense of staying in the same hotel, but his mother clearly believed Lottie over him.

'I don't suppose you've admitted this incident to Ancret? She wouldn't believe you if you did. That girl is the niece of the man who was your partner, how could you have been so cruel?'

'How can you not believe me?' he asked softly. 'Ancret did.'

'You owe Lottie something, at least her job.'

'We stayed in the same hotel, but in separate rooms.'

'That isn't what she told me.'

'It's best that she goes.'

'Poor little thing.'

'Mother, everything that happens in the office is my concern.' He spoke calmly but he was angry. This was an ugly situation. There was nothing to stop Lottie from repeating her lies and innuendoes. If she convinced his mother then she could do the same to others. Businesses like his, taking him into people's homes, depended on image. He had to be solid, reliable, trustworthy and decent. Stories of him seducing then abandoning a young woman who worked for him would be enough to seriously harm that image.

'I'm going out,' he said, reaching for the coat he had so recently discarded.

'What about your supper?'

'My appetite has disappeared.'

Ancret was sitting beside her mother, both eating salad, cold meat and crusty bread, fresh fruit and wine from trays. A knock at the door disturbed them and Loraine sighed. 'Why won't the man ever leave you alone?' she muttered, putting aside her tray.

Jonathan waited while Ancret offered food. 'I sacked Lottie,' he began, 'but I'll have to reinstate her, she's spreading malicious stories. She's already convinced my mother, and I can't cope with that.'

'So, she's rewarded for her disgraceful behaviour?' Loraine asked.

'Temporarily.'

'Unless her story is the true one?'

'Come on, Loraine! Whatever you think of me, you can't imagine I'll do something as stupid as seduce my assistant? I love Ancret, there's no place in my life for even the briefest of affairs.'

'I'm sorry,' Ancret said, handing him a plate of food. 'I thought her leaving would be for the best. I was wrong.'

While Loraine was putting the dishes in the washer, Jonathan said, 'Marry me. I'll take her back and play everything with great caution. If we were married she would change her view of an affair with the boss. It's because she thinks I might be available that makes it exciting. It's just a game. She'll tire of it when she meets someone special, but until then she could create problems.'

'It's the timing that's so wrong, darling. There's so much going on, the shop will demand all of my energy. If I marry you it has to be at a time when I can give you my full commitment.'

'And when you're sure that your grandfather wasn't a murderer or a child molester or a mentally ill monster?' He ignored the implication of the word, *if*.

'Please, darling, let's leave it until at least one of my problems has been sorted.'

He put his arms around her and said reluctantly, 'All right. Let's give it six months.'

'Let's say Christmas, shall we? Then if it's still what we both want, if we think it will work, we'll make our plans for the most wonderful wedding and dedicate ourselves to the well-being of the toads of Toad Hall.'

There was a message on his answerphone when he reached home. His offer had been rejected and someone else had bought Toad Hall. He was not pleased to learn, later, that the purchasers were the family of Edmund Preese.

Caroline Power, known as Mrs Pen-Marr to most, had known from the moment they had met that she would never like Ancret. She found her distant and far less demonstrative of her feelings for Jonathan than a young woman should be towards the man she purported to love. Going over Lottie's story, she began to wonder whether the younger woman might not be the perfect daughter-in-law. Malleable, young, unambitious apart from an interest in Jonathan's own business, she would be a better wife and certainly a more affectionate daughter-in-law. She sat for a long time wondering what, if anything, she could do about it.

Talking to the girl would be an innocent enough start; after all, she had come to her when she was in trouble, hadn't she? But how could she arrange to meet her? It was useless going into the office. Either Jonathan or Lucinda would be there. She decided that a letter inviting Lottie to lunch or dinner on her day off would be seen as a kindly move and they would have a chance to talk. Inadvertently Jonathan helped.

'Mother, I've decided to reinstate Lottie, on condition she doesn't spread untrue gossip.'

'You owe her that much,' Caroline said primly. 'I'll put a little note in, shall I? Just saying how pleased I am that it's all being settled amicably?'

'That won't be necessary.'

'But I think I should. After all, where did she come when you upset her so badly? To me. I don't interfere with business matters, dear, but she came to me, and it would be rude of me not to respond to your decision.'

Reluctantly he agreed.


On Monday, Lottie asked for a lift home.

'Sorry,' Jonathan said at once, anxious to avoid a situation that could be misconstrued. 'I have to leave early as I have to go out again immediately.'

'You're going home then?'

'Yes, and I'm in a hurry. I don't have time to take you home. I'm sorry.'

'I don't mean my home, I mean yours!' She beamed at him. 'Your mother has kindly invited me to dinner.'

'What? When?'

'She put a note in with yours, the one in which you told me I was reinstated. She was so kind, telling me how sorry she was for my situation and inviting me to dinner.'

'Sorry for your situation?' he queried. 'What situation? I asked you to leave, then my mother persuaded me to give you another chance. Hardly a "situation".'

47

'I won't have time to go home and change, so I brought a dress and I'll put it on before we leave.'

'Sorry. I'm leaving now. You can lock up, can't you?' He hurried from the office and went to the hired car. This had to be stopped at once.

Caroline was in the kitchen when he reached home.

'You're early, dear. Is Lottie with you?'

'No, she isn't. And I want you to promise not to invite her here again.'

'Why? She and I get on so well, and I think she needs someone to talk to, someone who understands.'

'Mother, she was lying. I'm not attracted to her in the slightest. In fact, I'm beginning to dislike her. We depend on teamwork and if she doesn't fit in with Lucinda and myself she really will have to go.'

Caroline opened the packages of food from the freezer and began setting out plates.

'You can put one of those away. I'm eating out. And,' he added, 'I won't be back in time to take Lottie home. Right?'

Apart from the time she spent at Moments, Loraine rarely left the house. Ancret went out with Jonathan, or occasionally to see a film, but Loraine was always at home. When she visited the solicitor to see about the house sale and purchase, she made sure she knew Ancret would not call. She would never tell her daughter beforehand in case Ancret's curiosity overcame her honesty and she decided to search through her mother's private belongings. Loraine's bedroom door was usually locked whenever she expected to be out and there was a chance Ancret might return. A cleaner came once a week, but she wasn't allowed into the bedroom. Loraine's biggest fear was being ill and having to go into hospital, leaving everything open to prying eyes.

However, it wasn't an illness that eventually brought about the situation she dreaded, but an accident. Loraine always dressed formally – as though a visit to the shops was as important as an evening at the opera, Ancret used to joke – so wearing high heels was the norm.

The tip of a heel caught in a gap in the uneven paving. Shopping baskets flying, Loraine fell heavily into the road and was hit by a car. Fortunately it was travelling slowly and gave her nothing more than a glancing blow, but it was serious enough for her to be taken by ambulance into casualty.

Ancret went at once to the hospital, leaving Angela in the shop, and found her mother looking around her groggily, in a confused state. When she saw her daughter, Loraine's eyes darkened. 'Don't tidy my room,' she said. 'Don't search for clothes. Buy me some nightdresses and everything else I need. Promise me, Ancret.'

'I won't snoop. Mummy. I'll just put fresh sheets on the bed ready for when you come home.'

'No! Leave it, I'll see to it. Leave everything as it is. Promise me.'

Ancret left her mother in order to speak to the doctors, who told her they wanted to keep Loraine in overnight for observation but that she would probably be home the following day. 'There doesn't seem to be any serious damage, just some bruising and a few cuts. But we have to make sure she isn't suffering from shock.'

Jonathan was beside her mother's bed when Ancret returned and he was writing a list of things she needed. 'I'll go at once and get them,' he said, kissing Ancret and blowing a kiss to Loraine.

'That's kind of him, Mummy,' Ancret said.

'Maybe, but he isn't all he seems. Be careful of him, my daughter,' Loraine answered, her voice low, her eyes bright. Then the medication took effect and she slept. Ancret waited until Jonathan returned.

'I cheated,' he confessed in a whisper, as Ancret admired the silk top and smart trousers, the pretty underwear and night clothes. 'I sent Lucinda.'

They returned to the house and Ancret stood at the door of her mother's room. 'I'm so tempted,' she said.

'So am I,' he whispered, enfolding her in his arms. They kissed and he began to guide her towards her bedroom, but then he stopped.

'Why don't you find out what you can? There won't be a better time, will there? You needn't force any locks, but a look, just in case she's left anything informative on view, wouldn't do any harm.'

'I promised,' she said doubtfully.

'Just a look. You might never get another chance.'

Ancret peeped around the door. An envelope had fallen to the ground; half in and half out of it was a photograph, black and white and scuffed as though it had been screwed up and then rescued. She bent down and picked it up. The picture was of a man aged about thirty. He was tall, well over six feet measured against the doorway in which he stood, and very slim. Clearly a countryman, he wore riding clothes; jodhpurs and a check shirt and tweed jacket were visible under an open riding mac.

Tears blurred Ancret's vision as she stared at the photograph.

'Could he be my father?'

Jonathan hesitated. If she believed this man was her father, an apparently well-heeled country gentleman, would she relax in her search for him? Would it mean she would have enough confidence in his apparent respectability to marry?

'It's obviously been held and studied, so I think yes, it's very likely.'

Ancret stared at the picture, trying to read more than it could tell. Jonathan leaned across her and pulled the drawer fully open. He carefully lifted up scarves and from underneath pulled out a bank book. Ancret took it and saw that a payment had been made every month until her eighteenth birthday.

'So Mummy has been in touch with my father. So why am I not allowed to meet him?'

'He looks very respectable and I'm sure there's nothing sinister about his absence. It has to be something simple, like he and your mother couldn't get on. Or he could have been married,' he suggested gently. 'Have you thought of that?'

'Mummy wears a wedding ring and an engagement ring.' She stared at the photograph again. 'He looks respectable. But if he is, why haven't we been in touch? He must be a terrible person. There's no other explanation. What have I inherited? What's in me that I could pass on to my children?'

'Beauty and a loving heart?'

# Four

Jonathan had been very close to his Uncle Richard throughout his childhood. With his father working long hours and his mother following her career, he was often sent to the cottage outside Cardiff to spend time with Caroline's brother. But since leaving school and starting work – and, later, a business of his own – the need for his uncle had faded and now Jonathan rarely visited him.

Caroline was different. Whatever was happening in her life she always kept in close touch with her brother. It was rare for a week to pass without them meeting, either in town or at his home. One Sunday, when she had arranged to spend the day with Richard, Caroline decided to invite Lottie to go with her.

'A day in the country? That would be wonderful, Mrs Pen-Marr. Are you sure I wouldn't be a nuisance?'

'That you could never be, dear. And why don't you call me Caroline? We're past the need to be formal.'

Lottie drove, and they arrived as Richard was sweeping the path after clearing weeds from between the crazy paving. He was casually dressed in comfortable and rather worn trousers and sweater. Cut-down wellington boots covered his feet. His face, out of which blue eyes shone clear and welcoming, wore the rugged look of the outdoors man. His eyes crinkled as he offered his hand to Lottie. They took to each other at once, she seeing a kindly, gentle man, he a pretty, brightly intelligent young woman.

To Richard's delight, she wandered around the enormous grounds that included a small woodland and an acre or so of uncultivated grassland, asking questions and showing a little knowledge and a lot of interest.

They went to a nearby pub for lunch and the conversation

was lively, Lottie listening to Richard's stories about his and Caroline's childhood and relating some of the more amusing incidents that had happened at the office. They spent some time sitting in the garden in the shade of a mulberry tree which had a seat built around its trunk, and tea and cakes were served before it was time for them to leave.

'I'm sorry to see you go,' Richard said as he shook her hand. 'I hope Caroline will bring you again soon.'

As Lottie got into the car and Richard opened the door for his sister, Caroline said, 'Can I telephone Jonathan to tell him we're on our way, Richard?'

She dialled the number and Jonathan answered at once. His voice was sharp, as though she had interrupted something. 'I'm at Richard's, dear—' she began, when he interrupted, saying, 'All right, Mother, I'll be there in an hour.'

The phone was cut off and she stared at it. She made to press the redial, but stopped. It wouldn't be a bad idea for Jonathan to see Lottie here and notice how well they all got on, would it?

'Sorry, dears,' she announced when she went back outside, 'there's a bit of a mix-up. I think Jonathan was in a terrible hurry. He said he's on the way and now I can't get through, he's left the flat and shut off his mobile. So irritating. But we'll have to wait for him.'

They returned inside and Lottie went into the kitchen to clear the dishes. Caroline followed. 'Jonathan doesn't like coming here, not really. It isn't far from where his ex-fiancée used to live. Babs, she was called.'

'What happened?' Lottie asked.

'A difference of opinion about children. She desperately wanted children and Jonathan doesn't want a family, not ever.'

She watched Lottie's reaction when she said it, and was relieved when Lottie nodded. 'I'm with him there, I'd hate to be responsible for another life. I'm filled with admiration for people like you, bringing up a son to be so successful and well adjusted.'

'I admit I'm partly to blame for his attitude,' Caroline confessed girlishly. 'I was constantly complaining about how he dragged me down and spoilt my chances of a more successful career. He knows I love him, but there were regrets and I didn't hide them from him. Jonathan and I have always been honest with each other.'

'What happened to Babs? Has she married?'

'I don't know. She moved away. Not far, she lives somewhere in Cardiff. But we've never bumped into each other since they parted.'

'Pretty, was she?'

'Not as lovely as you, dear.'

When Jonathan arrived he was clearly annoyed at having wasted his time. 'Why didn't you tell me you had transport? Why phone me for a lift?' he demanded.

'You didn't give me a chance, dear,' Caroline scolded. 'Slapped the phone down before I finished a sentence. Then I couldn't get through.'

He had a brief look around the garden at Uncle Richard's invitation, listening as the year's plans were explained. But his lack of interest clearly showed in his irritable movements and vague responses.

He apologized to his mother, explaining that he had been involved in the end-of-month accounts. But when they left, Caroline travelling with Lottie and Jonathan on his own, he overtook them and was soon out of sight. He drove too fast, angry with his mother for her friendship towards Lottie, and with Uncle Richard for the pleasure he found in her company. He should never have been persuaded to take her back.

'That was an unfortunate end to a pleasant day,' Caroline sighed. 'Forgive his bad mood. He's such a busy man and I did inadvertently waste his precious time.'

'It didn't spoil it, though. I don't know when I was happier,' Lottie said, and Caroline smiled contentedly.

When Loraine came home from hospital, Ancret watched as she checked everything in her room, making sure it was all exactly as she had left it. Ancret smiled a little, aware that this time her mother's suspicions were justified, although her careful searches had revealed little to help her find her father. The move to the flat was imminent, so she begged her mother to rest before the inevitable disruption began.

'I need to be involved,' Loraine said, shaking her head. 'I don't want you to sell any of the furniture without my knowledge.'

'Mummy, as if I would. But we have far too much for the flat, some things will have to go.'

'No, daughter. We have to keep it for when we get a decent house.'

They spent the following hour moving from room to room, arguing about what they would leave behind. 'The furniture is too large for this house, and it'll look ridiculous in the modern flat,' Ancret protested. 'We wouldn't be able to move around. It would be impossible.'

'It won't be for ever. We'll move out as soon as we can. Until we do we have to put up with it. It all holds memories for me.'

'Memories I'm not allowed to share,' was Ancret's muttered reply.


Jonathan bought paint and arranged for workmen to go in and freshen the walls of the flat with a light colour chosen by Ancret. He took Ancret and Loraine to buy curtains, leaving them at the store on Sunday and promising to return for them in an hour. They waited an extra thirty minutes, then found a taxi, which pulled up at the same time as Jonathan outside their house.

'Sorry,' he explained as he hurried to help them out with their purchases. 'Mother had to go somewhere and I misjudged the time.'

'If he can't tell his mother no when the alternative means letting you down, where does that put you?' Loraine muttered as they went upstairs with their packages.

The place was difficult to live in as moving day drew near, and when Jonathan invited them both out for a meal Ancret eagerly agreed. 'Thank you, darling, that's a welcome invitation.'

'Anything to get away from this chaos,' Loraine said less politely.

A music festival was taking place in the city and the thoroughfares were thronging with crowds come to see the open-air entertainers. All the cafés and restaurants seemed to be full. The streets echoed to music from many sources, while locals and visitors alike were encouraged by the atmosphere into good-natured camaraderie.

'Shall we go further afield, try to find somewhere quieter?' Jonathan asked.

'What, and miss this? Not a chance!'

They finally found a table on the pavement outside a busy restaurant, where they sat and ate while enjoying the carnival mood around them.

'Wonderful,' Loraine said as a group of musicians in Spanish gypsy costumes stopped and played to them. Jonathan looked slightly embarrassed, but Loraine and Ancret gave the performers generous applause.

The atmosphere was like an enormous party. Everyone seemed to be a friend of everyone else. The mood of the city filled Ancret with excitement. 'Isn't this wonderful, Mummy?'

'And he thought you'd want to live in a lonely place like Toad Hall?' Loraine whispered, gesturing to point out Jonathan's less than happy face. 'He doesn't know you at all.'

In spite of the crowds all around her, and the music and laughter, Ancret felt momentary sadness as she imagined living in that beautiful old house. Nothing more than a dream, although the dream didn't include Jonathan.

People began to dance and when Jonathan shook his head, a voice said, 'May I have the pleasure?' Ancret looked up to see Edmund of the Toad Hall encounters offering his hand. Urged on by Loraine, she stood up and slipped into his arms, giving Jonathan a wide smile.

'Don't you like him?' Loraine asked innocently as the frown deepened on Jonathan's face.

'He's the one who bought the house I wanted for Ancret and me.'

'Oh? He must be rich as well as good looking.'

'His parents, more likely. He's little more than a driver-cum-errand boy, from what I've heard.'

'Handsome though.'

Dancing with any kind of style was impossible as several kinds of music filled the air, and people pushed and interrupted, but Ancret and Edmund held on to each other's hands and somehow managed to stay together. When they returned to the table, Jonathan stood. 'Sorry, darling, but it's time to leave. You and Loraine have a busy day tomorrow.' He turned to Edmund and added, 'They're moving house, you see.'

'Not far, I hope?' Edmund stared admiringly at Ancret, waiting for an answer.

Jonathan wanted to ask, What business is it of yours? But Ancret said, 'Not far. Mummy and I will be living over the shop for a while.'

'So they have to leave early.' Jonathan held out a hand to Ancret, which she ignored.

'Get us another drink, will you, Jonathan?' asked Loraine, moving up to allow Edmund to sit beside her. 'What will you have, Edmund?'

With ill grace, Jonathan supplied drinks and listened to Edmund telling them about his busy life caring for visitors to his parents' hotel. He was aware of Edmund's admiring glances towards Ancret, and none too pleased with the way Ancret responded to them. As soon as he could, he led them away.

'I like Edmund much more than Jonathan,' Loraine said when they were home.

'Mummy,' Ancret scolded, 'you like everyone more than you like Jonathan!'

'He's straightforward, no hangups. And,' she added, 'his parents now own Toad Hall.'

'Really? I wonder why Jonathan didn't tell me?'

'What a wonderful combination, daughter. Edmund, and Toad Hall. I wonder why he isn't married?'

'Stop it, Mummy,' Ancret said with a laugh.

'He was married once.' Loraine saw Ancret's face light up with interest and went on, 'She jilted him, then they married a few months later and after two years she grew tired of the family business and left. He divorced her, citing an employee with a small guitar.'

'Mummy, for someone who doesn't go further than the shop, you manage to keep well informed!'

\*　　\*　　\*

When the removal van arrived, Loraine stood beside her sealed boxes and insisted they went on last so they could be taken off first. As the final item was carried out, Jonathan organizing the men like a general with his troops, Ancret stood and looked around the empty rooms with regret. She and her mother had lived there for a long time and it was sad to say goodbye to a place where she had been happy.

'Shed a few tears for what's gone, darling, but remember, the best days are to come,' Jonathan said, holding her in his arms. 'And I'll be there to share them.'

Moving into the flat was extremely difficult; too many possessions crammed into too little space. Jonathan and the removal men had to stack several areas with some of the smaller pieces and most of the boxes had to be stored in the garage, which fortunately was empty. The only room left relatively uncluttered was the kitchen, and it was there they spent the first few evenings between struggles to manoeuvre the furniture around, trying one arrangement then another in an attempt to allow them space to move.

Jonathan came straight from the office the following day and again invited them out to eat, as the search among the unending piles of boxes had failed to produce any utensils. 'It's a pity I sold the old office,' he said. 'It would have been useful as storage.'

'I want my things here, where I can make sure they're safe,' Loraine replied. 'And what a useless remark anyway.'

Loraine's bedroom was the most orderly, as Ancret and Jonathan had dealt with it first. All Loraine's personal possessions were sealed tightly and so far none of them had been unpacked.

'She's determined to keep her secrets,' Jonathan remarked with a wry smile. 'I don't think she'll open them until she has a locked cupboard ready to keep them in.'

'If only she'd talk to me. I thought I'd be told when I was eighteen, and then twenty-one and now I'm twenty-four. How much longer will she make me wait?'

'I found this when we emptied her bedroom,' Jonathan said, holding out an envelope. 'I slipped it into my pocket and forgot it. D'you think she needs it?'

The envelope was empty, the name and address on it

unknown to either of them. As she hesitated, Jonathan said, 'We could go and find it? There might be someone there who knows something about your mother.'

Making the excuse of a need for fresh air and a walk, they went off in Jonathan's car to search for the place. Ancret's heart was racing as they drew near. Perhaps, today, she would learn something to lead her to her family, tell her who she really was. They eventually found it, only to discover that the street was now divided into a children's play area, a small park and a car park.

'Something is telling you to give up,' Jonathan said, aware of her disappointment. 'Darling, don't keep putting yourself through this.'

'I have to know,' she said, trying to hide tears of disappointment.

The dress shop had been busy as spring moved into summer. Ancret was finding it difficult to find sufficient time to work on her designs. She missed Helena, and although Angela was intelligent and quick to learn, Ancret soon realized she had to be in the salon most of the time; Angela still needed her on hand to help. It added to the stress of her workload. She would settle to work on a hat for a client, and then the shop doorbell would jingle and she would be distracted at once. So after she and her mother had eaten she would frequently return to the workroom and stay there until bedtime. Loraine understood and would often sit with her, helping with the work, discussing what Ancret was doing and on occasions offering suggestions.

She was working on an unusual commission, a hat to be worn in a carnival by someone for whom she hadn't designed before. The client, Mrs Piper-Davies, was a well-known charity worker with enough money to indulge herself when it came to special occasions. Ancret was not aware of the woman's friendship with Jonathan's mother. She did know that, if she was pleased with the first hat, besides further orders from the woman herself there would be introductions to many of her friends. Although it was little more than a joke hat, she had to make it as professional and appealing as possible. She wished the commission had been for something more conventional and she also wished she knew Mrs Piper-Davies better. Sometimes a little extra information about a client helped with how she saw and worked the design.

She had been asked to make a colourful felt bowler and even though it was very time-consuming, she had spent two weekends and several evenings on the project, starting from the beginning and making the felt from a good-quality merino fleece. Fortunately her mother did the preliminary washing, sorting and carding. Interlocking the fibres with soap, water and hand pressure was tedious and messy, but as it was something she hadn't done since college, Ancret enjoyed it with a childish pleasure.

She chose a random pattern of reds and pinks and greens and blues on a black background and now, at the shaping stage, she was pleased with the result. In an attempt to ensure she pleased her client, she had actually made two hats, each with a different colour scheme in case the first didn't please. She wanted this customer to be satisfied, she needed to be a first choice when she or her friends needed a hat for a special occasion, although she hoped that her willingness to accept this project wouldn't mean they'd think of her as solely a joke-hat designer.

On the day Mrs Piper-Davies was due she cleared the clutter from her workshop and displayed some of her better hats on stands around the room. The lighting in the workshop had been improved and the electrician had set up adjustable spotlights to enhance the effect of her displays. With luck she might be able to talk to Mrs Piper-Davies about her work and show some of her first-class workmanship.

She was nervous when the time for the appointment drew near. Loraine came down with a tray set for coffee, promising to bring the pot down as soon as the client arrived. 'Talk to her, daughter. Make sure she stays long enough for you to show your finest handwork. Try some on her and tell her how wonderfully they suit her.'

Mrs Piper-Davies rushed in precisely on time, her voice loud, making it clear that she was an important person in a hurry. Ancret took out the beautifully finished bowler, and watched with dread as the woman's mouth curled in obvious doubt.

'I'm not sure,' she said as Ancret carefully placed it on her head and offered her a hand mirror. 'Isn't it a bit dark?'

'You did ask for a base colour of black,' Ancret said, rustling through pages of her order book to find her initial notes.

'I know what I asked for, I know exactly what I asked for. My request was simple enough for a child to understand. It's for a carnival in which I am taking part, opening it in fact. Surely you understood that a carnival is an occasion for lightness and cheer? I thought you would know such things, I didn't realize I had to write everything down in minute detail.'

Staying calm with a great effort in the face of such rudeness, Ancret lifted some tissue paper and showed her the second hat. This one was similar to the first but with larger patches of bright colour, plus some criss-crossing embroidered by hand. 'I made a second in case you were unsure about the black,' she said, removing the first hat and placing the second on the woman's head. 'And I have made some additional decoration for you to choose if you wish.'

This one seemed to please Mrs Piper-Davies more than the first and Ancret began to relax. Picking up a small tray, she offered up felt flowers, some on ridiculously tall stalks, and unlikely birds and other exotic creatures, besides jewels, mirrors and tassels. 'Do any of these appeal?'

At that moment Loraine came in with the coffee pot and placed it alongside the tray.

'You may pour me a cup, cream but no sugar,' Mrs Piper-Davies said, glancing pointedly at her watch without looking at Loraine.

'May I? How kind,' Loraine murmured.

Ancret glared at her mother, sure her customer had heard, although no comment was made until the delicate china cup and saucer was handed to her.

'No. I think not,' Mrs Piper-Davies said finally. 'For one thing, I don't like the idea of there being two. Surely that's most unprofessional? What if I met someone wearing the same model?'

'The second will be discarded, I promise you that,' Ancret said at once. 'I just wanted to give you a choice as it's the first time I've designed a hat for you.'

'No,' the woman said emphatically. 'Thank you for your time.' Pushing the cup towards Loraine, she picked up her bag and coat and swished out of the door.

'Mummy! How could you?' Ancret said tearfully. 'You know how many hours those hats took to make.'

'I'm sorry too, I really am. But no one should speak to you as though you're some stupid servant. I wouldn't have allowed her to talk to Angela with such condescension and, if you're honest, neither would you. Surely we don't have to depend on people like that for survival?'

'It looks as though I'm going to have to lower my sights and make cheaper hats, doesn't it?'

'No, I think not,' Loraine said, mimicking the recently departed customer. 'We have to give it more time and hope for customers who deserve a hat designed by Ancret.'

As the days grew warmer and towards their longest, Caroline took Lottie to visit Uncle Richard with increasing regularity. She began to help in the garden, listening carefully to his tuition and impressing him with her efforts. She had always enjoyed growing things and her expertise and interest increased. Jonathan pretended it wasn't happening, changing the subject whenever the visits and the growing affection between his mother and Lottie were mentioned.

In June and July there was a spate of weddings and the order book filled up satisfactorily, although few of the hats were really expensive. Ancret consoled herself by being thankful that her name was becoming increasingly well known, and tried to remain content to be kept busy designing and making hats. Slowly the business grew. As the emphasis fell increasingly on wedding dresses, and clothes for the brides' and bridegrooms' mothers and other guests, clients were beginning to expect to find a suitable hat at the same time.

Angela was now more confident, capable of working on her own. With Loraine available to deal with alterations and fittings, she managed the shop and was now herself assisted by a Saturday girl, enabling Ancret to use the whole weekend making her hats. Helena had helped generously, had advertised the fact that a top designer had taken over her premises as though Ancret's involvement was new, and as compliments flew, the word spread. The only problem was finding sufficient hours in each day.

Ancret had stood the two time-consuming felt carnival hats on a shelf, to remind her never to submit to such a foolish whim again. She would eventually sell them, at a fraction of their cost, to a team of acrobats performing in Cardiff when street entertainment once again brought a magical atmosphere to the city centre on August Bank Holiday weekend.

Before that, however, a sad event dampened the summer cheer. Jonathan was surprised one evening when he came home to find his mother crying and being comforted by Lottie.

'Mother? What's happened?'

'Your Uncle Richard. He's had a heart attack.'

'Where is he? I'll take you to see him straight away.'

'No need, dear, I've just come back from the hospital. Lottie came straight away when I phoned the office and took me there.'

'Why didn't you phone *me*? You have my mobile number.'

'I always try the office first. And Lottie came at once.'

'Mother, he's my uncle. Didn't you think I'd want to go too?'

'I didn't think, dear, and Lottie is so kind.'

'I'll go straight away. Will you come with me? We can drop Lottie off on the way.' He glared at Lottie, hoping she would take the hint and leave, but she tightened her grip on his mother's hands and looked away.

'I'll stay here and wait for you to phone,' Caroline said.

'Then I'll make you a cup of tea. And perhaps you can eat a sandwich? She didn't have any lunch,' Lottie explained, still without looking at Jonathan.

'Why wasn't I told?' Jonathan demanded, but as his mother began to cry again, he turned away, gathered his jacket and went out.

Really, that girl was becoming a nuisance. Such a pity he'd been persuaded to reinstate her. Before starting the car he phoned Ancret.

'I'll come with you,' she said.

She was waiting outside the shop when he drew up and she got in, kissed him and settled in her seat. 'A heart attack? He lives alone, doesn't he? He could have been there for days, unable to get help. Who found him?'

'No one. He walked to the corner and phoned for help.'

'Then it might not be too serious?'

'We'll soon find out.' He drove in silence for a while, then said, 'Darling, I know you'll think this is unfeeling, but he has a cottage and a large garden. If he dies it will be my mother's. With planning permission it could be worth a great deal of money.'

'You're right, I do think it unfeeling.'

'Sorry. But I'm wondering what to advise my mother to do. My company won't deal with it, of course. That wouldn't be ethical, conflict of interest and all that. But she could sell it as one lot, or piecemeal to developers.'

'Then don't give her any advice. Let her make her own decisions. She gave up her home to get you started and I think she might not want to sell. Oh, Jonathan,' she gasped. 'I'm as unfeeling as you! I'm talking about the poor man as though he were already dead.'

'I hope he's all right, I really do, but I can't help thinking about the possibilities.'

'She might want to live there. It was her childhood home, after all, and she's never been happy in the flat.'

'She loves the good address,' he said with a smile. 'That, and using the name Pen-Marr impresses her new friends wonderfully.'

She repeated what he had once said to her before. 'It's a harmless enough deception.'

Richard was sitting up in bed and looked better than they had expected. His white hair was thin and a shining pink head shone through, looking as though it had been thoroughly scrubbed. Bright blue eyes smiled a welcome in the highly coloured face. He was startlingly thin, and the scrawny neck stuck, bird-like, out of old-fashioned striped pyjamas. Hands knotted with veins clutched the edges of the pyjama coat together as though he were ashamed of his thinness.

'How are you?' Jonathan asked anxiously. 'Is there anything you need?'

'Toothpaste and soap and shaving stuff, but Caroline is bringing all that in tomorrow. I'm fine, son. Nothing more than a false alarm really. The attack was fairly mild. But they tell me I'll stay in hospital for at least a week. Try to fatten me up, one of the nurses said, but I think it was a joke. I'll have tablets to take but that's all.'

'You seem to have learned a lot in a short while,' Jonathan queried. 'I thought tests took days?'

'Some do, but although I didn't phone your mother until today, I was here yesterday evening and from what they did then, they seem happy about things,' Richard said cheerfully. 'I reckon I'm good for a few years yet.'

'I'm glad to hear it,' Jonathan said, giving him a gentle hug.

'I'm pleased too,' Ancret said. 'Now, can I go to the shop and bring you anything? Something to drink? Something to help fatten you up?' she teased.

While Ancret was away looking for the hospital shop, Richard said, 'Lovely girl. You ought to marry her before someone else does.'

'I'm trying to persuade her,' Jonathan said. He frowned suspiciously. 'I'm careful to keep her away from handsome and eligible men. In fact, I wouldn't trust her with you. That's why I didn't offer to go to the shop!'

Richard laughed, then grew serious. 'I'm worried about your mother, Jonathan. She's unhappy in the flat. I think I could persuade her to move in with me. How do you feel about that?'

'I don't think she should. I'll arrange some help for you, and she can visit for a few days at a time. But not permanently. She's too old to look after an invalid.'

'I don't mean to look after me. I can afford help. She'd be free to come and go as and when she pleased. I wouldn't object to her inviting friends to stay. The house has been too quiet for too long. She's always loved it and I think she'd be happier there than where she is now. She hated selling the house, you know. More than she told you.' He stared at Jonathan's frowning face, his breathing becoming faster in a way that alarmed Jonathan. 'Will you think about it?'

'I will. Now I think you should rest. Forget about Mother moving in for the moment, just concentrate on getting back your health.'

Ancret returned with drinks, fruit and a few magazines, and soon after, they left.

'Did you manage to talk to the doctor?' she asked as they reached the car.

'No, it seems it's too early for a prognosis. I'll come again tomorrow and try to get some information then.' He turned on the ignition and, before moving off, said, 'I feel ashamed. I shouldn't have thought about property. He's a nice old boy, and I have him to thank for much of the happiness in my childhood. And Mother's fond of him. Let's hope he'll be with us for a long time yet.'

'I hope so too.' She reached over and kissed him. 'Don't feel ashamed. You wear your estate agent's hat so much of the time, you sometimes forget to take it off.'

'Talking about property, although I've lost Toad Hall I'm still reluctant to forget it. Would your mother like to see it, d'you think?'

'I think she'd love to.'

'On Sunday afternoon then. The new owners haven't moved in yet, they're having an extension built and renovations done and I've been given permission. It was easy when that Preese chap knew it was for you,' he added ruefully. 'I hope they aren't ruining it. I admit I'm curious to see what they're doing.'

'So am I. Although I'll never live there, I feel quite proprietorial towards it and its toads and I'd hate to see it spoilt.' Part of the pleasure – although she tried to deny it – would be seeing Edmund Preese again.

The garden was a shambles, with a cement mixer and piles of building materials spread untidily in front and at the side of the house. A short distance away, a barn was being converted, piles of stones and stacks of wood ready for the restoration. Once they were inside, the place didn't look very different from their previous visit. The carpets and curtains were the same. A leather suite and two fine old armchairs plus a long dining table and eight carved chairs were in situ; the patina developed by years of loving polishing had made the wood glow. The sun shone through the leaded windows and the place looked at its most attractive. Although there was very little else, the place didn't have the neglected and unloved look that often greets a new owner.

Upstairs the bedrooms were simply and comfortably furnished and the only upheaval was the plumbing, which was adding extra bathrooms and shower units to the largest rooms. Ancret showed her mother around as though it were her own and Loraine loved it. She began imagining how their over-large furniture would look in these more suitable surroundings, and followed Ancret from room to room like an excited child.

'I could imagine us living here,' she whispered to Ancret as they looked again at the bedrooms. 'Only it would have been with Jonathan. And even with this to offer he isn't the man for you.'

'Hush, Mother, he'll be a wonderful husband and father.'

'Don't let dreams of a house like this tempt you to rush into anything. Who knows what's around the corner?'

'Around the corner is the main, family bathroom,' Jonathan said as he followed them up, having heard the last few words. He didn't understand why Loraine and Ancret laughed, or why neither bothered to explain.

Reluctantly they left the house, locking it securely, and set off towards the car.

'Can I help you?' a voice asked. 'Oh, it's you again.'

'Hello, Edmund,' Ancret said. 'You remember my mother?'

'Of course.' Edmund looked at Jonathan. 'You do realize the place is sold, don't you?'

'Of course. I arranged with a Mr Preese to show Ancret's mother the place, as Ancret was rather taken with it.' Jonathan spoke sharply, a smile barely disguising his rudeness.

'I am Mr Preese. You must have spoken to my father.'

'It's lovely,' Ancret said. 'Lucky you.'

'Come whenever you wish,' he said. 'I'd be pleased to see you and your mother any time.' Without being more specific, he excluded Jonathan from the invitation. He walked them to the car.

When he'd gone, Jonathan said, 'Superior sod, showing us off the premises like an old retainer!'

'No, more like the new owner!' Ancret and Loraine laughed. Somewhat grudgingly, he joined in.

Richard was told he could go home after a few days. When Jonathan asked if she would like to move in and look after him, Caroline was delighted.

'Don't do too much, Mother, there'll be no need. Uncle Richard is arranging for extra help and you'll be there as a guest.'

'I'll enjoy looking after him, dear. He and I always got on well, and I love the house, it has so many memories. Nostalgia is so warming.'

She took several suitcases and a box or two and, on the day Jonathan brought Richard home, she was there. The house shone its welcome, the kitchen issuing forth the delicious smell of freshly baked cakes – an indulgence she had no intention of repeating.

After making sure they had all they needed, Jonathan left them to settle in. He went back to the flat, already dulled and less welcoming without his mother's bright presence. As he began to loosen his jacket he saw Lottie sitting on the couch.

'Shall I make you a cup of tea, Jonathan? You must be exhausted,' she said, getting up and helping to remove his jacket.

He jerked it back on to his shoulders. 'What are you doing here?'

'I left my camera here when I came yesterday,' she replied.

'Sorry I can't stay and help you search, but I have to go out. When you leave, will you leave your key on the table? My mother isn't staying here at present so you won't be needing it, will you?'

He drove to Moments and knocked on the door, his anger apparent in the fury of his fist's demand to be let inside. 'That damned woman was at the flat when I called to shower and change,' he said as Ancret opened the door.

'At what stage did she arrive?' she teased.

'Thankfully I'd only begun to remove my jacket,' he replied, before kissing her. 'She was sitting there completely at home, and got up to help me. It would be creepy if it weren't so annoying.'

'You should have let her go when you had the chance.'

'My mother is fond of her, and she's my ex-partner's niece.'

'Those aren't reasons. Some people are trouble and I have the feeling that she'll get worse rather than better. Make sure she returns the key – and without having another one cut!'

'She wouldn't!'

'She might.'

'There's only one solution. Marry me.'

'One day. Maybe.'

They went out for a walk around the busy city streets. Cardiff was buzzing with groups of young and old, some sitting at the cafés enjoying the last hours of a pleasant late-summer day, others dressed in blatantly sexy attire, heavy make-up and face-piercing jewellery, dashing along to the excitement of the nightclubs. Taxis spilled out more laughing groups of young people. Ancret confessed to feeling rather ancient.

'Yes, you're old enough to settle down to boring domesticity,' Jonathan joked.

'You wish!'

'But I don't. I want you to continue doing what you enjoy. You have a talent which shouldn't be wasted and today there's no reason you can't have both.'

'I know it's difficult for you to understand, but I'm still blocked from committing myself to you because of the secrets my mother holds.'

'If you really want to know, why haven't you been to St Katherine's records office?'

'I don't even know where I was born. I even doubt whether my birth date, October the twenty-fifth, is correct. Mother was so determined to cover her tracks I have nothing to go on, nothing at all.'

'Then forget it.'

'I can't.'

They went to see Caroline and Uncle Richard several times during September and Caroline showed no great desire to return to the flat. On their first visit it was clear Caroline had been shopping. The living room had been transformed from dowdy browns and greens and was scattered with cushions of every hue, mainly pinks. Caroline was dressed in what she considered country wear. A skirt of rust and brown and gold, a hip-length gold top edged with dark red, on which she wore six or more gold chains. Gold earrings dangled and tinkled as she moved, a hair decoration sporting more touches of gold. As always, finding the colour irresistible, she had a stole wildly patterned in gold and shocking pink. Nothing matched, nothing blended, but to Jonathan his mother was a beacon of light and happiness that made him aware of how much he missed her every time he returned to the flat.

'Would you mind if I stayed a while longer, Jonathan dear?' she asked one Sunday when they had been invited to lunch.

'If you want to stay I have no objection. I just want you to be happy.'

'Then I think I would like to make it permanent.'

'As long as it isn't too much for you.'

'Too much? I don't have to do a thing, dear. The daily help and the handyman-cum-gardener keep everything running smoothly between them, and Richard and I go for pleasant walks and eat out when the weather tempts us. I'm enjoying the company, and the reminiscences. I couldn't be happier – just as long as you're managing all right without me.'

'I'm fine. And you know the flat is there if you ever want to come back,' he added, aware that if Richard were the victim of another attack, everything might change in a brief moment.

Moments continued to be busy. To Ancret's delight, Helena came back permanently to help out part time, Jeremy's health having improved. She had been thankful to return to the shop she had once owned.

Summer had ended with garden parties and a surprising number of weddings and christenings. Ancret worked long into the night on occasions, Loraine alongside her, their nimble fingers working at designs that were sometimes carefully planned and at other times evolved as they played with the material.

Ancret was sometimes aware of her mother staring at her and once or twice they had spoken at the same time. On those occasions Loraine always insisted on hearing what her daughter had been about to say. 'It's bound to be more important than anything I can tell you.' Ancret was always filled with an aching disappointment, believing she had been about to learn something of her past and that the imminent confidence had been spoilt by the coincidence of their thoughts. Try as she might, she had never succeeded in persuading Loraine to talk.

To her surprise she opened the door one day to see Mrs Piper-Davies standing there.

'Sorry,' Loraine called. 'Ancret only sees people by appointment.'

Stifling a chuckle, Ancret apologized and offered a card with her name, address and phone numbers on it. 'There aren't any appointments available for three weeks,' she said almost gleefully. 'But if you'd phone after that time—?'

When the woman walked away, Ancret and Loraine hugged each other. 'Daughter,' Loraine said, 'I think you've arrived!'

A few days later they saw Mrs Piper-Davies outside with another well-dressed, fashionable woman. They had stepped out of a car and were looking at the window. Ancret heard her say in her penetrating voice, 'Her reputation might be growing, but I couldn't buy from a sad little place like this, could you?'

'Her prices are very good, I understand,' the second woman said.

'So what? To know they're cheap doesn't exactly add to their appeal.'

'Oh, they're far from cheap, dear,' the woman protested as she was encouraged somewhat hastily back into the car.

'She's coming round,' Loraine prophesied. 'She might be feeling a bit put out but she's coming round.'

With Angela and Helena able to handle everything that happened in the clothes department, Ancret and her mother now dealt solely with hats. The prices she now charged were more in keeping with the quality and designs and the business was already beginning to turn around from its slow beginnings. This year she had missed Royal Ascot as she had not been sufficiently well known for people to trust her, but next year would be different. Large numbers of men and women travelled to the prestigious race meeting from Cardiff and the surrounding area, and women went in coachloads for Ladies' Day. They all needed a special, and if possible a unique hat.

When Ancret had a preliminary discussion with her accountant, everything looked on course for a good year. Her life was working out perfectly; exactly as she had hoped. It was then she discovered she was pregnant.

It was the lateness of her period that first made her curious. There was no sickness, and no other symptoms apart from an unusual tiredness that prevented her from spending time on her hats so late into the evening. She had put that down to overworking and the need for a rest.

The possibility came as a heart-racing shock. Surely it wasn't possible? She took her pill without fail, conscious of the importance of avoiding a pregnancy before she was ready for it. But a testing kit from the chemist, bought somewhere she was unknown, confirmed it.

She sat on her bed, feet jammed between the bedside table and a box of books, and looked around her. How could she have a child? She didn't even have a proper home. And marriage to Jonathan under these circumstances was absolutely out of the question. He mustn't even know. At least, until she had decided what she would do.

Making a decision was difficult. Her thoughts were unclear, contradictory. One minute she wanted to run to Jonathan, the next she wanted to run away and hide her head, ostrich-like, in the hope it would all go away.

She needed to talk to someone, but she stubbornly held back from saying the words that would make it official. The outcome would be inevitable – marriage to Jonathan, a child to put before her career and for whom she would be respon-sible for ever, a lifelong interference with her plans. She couldn't marry for the wrong reason. She couldn't, wouldn't.

She went out for long walks alone, often late at night, making the excuse that she was stale and stiff after long hours of the close work. September ended as her limited choices swam in front of her mind. She didn't visit a doctor until she had made up her mind that an abortion wasn't the solution, and neither was bringing up a child in the cramped flat above Moments.

'Your baby is due in March,' the doctor said after examining her and making copious notes. She guessed the young woman was not completely filled with joy at the prospect of motherhood.

'I haven't made up my mind about keeping him,' Ancret said.

'You realize it's getting late to consider a termination, of course?'

'I hadn't thought—'

'It's due in March,' the doctor reminded her gently.

Ancret began counting, her slender fingers moving with her lips as she chanted the months. 'That's five months' time? So soon?' She thought of her absentmindedness with deep regret. She had been so busy, the hours and days and weeks melting into a haze of dress shop and workshop and struggling to live in the overcrowded flat, that she had allowed all this time to pass without realizing what a child could have worked out.

'You have plans for when the baby is born? There are people you can talk to if you envisage problems.'

'I'll need someone to look after him, but I can deal with that myself.' Ancret spoke, but her voice sounded far away and as though it belonged to someone else.

'Don't struggle on your own. Come back if you need any help. You'd be amazed at just how much is available.'

'There is one thing.'

'Yes?'

'Please don't tell my mother. I'll tell her myself when the time is right.'

'Of course. But mothers are a wonderful support, and any initial disappointment they might display quickly fades at the prospect of being a grandmother.'

Ancret didn't disagree, she just thanked the doctor and promised to deal with all the necessary tests, then left.

The doctor stared at the closing door. There was something unusual about this pregnant mother. A distinct lack of either excitement or dismay. She had a feeling that she might not see her again. Both Ancret and her mother were patients who kept themselves private, none of the usual chatter when they visited the surgery. She was a little worried but, with her promise to Ancret, she couldn't call and enquire on her progress. She jotted down her notes and hoped the girl would come back to talk to her. Whatever the problem, Ancret seemed in need of a friend.

Ancret went to see Jonathan, but with no clear intention in mind. While they sat drinking coffee in one of the pavement cafés, the words came at once, almost of their own volition. 'I might be pregnant.'

His reaction was frightening. 'No, you can't be! I've been so careful. You mustn't have this child. I can't allow it, not under any circumstances, d'you understand?'

'Jonathan, what's so terrible about a child? I know we decided not to think about it, at least for a few years, but—'

'Not ever. I can't have a baby. If you're pregnant you'll have to arrange an abortion. Now. Let's go and see a doctor now, get it settled before you begin to feel emotional.'

'Jonathan. What's the matter?'

His face was pale and his eyes wider than normal in his anxious face. 'Tell me it isn't true?'

'I don't understand.'

'I was engaged to Babs but she became pregnant. Twice. Even though she knew I never wanted a child.'

'What happened? Where are the children? Are you telling me you have children and haven't told me?'

'She had an abortion. I couldn't let her have my child, you see.'

The shock and disbelief silenced her and she stared at him, waiting for him to tell her it wasn't true, that she had misunderstood him. He had forced Babs, a woman he loved, to abort two babies? Destroyed two lives?

'Tell me it isn't true, Ancret,' he said in a low voice. 'I couldn't bear it, not again.'

'It isn't true.' Her voice was flat, toneless, as though it was coming from someone else. 'I had a brief scare, that's all. It's over now. I was teasing, that's all, making you suffer the same fright as me.'

He stood up and walked away from her without looking back.

So, the decision was made. She was on her own with this child and Jonathan would never know. She hurriedly left the café, head down to hide the tears that she couldn't stop from rolling down her cheeks.

'Ancret? What's the matter? Can I help?'

She looked up to see Edmund in front of her, offering a large white handkerchief.

'No, there's nothing anyone can do,' she said between sobs.

'I saw Jonathan storming off, so I presume you've had a quarrel. Please, Ancret, don't marry a man who makes you cry.'

She held on to his handkerchief and hurried away.

Using the excuse that she needed a break, Ancret left the shop in Helena's care. She visited several agencies and those agencies passed her on to others. Her enquiries led to dead ends, and after a week during which she got exactly nowhere she was exhausted. Another week passed and she was on the point of telling Loraine and Jonathan the truth.

There seemed nowhere to turn for the kind of help she needed, yet it must be out there somewhere. Everyone said that it was possible to work and have a child in the twenty-first century. So where was this wonderful network of problem solving to be found?

She needed at least to find the information to allow her to consider the best arrangements. She had to have her answers ready in case her mother guessed. Loraine was shrewd and had flashes of knowledge without explanation. This was her baby, her problem, and no one must be allowed to persuade her to do something against her will.

Then one day, while Ancret was at the hairdressers, Loraine came across a magazine on which several addresses had been ringed. She knew that her suspicions were confirmed. Ancret was carrying a child. She felt the sadness of isolation. Why hadn't Ancret confided in her?

The addresses referred to fostering. She tore up the magazine. They wouldn't need help from strangers. They would cope; she'd dealt with worse and survived. Her daughter would manage as efficiently as she once had.

Although she hoped that Jonathan providing financial help wasn't part of any plan. No, enquiries about fostering suggested she wasn't going to tell him. That at least was good news.

She went to the library and searched the papers and magazines for a child-minding service. One of the names listed brought her leaping out of her chair. A phone call, during which she didn't speak, and the situation was confirmed. She took the paper, tucking it under her coat as she walked past the librarian and hurried home. She threw the paper, open at the relevant page, on to the table. The rest was up to a quixotic fate.

Ancret walked around the streets at night, considering first one possibility then another until her head ached. Whatever she decided, Jonathan would not be considered. After the way he had treated Babs he hadn't the right. Adoption was not a consideration. This was her child and nothing would make her part from him. But child-minding was a possible solution. If only she could find the right family, they could care for her child until she was able to bring him home with a story of having adopted him.

The more she thought about it, the more it seemed the right way forward. It would be expensive, but thank goodness the business was beginning to grow and should be able to stand it.

Avoiding Jonathan was fairly easy, but keeping her problem from her mother was difficult. She knew Loraine was beginning to worry about her regular absences and vagueness, and she longed to tell her. But until she had reached her own decision she would keep it to herself.

The advertisement was small, but something led her eyes to it. She made an appointment to see Mr and Mrs Flowers. They lived a double bus journey away from the shop but, having checked on transport, she was confident of getting to them without difficulty.

'They greeted her warmly, introduced themselves as Marguerite and Simon, called their two sons down from their playroom to be introduced, and showed her around their pleasant home. Every room was bright, cheerful and clean, and after checking every reference they gave her she decided that she would employ them to look after her child.

The house was at the edge of the city; fields behind it led up to a hill bordered by a farm and woodland.

'We used to play up there when we were children,' Simon told her. 'Gypsies camped there every year and worked on the farms around.' He laughed. 'Don't worry, we won't allow your baby to wander. Times have changed and we rarely see the gypsies any more.'

As she sat in the taxi back to the railway station she touched the scar on the side of her left hand where a tiny, residual finger had been removed at birth. She wondered if her child would have the same small disfigurement and hoped he would. There was something about sharing such a distinctive scar that would give her a strong sense of belonging. She wondered sadly if, somewhere, she had relations with the same distinguishing mark.

Her next problem was how to get through a pregnancy and birth without her mother knowing. At first consideration it seemed an impossibility, but slowly an idea formed. The flowing, loose-fitting garments she usually wore were a distinct advantage, she thought with a smile. She might get away with a couple more months before she needed to disappear.

'Mummy,' she announced one evening as they sat eating their meal in the uncomfortable kitchen. 'D'you think you, Helena and Angela could manage for about eight weeks without me?'

'Eight weeks? What on earth will you be doing for eight weeks?'

'I've been asked to run a course on design and it's in North Wales. I wouldn't be able to get home as there'll be weekend students as well as the day and evening courses.'

'You can't disappear for eight weeks. What will happen to your business? That's a very long time.'

'Luckily it's the right time of year. From now till Christmas and through till April is traditionally quiet. I'll be back in time for the build-up to the spring weddings – and hopefully Ascot, this year.'

They discussed it for a long time until most of Loraine's concerns had been dealt with.

'What does Jonathan think of you leaving him for two months?' was Loraine's final question.

'I haven't told him yet. D'you think he'll be upset?'

'I doubt he'll be thrilled. But it won't be a bad thing, you having time apart to think about how you really feel about him.'

'I know how I feel about him, Mummy. I think I want to marry him one day, but not yet.' She was lying. She could never trust him after his revelation about Babs and her two lost babies.

'Passion is sadly lacking if you can wait without a reason.'

'I want to be really established before I commit myself to marriage and all that entails.'

'Children?'

'Children,' Ancret replied slowly. 'Now there's a thought.'

# Five

Jonathan stared at Ancret in utter disbelief. 'What on earth are you talking about? Going away for two months? Where? And why?'

'It's a favour to a friend from college. She has to go abroad with her husband and she wants me to stand in for her.'

'But you can't. How can anyone expect you to leave your growing business to save her job? Ancret, this doesn't make sense.'

'All right, if you want the truth, I need to get away for a while and this seemed a perfect opportunity.'

'If you want a holiday I'll arrange one. Where d'you want to go? Tell me where and when and leave the rest to me. You only had to ask and I'd have done whatever you wanted, you know that. There was no need for all this rigmarole. I wouldn't need persuading. And it isn't like you to play games.'

'This isn't a game. I'm going to take over from Mary and I don't want to discuss it. It will give me a chance to sort out my feelings for you and to decide what I want to do with the rest of my life.'

They were sitting in the car outside Moments, having returned from an evening at the cinema and supper at one of Cardiff Bay's favourite eating places.

'Ancret, please tell me this is a joke.' He placed a hand on her thigh and she pushed it gently away. The telltale swelling of her burgeoning pregnancy was becoming too obvious to conceal. She had to avoid intimacy and get away soon, or he would guess.

'I have to go in. Mummy won't sleep until I'm home.'

'For once Mummy will have to wait,' he said, anger rising. 'I want you to tell me why you're doing this. You can't just leave without an explanation.'

'No, you're right, I can't. But can we talk about it another time? I'm very tired. I was up at six and working before half past, it's been a long day.' She opened the door and stepped out of the car. He called something after her, but she didn't hear as she hurriedly let herself in through her door.

She lay in bed and thought through what she had planned. The arrangement for Mr and Mrs Flowers to care for the child seemed satisfactory, although she would have to visit often in the first weeks to assure herself that all was well, and contact the doctor and clinic in their area. Social Services needed to be informed and they would make their own investigation to ensure the safety of the child, even though it was a private arrangement. So far as arrangements for the child were concerned, everything that could be done had been done, but the more she thought about the imaginary work in North Wales the more impossible it seemed.

How would she contact her mother and Jonathan without telling them her address? Phoning was easy – dialling 141 before a call would ensure the number was withheld. But what if she forgot? Jonathan would discover where she was and come to find her. Or if there was an emergency and they needed to contact her urgently? What if her mother were ill, or had an accident?

She slept fitfully, more problems presenting themselves each time she woke. She rose at six o'clock convinced that she would have to tell Jonathan and her mother about the baby. For her to be able to keep it a secret she would need help, and who could she turn to for that? She wallowed in self-pity for a while, imagining having a family. Brothers, sisters, cousins and aunts, the support team taken for granted by so many. Something she would never have.

She slipped on a dressing gown and went quietly down the stairs, hoping not to disturb her mother. But Loraine was already up, dressed, and with a cup of tea at her elbow was sitting at the table going through the order book and noting delivery dates on a separate list. She put down her pen and stared at Ancret. 'Have you told him?'

'Yes. I'll be leaving straight after Christmas.'

'Christmas,' she said thoughtfully. 'And when do you intend telling me the truth?'

'Mummy?'

'I've known for weeks and I've been waiting for you to tell me. Do you intend to?'

Ancret collapsed into a chair. Resting her elbows on the table, she slumped forward, her chin in her hands, staring in disbelief at her mother. 'You know?'

'I know you're expecting a baby. And as weeks have passed and you haven't disappeared for an afternoon and returned looking upset, I presume you haven't aborted my grandchild?'

Ancret burst into tears. Her mother sat waiting silently, her dark eyes showing no emotion, until the tears subsided and Ancret relaxed.

'Do you intend to have the child adopted?' Loraine asked calmly. 'I'd like to know. I imagine, as you haven't told Jonathan that he's about to become a father, that you don't plan to keep it.'

'Mummy, I'm sorry. I should have trusted you.'

'Yes, you should. You should have known that I'd support you whatever you decide. In the present instance, I certainly wouldn't persuade you to marry the father.'

'What do you have against Jonathan? He's kind and loving and I know he'd be a good husband.' She looked away from her mother's knowing eyes, remembering Jonathan's confession that he had persuaded Babs, a woman he purported to love, to abort his children.

'I've always had a feeling that there's a veil in front of him, a barrier keeping people out. If you were completely sure of him you wouldn't be making up lies yourself, would you? He's going to be a father and that's a huge secret to keep from him. When will you tell him? When the child is five years old and going to school? I don't think you've thought this through at all, my daughter. You can't suddenly present him with a child and say, Oh, by the way, this is your son, can you?'

Ancret made some fresh tea. As they sat drinking it, she said, 'What can I do?'

'Either tell Jonathan, or have a row with him and finish it. That way, if he does learn about the baby he just might be able to excuse you for keeping it from him.'

80

Ancret stared at her mother. This was not how she expected her to behave, to be as dishonest as she herself was planning to be.

'You mean that I might be excused for not telling him by the fact that we were estranged? That's just as dishonest and even more devious.'

'But it gives you a better way out – or rather back in – if you need one.'

Ancret began by pretending, to Angela and to the few customers with whom she had developed a friendship and who might notice, that she was overeating. 'Comfort eating,' she explained, 'probably overwork. And Jonathan and I aren't getting on too well.' She was fortunate in that she was not putting on a lot of weight. With her usual loose-fitting clothes, her pregnancy was still not apparent.

Lottie visited Jonathan's mother and Uncle Richard quite often, having promised to keep an eye on Jonathan and report any problems.

'I don't think he's in the flat very much, but I do wonder whether he deals with the laundry as he should,' she told Caroline on one visit. 'One day last week he was wearing the same shirt as the previous day. That isn't like him, is it?'

'There's no need for him to do that. He has a very extensive wardrobe.'

'I know. He usually looks impeccable. That's why I was worried.'

'Would you go to the flat and make sure everything is all right, dear?' Caroline asked. 'I don't like leaving Richard for long. He seems well enough, but he still gets very breathless at times.'

'I can't just go in without an invitation,' Lottie protested. 'Besides, I don't have a key any more.'

'That's easily remedied. I can get a spare cut from mine. Please, dear. I do worry about him, even though he's a grown man. And I trust you to be discreet. Go after work when you know he and Ancret are eating out.'

'All right.' She sounded reluctant. 'Although it isn't that easy. You see, I don't think they're as close as they were. I think there's a distinct cooling off in their relationship.'

'Oh, what a pity,' Caroline said gleefully, raising her hand to show crossed fingers.

'There's something else,' Lottie said, and Caroline moved closer in the hope of interesting gossip. 'Lucinda told me that Ancret is going away for a few months, North Wales I understand, to some college where she'll teach design. Fancy leaving Jonathan alone for all those weeks. And she isn't even coming back at weekends.'

'What an unkind thing to do. She can't care for Jonathan or she wouldn't be able to contemplate such a thing.'

'Don't worry, Caroline. I'll be there for him and I'll do anything I can to make sure he's not lonely.'

'Thank you, dear. He doesn't deserve a friend like you.'

Lottie went to the flat the following lunchtime, gathered up some shirts and towels and put them through the washing machine. While the first programme ran she tidied up and pushed the cleaner over the carpets. She went back at five thirty, folded everything and put it away. The shirts were ironed and on hangers outside the wardrobe in Jonathan's bedroom. She was gone before he returned.

Lottie was pleased with the way things were going. She knew that the way to Jonathan's heart was via his mother. No such thing as being indispensable? she mused. Well, she would be as close to that as possible. Caroline liked – even needed – people running around after her, spoiling her and making her feel special. She also needed to know what was happening in her son's life. In fact, Lottie thought, Caroline was slowly being revealed as the kind of mother who wanted to take over her son's life completely, giving herself a role greater than that of wife. She was gently demanding, in a way that made it impossible for Jonathan to refuse any request she made. Young as she was, Lottie had worked out that the only way to have a successful relationship with Jonathan was to become his mother's trusted partner. With Ancret out of the way, she would make sure Jonathan and Caroline realized how suitable she would be for the role of wife to a successful businessman.

Jonathan looked around at the freshly vacuumed carpets and the evidence that the laundry had been dealt with, and smiled. It must be Mother, he decided, and dialled her number.

'I don't have to follow you around to make sure you're being looked after,' she said enigmatically.

Ancret too had a key to Jonathan's flat. She went along one Sunday morning resolved to settle the situation. He invited her inside but she moved away as he tried to kiss her. 'I can't stop, I have a hat to finish before Tuesday,' she said, throwing her handbag on the armchair. Best to stay away from the couch where he could sit beside her.

'Then you have a reason for the call?' he asked with a forced smile. 'Do you have time for lunch somewhere? Or a drink? Or even a kiss or two?'

'I've come to tell you I'll be leaving at the end of December. I don't have an address but I'll phone as soon as I'm settled.'

'If you have time!' he retorted. 'I understand how unimportant I am. This woman whom you met at college and haven't seen since, or even mentioned as a one-time friend, is far more special than me. She even manages to make you neglect your precious business. I wonder where I went wrong?'

'Stop this, Jonathan.' Ancret stood up. As she reached for her handbag, her fingers touched something at the side of the cushion. She tugged at it and out came a woman's evening bag, gold with a chain handle.

'Yours?' she asked sarcastically. 'How surprising.'

'It must be one of my mother's.'

'It's certainly her style,' Ancret said. She opened it and saw the credit card wallet inside. Two cards were tucked into its transparent slots and one showed backwards. 'Lottie's,' she said, throwing it towards him. She had come with the intention of creating an argument, and this was a gift. 'So who does she come to see, now your mother isn't here? Sorry for you, is she? Poor, lonely, helpless bachelor?'

Jonathan frowned, ignoring her apparent anger. 'So that's it,' he said slowly. 'Mother has arranged for her to come in and clean and deal with the laundry.'

'Oh, really?'

'Yes, and I'm quite capable of coping with it myself. If there's something I can't or won't do, I can pay for help. I thought Mother had been here but she must have asked Lottie to come. Damnation, that girl is a pain.'

'An evening bag with perfume and a lipstick and nothing else. I wonder where she could have been going?' She felt silly making a fuss about what was obviously an honest mistake, but it would be difficult to find a better opportunity. She opened the door and hurried out, ignoring him as he called her name, first pleadingly, then with a tinge of anger.

She felt ashamed of her childish behaviour, but her guilt was eased when she reminded herself of his behaviour towards Babs. Better this stupid nonsense than face a humiliating situation like that poor girl had gone through. Engendering dislike was easy when she imagined the distress Babs must have suffered.

'Well, Mummy, I've created a row and walked out. Such a childish argument about that stupid girl in his office. I felt about twelve years old and a backward child at that! Now I have to leave before he comes here and tries to make it up.'

'You don't have to go to North Wales,' Loraine told her. 'I've found a house with two rooms to let, with a large kitchen in which you might be able to work. I can take orders, do the basic measurements, collect the hats and bring them here.'

'But isn't that too close to home?'

'Who will see you? I doubt whether you'll be going out much. I'll keep you too busy for much socializing. You have to get a stock ready for the spring weddings when you come back.'

'Oh, Mummy, what have I done? Why did I dig myself this hole?'

'Better than burying yourself in an unfortunate marriage.'

'Why did I not tell him about his child?'

'Love is unconditional. If you loved him you would have told him the minute you knew.'

'I tried,' she admitted. 'Mummy, he went a little crazy, out of his mind with shock. He said he never wanted a child. Ever. Babs wanting one was the reason they ended their engagement,' she lied. 'But although he insisted he'd never

84

want a child, he offered no explanation and it seemed so irrational. Not like Jonathan at all.' She looked at Loraine sadly. 'I'm afraid for myself too. Committed to Jonathan for life, that's what this baby would mean if I told him.'

'Did you think of having an abortion?'

'It was already too late before I realized it, and got around to facing it and thought about actually doing something. But no, I couldn't have destroyed a life.'

'So it's Jonathan you're rejecting?'

'I suppose it is.'

'Something is telling you not to commit yourself to him. Maybe, over the next few months, you'll understand why.'

'But an argument about that stupid Lottie, of all things. She's a child. Years younger than Jonathan. How pathetic I sounded, accusing him of seeing her in his flat. His explanation was so obviously true. I was so—'

'Hormonal, as he'll realize when – or if – you eventually tell him about the baby.'

Jonathan phoned several times over the next few days, and either Loraine or Ancret quickly replaced the receiver. He knocked on the door when the shop was closed, and tried to get through the shop when it was open. Angela apologetically refused to unlock the door leading to the living area. After a week all attempts at contact ceased.

Ancret was confused. She was unreasonably hurt at his lack of determination, while at the same time she counted the days before she could escape. With winter darkening the days and giving a chill to the air, she rarely went out. Hats in their early stages, various crowns and brims, and dozens of trims prepared for the final decoration, filled every corner of the already overcrowded premises. As Christmas approached she was filled with dread.

Facing this alone was not going to be easy. Several times she was tempted to call Jonathan and tell him about the baby. But something held her back, and by this time she was no longer sure what the reasons were for her deceit.

Lottie continued to work in the office and became a go-between for Jonathan and Caroline. He was unable to visit his mother and Uncle Richard often, but Lottie went on her day off and sometimes on Sundays as well. She continued to check on Jonathan's flat too, reporting to his mother on the boxes of ready meals she regularly found in the waste bin. This had Caroline tut-tutting as though she were the kind of mother who cooked fresh food daily, something she had never done.

Lottie spent one whole day at Richard's home during the week she was on holiday. While Richard advised and occasionally helped out, she cleared the weeds from an overgrown flower bed. She was tired but happy when she left to drive home, and promised to go back the next day to finish the digging. 'Don't you try and do it,' she warned Richard.

'Don't worry dear, I won't let him do too much,' Caroline said as she kissed her goodbye, but Richard was already carrying heavy forkfuls of vegetation from the neat pile Lottie had left, to the bonfire site further away from the house. The following morning he was unwell and the doctor called and arranged for him to go back into hospital.

So it was from Lottie that Jonathan learned of his Uncle Richard's second heart attack. He drove down and found his mother tearfully getting ready to go to the hospital. Lottie arrived a few minutes later.

'Why have you come?' Jonathan asked, politely, due to his mother's presence. 'There was no need. And you should be helping Lucinda in the office.'

'I asked her to, dear,' Caroline explained. 'She's so good at keeping me calm.'

'Lucinda will stay for the last hour, her mother is coping with the children,' Lottie added, putting an arm around Caroline's shoulders and leading her away.

'It needs more than one person,' Jonathan called, but there was no indication they had heard.

Lottie led the distressed woman into her bedroom and helped her choose something to wear. She understood Caroline's tastes by this time and when Caroline's fingers hesitated on a dark blue, formal suit, she pulled out a more cheerful one, rosy pink with an apricot scarf. 'You don't want to look sad and miserable when you visit someone in hospital,' she said encouragingly, as Caroline hesitated.

'I was thinking the blue would be more suitable,' she said,

pulling out the skirt from the over-filled rail. 'But you're right, as always. I don't want to look as though I'm in mourning, do I?' She held up the pretty suit while Lottie searched through her shoes for a suitable colour. 'It will cheer me as well as my brother.'

The three of them waited at the hospital while Richard was made comfortable and then they were advised by the doctor to go home. 'Come in tomorrow, we'll know more then. Try not to worry, we'll do everything we can. And if there's a change we'll telephone you.'

'That doctor didn't sound very hopeful,' Caroline said, holding back tears. Jonathan stayed with his mother, knowing how she would hate being alone in the house, dreading a telephone call summoning her to Richard's bedside.

Lottie came at the weekend and worked on the flower bed, digging and clearing the roots. 'I'm determined Richard won't do anything so silly again,' she told Caroline.

Richard came home a week later. Lottie arrived as he was getting out of Jonathan's car and, leaving the two of them to settle him in, she went out and cleared the last of the rubbish and started a bonfire. She genuinely enjoyed clearing the untidy areas and seeing the earth neatly dug ready for the spring planting. And there were pleasurable yet inexplicable childhood memories in the smell of wood-smoke.

Jonathan came out as she was covering the flames with turf to encourage the fire to burn at its heart. 'It should last all night and there won't be much left for Richard to worry about,' she explained.

'Thank you, Lottie. You've been so kind to my mother.'

'I like her,' she said simply. 'I enjoy her company and unless she hints that she's had enough of me, I'll continue to visit – if that's all right with you,' she added with a frown.

'It's fine, just fine,' he said, leaving her hastily and returning to the house. How could he be polite to her and at the same time avoid her thinking there was something more in his manner? Where was Ancret? Why had she left him at such a time, and after that stupid quarrel?

On impulse, he telephoned again. Loraine told him Ancret was out. 'Just out?' he asked. 'Or out of my life, for good?'

'How would I know that?' Loraine asked. She looked quizzically at her daughter, who shook her head vehemently, and replaced the phone.

Jonathan took Uncle Richard, his mother and Lottie to a nearby pub for a meal. During the lull as they waited for their food to arrive, Caroline said, 'Is it true that Ancret has to go away, dear?'

'Has to? No. She's chosen to.'

'It seems you and she have reached the end of the road, then?'

'Of course not, Mother. Ancret has ambition and I admire her for it. It creates difficulties but nothing we can't overcome. She works very hard and I support her in what she's doing. If that means we have to be apart for a while, well, I'll accept that.'

'I did wonder. I'd expected her to come and see me, or at least ask about poor dear Richard, but she hasn't been in touch.'

'She doesn't know. I didn't want her to change her plans and not go away, as she might if she heard about how ill he is. She'd be letting people down. I thought if that could be avoided it was for the best.'

'But even if she didn't know about Richard, I'd expected her to phone me,' Caroline insisted.

'All right, we've had a disagreement.' He was about to point out that she was responsible, having allowed Lottie to go into his flat, but held the words back. The less Lottie knew about things the better. He was beginning to realize that Lottie was capable of using everything she gleaned. He looked at her as she ate her food, apparently unaware of the conversation. What she did miss, his mother would fill in for her, he thought with some irritation.

'Is it serious?' Caroline asked.

'No it isn't, and I don't want to discuss it here.' He gestured towards Lottie, who looked up as though suddenly aware of them, dragged from a daydream, smiling guilelessly.

It was ten o'clock when, assured by Caroline that she and Richard would be all right, Lottie and Jonathan prepared to leave. Amid goodbyes and promises to meet soon and keep in touch, Lottie's car wouldn't start.

Jonathan tried and the engine at once flared into life. But when Lottie got in, it stopped.

'It's been doing this for a few days,' she said. 'Suddenly stopping and refusing to start. It did it once on the way here. I hope I don't get stranded in some out-of-the-way lane at this time of night. That would be scary.'

Jonathan started the car but again, as Lottie began to move off, it stalled. Barely hiding his irritation, he said, 'Are you using the clutch properly?'

'Jonathan, I've been driving for ages!'

'All of a year!' he retorted. He tried again and stalled it himself before he reached the gate.

'Look, you'd better let Jonathan drive you home. Tomorrow we can get the local garage to have a look,' Caroline said.

'I can't let you go so far out of your way,' Lottie protested mildly. But Caroline insisted, and Jonathan accepted the inevitable with less than good grace

Waving at Caroline, and up at the bedroom window where the frail figure of Richard could be seen, they set off. Jonathan spoke very little on the journey and dropped her off at her parents' home with a curt 'Goodnight.'

Ancret had been informed that Social Services had made their investigation and were planning occasional visits to assure themselves that the baby would be properly cared for. Notes and phone calls passed between all parties until they were satisfied that the privately arranged fostering was acceptable and that Mr and Mrs Flowers were considered suitable people to care for her child. That aspect of the plan was ready for her departure.

She looked at her mother and felt ashamed at the way she was leaving her alone, although Loraine seemed unworried by the thought of sleeping in the rooms above the shop. Everything was as secure as they could make it and unless a very determined burglar broke in, she would sleep undisturbed. And what burglar would steal wedding dresses and highly distinctive hats?

It was only her mother's upsetting dreams that made her uneasy. When her mother suffered one of these frightening nightmares she had always been there to soothe and comfort her, and for the next few months Loraine would be alone. Ancret was still very tired. Sometimes she rested during the day, but at night her thoughts kept her awake as she mulled over the effect of her apparent disappearance on her mother and on Jonathan, who was being kept so cruelly in the dark.

Coming downstairs after a rest one lunchtime and walking into the kitchen, she saw at once that her mother was upset. Loraine was reading something in a newspaper. But when she saw Ancret, she thrust it from her and hurried out, pushing her way through the shop, blindly unaware of a group of people who stood admiring a young girl wearing a wedding dress for their approval.

Ancret followed, but stopped when she saw her mother outside talking on her mobile, moving in agitation from one foot to another, then pacing around unable to stay still. She swept an arm across her face in a gesture of despair, then the arm was flailing the air, gesticulating to unheard words.

She went inside and waited. But when her mother returned she said nothing, and the expression in the dark eyes and the strained face forbade questions. Later, Ancret found the newspaper screwed up and crammed into the litter bin. While her mother was out posting a letter, she took it out and tried to guess which news item had upset her mother so badly.

One describing a gypsy funeral? That was hardly likely. A golden wedding celebration? Possibly, as it was something her mother would never know. Much of the page held foreign news; then, at the bottom of the page, was a piece about a woman made homeless who, with her two young children, was sleeping in a van while the local authorities argued about who should accept responsibility for them. It had to be that. But who was she telephoning? And why? The woman lived miles away and couldn't possibly be known to her mother.

That night when her mother began to moan and then call and cry, Ancret was at her side in moments, aware that Loraine was suffering the recurring dream. She glanced at the bedside clock and saw it was three o'clock, the usual time for these dreams to disturb her sleep. It must have been the piece in the paper about the homeless family, she decided, as she watched over her mother and waited for the horrors to pass.

As before, Loraine was apparently nursing a child, sitting up in bed, her face red and blotchy with crying. 'Don't! You can't do this,' she pleaded in her high-pitched dream voice. 'You can't,' she wailed, pitifully begging someone to change their mind. Most of the words were unclear, but between the unrecognizable mutters and the cries, Ancret heard some clearly. 'She's yours. She's yours. Don't send us away! How will I—? Oh no, please . . .' The word was elongated and filled with despair. Then, 'My daughters— No, I won't, you can't— It's wicked— No, no, no!'

Words became groans, so jumbled as to be indistinguishable. Sweat formed on the woman's brow, running down her cheeks. Unable to decide what to do, Ancret held her mother's hand as Loraine writhed on the bed, the sheets twisting around her as they clung to her sweat-soaked body.

Gradually the terrors receded and Loraine opened her eyes to see Ancret's tearful face beside her. She couldn't speak for a while, appearing confused about where she was as she returned from the dream world she had been occupying. Then she said, 'Sorry if I woke you, daughter.'

She lay quietly for a while, then Ancret asked if she wanted a drink. 'Something cold, or a cup of tea?'

'Make me a pot of tea, then we can share it.'

'I don't think I can go away,' Ancret said as she sat watching her mother slowly recover. 'I can't leave you to face this alone.'

She helped her mother to sit up, then, wrapping a blanket around her shivering form, she moved her to a chair. While she sipped her tea, noisily, like a child, Ancret put fresh sheets on the bed, cool and sweet smelling, to help Loraine to return to sleep.

'I'm always relieved to see you sitting there beside me, when I wake from one of the bad dreams, but I don't have them very often. If I have one while you're away, I'll just get up and make my own tea instead of waiting for you to do it for me.'

'It was a stupid idea. I'll cancel everything and—'

'No. You must go.' She reached out and touched the wicker basket, stroking it as though it were a living creature that needed her love. 'Always do what your instincts tell you is right. We won't be far apart and I'll phone you if I need anything.'

'Will you promise me you'll phone even if it's the middle of the night? I can talk to you at least. Promise?'

'All right, I promise.'

This time the dream had lasted longer than usual and more words had been recognizable. *My daughters?* Did that mean her mother had other daughters somewhere? That she, Ancret, had a sister? Or even a brother? In her emotional state, after watching her mother endure the agony of the dream, she cried silently, not wanting her to hear. She cried for the people she might have known, people who were living somewhere, perhaps not that far away, brothers, sisters who would have filled her childhood and made the world a happier place. What on earth had happened for her mother to deprive her of all that?

The more she thought, the more convinced she was that it had been a criminal act so terrible she was never to be told. But if the villain had been her father, what had happened to the sisters her mother pleaded for in the dream? Was she the child her mother nursed so desperately? Or was it someone else?

After a strange, quiet Christmas she left to begin her sojourn in an unfamiliar place, for the first time completely alone.

Having said a tearful farewell to her mother, she went by taxi with the few belongings she needed. The rooms were comfortable and the kitchen was a large one. An old pine table covered in heavy plastic cloth was a perfect area on which to work. Once she had unpacked and spread her few possessions around the two rooms, she sat and stared at a wall. Besides the feeling that the place was alien, that she didn't belong here, she had no idea what to do to fill the time. Whereas at home she was never still, her hands constantly occupied, here she was faced with a need to fill the hours and she didn't know how. Until her mother had brought the materials, she couldn't even begin to make hats. And besides, with the limited tools and materials she could collect and store, there were few styles she could make in just one room that had to be used for other things.

She took out her sketchbook, but no ideas came and she felt tears beginning to swell. What was she doing here? Why had she made such a stupid decision? Picking up her mobile she began to dial Jonathan's number, but stopped and threw it aside. It rang almost immediately. She shrank from it, half convinced she had dialled the full number and Jonathan was ringing back. She looked at the VDU and saw her mother's number. 'Mummy?' she said. 'I'm all right, just a bit restless.'

'Jonathan left a message on the answerphone asking you to ring him.'

'I almost did, just before you rang. It's so odd, sitting here in a strange room with nothing to occupy my hands.'

'Write a list of what you have to do tomorrow,' Loraine suggested. 'Make an appointment with a doctor, buy food and anything else you need. Feed the ducks in Roath Park.'

'No, not that,' Ancret laughed. 'I might bump into Jonathan!'

Within a few days she had settled into a routine. Loraine had delivered boxes of materials and more were on order. The sketchbook was filling up with ideas. Abandoning the larger hats she so loved, she had decided to concentrate on smaller, frivolous 'confectionery' – her personal name for these light-hearted designs. Using the smallest disc of plaited material as a starting point, she allowed her imagination to fly; sequins rained down on net so fine it was hardly visible, feathers curled extravagantly, and beads and pom-poms displayed themselves outrageously, apparently defying gravity.

In that unimposing room on the kitchen table she made small hats with little more than saucer-sized crowns, token brims hidden by delicate decorations made from feathers and fur and fake blooms that represented no flower that ever grew. Time-consuming, outrageous, light-hearted hats that gave her joy to make and which she knew would bring customers begging for more.

The boxes that seemed so large for such small items were sent back to Loraine, and either stored ready for her spring collection or sometimes sold to clients needing something light and cheerful for a charity lunch or wedding.

Time passed. With her pregnancy well advanced, Ancret marked the dates on her calendar and counted the days remaining before the beginning of March. Visits to the doctor and the clinic, which she had imagined would be a nuisance and a waste of time, were welcome for their reassurances that all was well.

She kept in close contact with her mother, and Loraine visited most weeks, usually to take or collect work. Large boxes went to and fro by taxi. Ancret saw the books every week so she didn't feel isolated from the business, which, regardless of her absence, was coping well enough during this quiet period of the year. Helena sent messages of affection, assuring her that there were no serious problems, and no one suspected the truth.

Of Jonathan there was no word. Although it was not what she really wanted, the fact that he wasn't even trying made her perversely disappointed.

'I do, I don't. I will, I won't. I'm all over the place,' she complained to her mother.

'Blame your hormones,' Loraine said pragmatically.

Jonathan gradually got into the habit of taking Lottie when he visited his mother and Uncle Richard. Caroline was so obviously pleased to see her that he couldn't complain. He had insisted that the key to the flat was returned, so Lottie no longer went there to check on his needs. But, working together and aware of the strong friendship between the two women, it would have been churlish not to accept it and take her with him.

The cultivated garden was cleared of weeds, and under Richard's supervision, Lottie planned displays of daffodils, tulips and other spring bulbs. She had planted most of them where he would be able to see them from his bedroom window. The garden was full of birds and she began to recognize the various visitors, joyfully discussing them with Richard and poring over his books to learn more.

'I'll miss her terribly if she tires of us,' Richard told Jonathan one day. 'I hope she doesn't find a regular boyfriend and stop coming to see us.'

'I don't think she will. She's very fond of you and Mother.'

He didn't add that he was Lottie's choice for a boyfriend and that she refused to accept that he was not interested; it would have sounded vain. He did admit, though, that he'd miss her too.

'I found her a bit of a nuisance at first. She was so pushy, forcing herself into our lives, but she's made a niche for herself and I can't imagine this place without her enthusiastic chatter.'

One Sunday he went alone, as Lottie was committed to attend a family party. The place seemed less cheerful without her. When Richard asked Jonathan to take him up on Miller's Hill so he could look at the view and perhaps go for a short stroll, Jonathan readily agreed. After Caroline had wrapped her brother in warm clothes – 'Like I was a child,' Richard had light-heartedly complained – they set off.

'Not too far,' Caroline warned. 'I'll have lunch on the table in an hour.' She watched them anxiously as Jonathan settled his uncle into the passenger seat and started the engine. She tapped on the driver's window. 'Don't walk him too far, and keep out of the cold wind.'

'I'll take every care, Mother,' Jonathan said, sharing an amused glance with his uncle. He patted Richard's shoulder, joking, 'Are you ready, son?'

'Yes. The roles are reversed, aren't they? Me looking after you all those years and now you looking after me!'

For February the day was a pleasant one. There was no wind and the air was still, hinting at the warm weather to come. The trees were bare, stark against the sky, offering better views than in summer when so many climbed the hill to admire the panoramic views over the huge spread of the city sprawled next to the sea, and Penarth with its top hat of a church on the hill above the town.

Jonathan drove up the steep incline as far as he could, leaving only a short, level walk to the top. Ignoring notices to the contrary, he took the car through a gate, which he carefully closed after passing through, over a field and through a second gate, along a route taken by farmers when their flock needed attention. There were bare, overgrown hedges on one side, the remains of an old dry-stone wall on the other.

It was colder than they expected when they stepped out of the car, the air sharp, a frosty edge to each breath.

'I don't think we should stay long, Uncle,' Jonathan warned. He knew that some heart patients found cold air difficult, even dangerous, although he said nothing to worry the man.

'We'll just go to the top, then back for lunch,' Richard promised. 'I've wanted to come up here again for such a long time.'

Taking Richard's slow pace, they strolled to the viewpoint and stood for a moment looking down at the city below. Richard looked around, memories rising bright and as fresh as yesterday, then fading to make room for others. Jonathan saw he was smiling with pleasure.

Jonathan looked down, imagining how under so many of the roofs there was a man with a family – with worries and joys, tears and laughter – and was sad knowing he would never, ever, be one of them.

Where was Ancret? Why had she so mysteriously vanished after creating that stupid quarrel? He had given up trying to contact her; Loraine was as efficient as a gaoler in keeping her away from him. But why?

He was so wrapped in his frustrated thoughts that he wasn't aware of Richard's discomfort until he felt the hand on his arm tighten its grip and turned to see a grey-faced stranger beside him, holding a hand across his chest.

'Uncle! What is it? Let's get you home.' He tried to keep his voice calm but inside he was panicking. It was soon obvious that Richard was unable to walk. Gently he lifted the man into his arms and although the temptation was to hurry, walked slowly and carefully across the field to the car. He tried not to lose his footing on the uneven grassy hummocks, to stagger with his burden and cause the sick man any distress.

He drove carefully, headlights on, until a policeman stopped him and he was able to explain the situation. With the police car in front they went swiftly to the hospital and help was waiting for them as he drew up.

Caroline arrived within the hour. Richard died soon afterwards.

There was confusion for hours. The police wanted to know where Jonathan had taken the sick man and why. Jonathan told them exactly what had happened, how brief the walk had been. They interviewed Caroline and she explained that it had been Richard's wish. For the moment they appeared satisfied, although they said they wanted Jonathan to take them to the spot where it happened and point out every detail.

When they were finally back at the house, the doctor persuaded Caroline to take the sleeping tablets he had prescribed and go to bed. Shock, sadness and a great sense of loss invaded Jonathan's heart and mind. It was a situation when someone or something was needed on which to lay blame; as there was no one and nothing else, he blamed himself.

In impotent fury, he rang Loraine. 'Tell Ancret, Uncle Richard died today – if she cares a damn.'

# Six

'Mummy, I can't go to Uncle Richard's funeral like this!' Ancret smoothed her dress over her swollen figure and sighed. 'I don't know what to do. I was fond of him and I know Jonathan loved him dearly. He was close to Richard, he depended on him during his childhood when his mother was absent – and that was a lot of the time when Jonathan was young.'

'I'll go in your place and explain that you're unwell,' Loraine said. 'Don't worry, I'll make sure he and Caroline believe me.'

'When I decided to disappear for a while I couldn't have imagined some of the problems. This is the worst, not being there to say goodbye to Richard. I know Caroline has never liked me, but she'd be glad of my presence at this time, I'm sure of that.'

'I expect Lottie will go. She seems to be a regular visitor to the house, from what I've been told.'

'Where did you hear that?' Ancret demanded.

'I met Lucinda and she told me that Lottie and Caroline are friends.'

'I see.' Ancret again felt unreasonable jealousy. She had left Jonathan without even giving him the means to get in touch, she was keeping from him the fact she was carrying his child. So why should she expect him to stay loyal? But the thought of him with Lottie caused her considerable pain.

'Write him a letter, and one to Caroline,' Loraine suggested.

'How can I? The postmark won't be from North Wales, will it?'

'No envelopes, just the letters. I'll tell them they were included in mine as you weren't sure of Richard's address.'

'So many lies and complications.'

'Deceit is never easy.'

Jonathan drove through the streets towards Ancret's home and parked nearby. He stared at the shop front. He couldn't stay away from Moments. His grief, for his uncle and for the loss of Ancret, created a need to be as close to her as he could. He sat and watched as people came and went through the doors of the busy bridal salon, but he didn't go inside. He sat in the car and stared, wondering what had gone wrong, what was the truth behind Ancret's so obviously contrived quarrel and disappearance.

Had it been his over-reaction when she joked about being pregnant? Perhaps he should have been honest and explained his reasons. That thought took him to Babs, his earlier love. There were times, like today, when he bitterly regretted losing her. Babs had no burning desire to be successful. She was the kind to settle, contented, into domesticity, filling her days with voluntary work, supporting charities and caring for him as a wife ought. A home and—

There it was again, she would have wanted to fill that home with children. Motherhood was such a strong need. But surely it wasn't impossible to find a woman who'd settle for him alone?

He silently grieved for Babs as well as Ancret. In his melancholic mood he felt he was a man doomed to loneliness punctuated by brief, meaningless romances.

Sitting there, he glanced at the people who passed, wishing he were one of them, these anonymous strangers who seemed to have it all, their faces showing none of his misery. Teenagers with hope in their hearts, young women, inevitably with children, and older couples whose pockets, he imagined, contained photographs of their grandchildren . . . He felt as isolated as lepers must once have done.

He had started the engine, preparing to return to the office, when he saw Loraine leaving, carrying several boxes. She got into a taxi, and on impulse he followed. She was probably going to the post office, but there was a chance she was heading somewhere that would offer him a clue to where Ancret could be found. Although she'd hardly be visiting her. North Wales was too far to go without luggage.

Following the taxi was not as easy as it looked on television. The experienced taxi driver nipped in and out of places where Jonathan would hesitate to go, always managing to be in the correct lane, while Jonathan, who had no idea where he was going, did not. Twice he lost sight of the taxi but consoled himself with the thought that at least Loraine wouldn't be aware of being followed, even if she were looking back expectantly – which was unlikely. Horns proclaimed their protest once or twice when he cut across the traffic without warning. If he heard, he didn't react. Ten minutes passed and the taxi was still in sight.

They left the city far behind and were on the road heading for Newport before the taxi stopped. He parked close by and waited. An elderly woman got out, carrying a small dog. Somehow he had lost the taxi he'd been following and begun tailing another instead. Dejectedly, he tried to think where the error could have occurred and went back to the last set of traffic lights. It must have been at this point, when his quarry had gone through and he thought he had caught up, that the second cab had taken its place.

Without much hope, he cruised around the streets before heading back to the office.

In the front window, protected by a lacy curtain, Ancret stood watching in disbelief, her mother beside her.

'He must have followed you!' she said, smiling in relief. 'So he still cares.'

'But won't all that end when he finds out about your callousness in hiding your pregnancy from him?'

'Callous? Is that what I am?'

'What d'you call it, daughter?'

'Buying time, that's all.'

'For a daughter of mine you seem to find it difficult to make a decision.'

'Are you feeling sorry for him now? I thought you didn't want me to marry him?'

'He's not the right man for you, there's something about him that makes me uneasy. But I'm beginning to regret supporting you in this deception.'

'It's too late to change my mind now.'

'But you already have. You didn't want to marry him and that was why you didn't want him to know about the baby – it would just add to the pressure. But all the time you've been away, you've been imagining him coming back into your life, haven't you? What's that if it isn't changing your mind?'

'Sometimes I think I love him, but I don't want to marry him. There'd be pressure for me to give up the business and I can't do that. He's adamant that I'll stay home and be a full-time housewife. And whatever he feels about a child at the moment, he'll want a family one day. I want to make hats, not babies.'

Loraine looked at her and smiled. 'That's hardly convincing from where I'm standing!'

When Jonathan returned to the office, a jubilant Lottie greeted him. 'Jonathan, I've sold the Harding Road semi!'

The house in Harding Road had been on their books for several months. The vendor had tried three other estate agents without any luck and there seemed no hope of the Pen-Marr agency changing the pattern of failure. The house was dark, dingy and in need of complete refurbishment. Few viewers went further than the downstairs rooms.

'Well done.' Then he found himself hugging her. The way she ran towards him, arms outstretched, made it impossible not to. He tried to push her gently away but she hugged him more tightly.

'Oh, Jonathan,' she said, her breath touching his neck, her cheek against his. 'What a team we make.'

He tried to free himself by starting to remove his coat, and repeated, 'Well done. I'm really delighted.'

'What a spiel! You'd have been proud of me,' she said breathlessly, her blue eyes still close to his own and sparkling with excitement. He noticed how clear they were, and was fascinated to notice that the whites had a hint of blue. He released himself and moved quickly away, prolonging the simple task of hanging up his coat.

'I am proud of you.'

'I talked about it as a sad little house just waiting for

someone with imagination and flair, and I painted a gloomy picture so the inside wasn't a shock. Then I showed him some sketches I'd made to demonstrate how it could make two well-appointed flats. I gave a hint as to the value of each flat – cautiously, mind, I wasn't specific – and he went in. Starry-eyed, not seeing peeling paint and drooping ceilings but pounds and profit.'

'Well done. I just hope the survey doesn't ruin your good work.'

'Oh, I warned him about how wary surveyors can be, how they have to point out the vaguest suspicions of structural damage, for fear of being sued for incompetence,' she said with a wide grin.

'I think we should send out for cream cakes to celebrate.'

'There's something else,' she said, reaching towards her desk while holding on to his sleeve. 'I've re-marketed New Grange. What d'you think?' She handed him some photographs and a page of details. 'It should have sold before now, it's a beautiful property and the price seems right, so I took photographs from a different angle and reworded the first paragraph. So far this morning, two passers-by have stopped and looked, then called in to make an appointment. I've arranged for you to meet them there. Mr and Mrs Poulton at two thirty and Mr Graham at four fifteen. All right?'

'You have been busy,' he said, studying the rewritten details and the photograph. 'It certainly deserves a cream cake.'

'Oh, is that all?' she said with a light frown. 'What about lunch instead? Lucinda will be in at twelve and I think I deserve it, don't you?'

'I'll get something sent in for the three of us,' he said, moving away and releasing his arm from her grip.

'Haven't I earned a little treat? Besides, Lucinda will have eaten. You know she has a snack before coming in at twelve on Mondays. I've been trying to think of ways to cheer you,' she added softly. 'I know how devastated you are by Uncle Richard's death.'

'All right. Lunch at Guido's, one o'clock?'

'That won't allow much time before your two-thirty appointment.'

'It'll be sufficient.'

'All right, I'll book it straight away.' She dialled the number, glancing at him, then smiled excitedly and blew him a kiss. When he heard her request a corner table for two, he knew he had made a mistake. Going outside, he rang the restaurant and asked for a centre table. 'I don't want a cosy corner,' he said with a forced laugh. 'This time I won't be with Ancret, just the young office girl who deserves a little treat.'

He spent the rest of the morning phoning friends and checking on arrangements for the funeral. He wished his mother hadn't chosen to stay at the house alone, but she felt she had to be there so Richard's friends, many of whom she didn't know well, could contact her. That evening after the office closed, Lottie called 'Goodnight' and went straight down to see her.

Before Jonathan left the office he had a visit from the police. He was questioned politely about everything that had happened on the day his uncle had died. When the questioning went over the same ground for the third time he grew impatient. 'D'you mind if we leave this now? My mother is alone in the house where her brother died and I have to go to make sure she's all right.'

'That's fine, sir. I might have to come back once more to confirm everything you've told me.' He laughed deprecatingly. 'We have to make sure everyone's statements match. Tedious, but then the case will be closed and we can put it aside.'

'Case?' Jonathan queried with a spasm of alarm.

'A death that's unexpected or that happens outside the home is always subject to careful investigation.'

'I see.' Jonathan frowned as he showed the policeman out.

He was thoughtful as he drove to join his mother. Putting the police questions aside, curiosity about Ancret's whereabouts and the reason for her departure, mingled with grief for the loss of a loved uncle, were foremost in his mind at the moment. He needed Ancret, wanted her sympathy. He ached for her presence in a way that was almost a grief in itself. But the visit by the police came back to him like a shocking, alarming shower of icy cold water.

Why were they asking so many questions? Was he

suspected of causing Richard's death? Were they investigating 'foul play'? This unbelievable fear drove everything else from his mind, even Ancret. He needed to talk to his mother, listen to her account of what happened, find out what she knew about the police enquiries and be reassured. So when he walked in and saw Lottie there he was less than pleased.

Caroline raised her face for a kiss before quickly closing the door against the cold February night. 'Lottie has been telling me how you took her out for a splendid lunch today. That was nice for you, dear, to have such charming female company.'

'It was only a small reward for selling a "sticky" property and re-presenting another, resulting in two interested prospects,' he replied, off-handedly. 'I try to be kind to my staff.'

'Well, I loved it,' Lottie said. She hugged Caroline and together they went into the kitchen.

'Dinner in ten minutes,' Caroline called.

'Is Lottie staying?' he asked pointedly.

'Of course, dear. She brought a delicious punnet of strawberries, some shortbread and some clotted cream for pudding,' Caroline called. 'Oh, and there are some letters for you to read, dear,' she added, as she disappeared into the kitchen. 'Including one for you from Ancret.'

He hurriedly thumbed through the pile of letters on the sideboard but didn't see an envelope bearing Ancret's large, scrawny handwriting. 'Where is it?' he called.

'It's open at the bottom of the pile. It was enclosed in one to us both from Loraine,' was the shouted explanation, hardly audible over the clatter of pots and pans.

The letter was disappointingly short. Sympathy, regrets at not seeing Richard more often, a reference to happy memories. Apart from being signed with fondest love and a couple of kisses, there was nothing to distinguish it from the many others.

As Lottie prepared to leave, Jonathan said he would stay the night. He avoided looking at her face, afraid of seeing disappointment. An offer of a lift home might have been what she was hoping for, then a lift to the office in the morning, and another lift back here to collect her car. Perhaps he was becoming paranoid, but he was beginning to 'read' her and he didn't like what he was learning. She appeared so often, had become such a loving friend of his mother, and – the mechanic had found nothing wrong with her car.

It wasn't much of a surprise, therefore, when once more her car struggled and refused to start. He went across and asked her to get out. He gave it a little choke and it started easily, the engine running as smoothly as a sewing machine. He drove it to the gate and then got out.

'Thank you, Jonathan, you have a way with my little car. And thank you for a wonderful lunch.' She ran up to him, and without warning reached out, put her hands behind his head and kissed him. He was so shocked that for a moment he froze, then pulled away. He was startled by his body's powerful response. Embarrassment followed, quickly changing to anger, tinged with guilt. Had he encouraged her in some way? Had she misconstrued his delight at her success in selling a difficult property? How else could he have acted? How ridiculous this was! He sighed with audible relief when the sound of her car faded and he and Caroline were alone.

'Mother, I do wish you wouldn't invite her here. Can you at least make sure she doesn't come while I'm here? She's got a childish crush on me and if it doesn't end soon I really will have to sack her.'

'I don't understand, dear. From what she's been telling me I thought you were, well, a little fond of her?'

'It's all in her mind.'

'She's such a sweet child.'

'So you won't encourage her any more?'

'I do like seeing her, she's so kind,' Caroline said regretfully.

'Besides making me feel uncomfortable, I wouldn't like Ancret to get the wrong idea.'

'I thought you and she were finished.'

'No, just parted for a while. It's only a temporary thing, she'll be back soon. March, she said, when the term finishes and her friend returns.' He didn't sound convincing, even to himself.

Lottie was in the office when he arrived the following

morning. 'I came early in case you were delayed,' she said, handing him a cup of coffee. 'Is your mother all right?'

'She's fine and very busy at the moment, dealing with the funeral and her grief, as well as the many friends who call. So I don't think you should bother her.'

'Nonsense, Jonathan. I'm not a visitor, not any more. I'm there to help. I'll go down after work and see what I can do.'

'There's no need,' he said, tight-lipped.

'Of course there's need, Jonathan. We've decided to bring some of the bedroom chairs down and rearrange the rooms to seat the guests who'll be coming after the service. And I want to get the front paths clean. It's amazing how fast the weeds grow, even at this time of year.'

'I can see to all that.'

'You know I'll do anything to help your mother. Or you,' she said, ignoring his mild protest, moving towards him and slipping into his arms.

Her hands moved in the hair at the nape of his neck. Almost before he was aware, her lips moved sensuously across his own. He pushed her away rather too roughly and she staggered against her desk.

'I'm sorry, but I don't want your help with my mother, or anything else. I think it's best that you leave.'

'Jonathan! I know you feel more for me than employee and employer,' she gasped. 'If not, why did you kiss me last night?'

'I didn't. You kissed me after trying the "my car won't start" routine again.'

He went out of the office. Seeing someone browsing through the display of houses for sale, he called sharply, 'Lottie, will you come and help these people?' before storming out.

Stepping from the cloakroom, Lucinda stared at the now tearful Lottie. She waved her hand, telling her to go back into Jonathan's office. After she had assisted the customers, taken down the details of what they were looking for and added them to the client list, she asked Lottie what had happened.

'Jonathan told me I have to leave,' Lottie sobbed. 'I thought he was attracted to me and we kissed and then this morning he became angry, accused me of goodness knows what and told me I had to leave.'

'Did he do anything except kiss you?' Lucinda asked. When Lottie shook her head, she added, 'Thank goodness for that.'

'I don't want to talk about it,' Lottie whispered, still shaking her head, the words less convincing than the gesture alone.

'You mean he did do more than kiss?'

'I don't want to talk about it.'

'Go home. He's upset at the moment with Ancret away, and now the loss of his uncle. Leave it until tomorrow then come into work as normal. It might have all blown over by then.'

At lunchtime, when Jonathan had still not appeared, Lottie took Lucinda's advice and left. She didn't drive home but went instead to see Jonathan's mother.

'But I thought you and he were, well, growing fond of each other?' Caroline said, soothing Lottie with tea and tissues.

'I thought so too. He was so thrilled with my work, and we were brought closer when dear Uncle Richard died. I don't need to tell you that I loved Uncle Richard too. In the short time I knew him he taught me so much. He opened up a new world to me, sharing the pleasures of growing things and creating a beautiful garden. I miss him so much. And you and I becoming friends, it was all so wonderful. I thought my life was perfect. But then he changed his mind, told me to get out, and now I've no job and I've lost you as a friend.'

Caroline held her in her arms and allowed the sobs to subside before she said, 'I'll talk to him, dear. I'll make him understand how cruelly he's treated you. And as for losing me as a friend, that's nonsense, dear. I'll always be here. Never forget it.'

Jonathan was sitting in a parked car outside Moments again. He watched as Loraine stepped out of a taxi, this time transporting three very large boxes. They had to be hats. Could Ancret be making them? If so, had Loraine collected them from a specialist transport company? That was unlikely.

Having seen many of Ancret's creations he knew they could so easily be damaged by careless handling. Could it be that Ancret was not as far away as North Wales? A taxi drive that took Loraine to the other side of Cardiff was feasible. That would also explain why her letter of sympathy came enclosed with Loraine's; a postmark was impossible to fake. He looked up at the windows of the flat above the shop as the lights went out one by one, leaving a faint glow where he guessed Loraine would read awhile before settling to sleep. He wondered whether Ancret was asleep – wherever she was – and if she dreamed of him.

Loraine stood at the back of the small country church, waiting for the funeral service to begin. Apart from a nod, Caroline barely acknowledged her. But when Jonathan saw her, he brought her forward to stand beside him.

'Is Ancret coming?' he asked, looking expectantly towards the door as more mourners entered.

'She intended to. She's very upset about your uncle, she was fond of him.'

'But she isn't coming to his funeral.' His voice was hard.

'She's unwell and can't make the journey. I think she'll write to you to explain why she can't be here. But I'm her representative and I come with her apologies.'

Jonathan stood up and went forward to greet the other arrivals, glad to escape. Among them, caught momentarily in a shaft of sun that darted through the window and on to her golden head, was his ex-fiancée, Babs.

A rush of pleasure flooded him with warmth. She didn't look any different from when they had last met, more than six years before. Blonde hair fashionably short, large greenish eyes still with that slow, gentle expression, uptilted nose, so heartbreakingly familiar. She had three children with her, a little girl aged about a year old, wriggling frustratedly in her arms, a little boy of about three – and a serious-faced boy with Down's syndrome aged about six, who looked around him with great interest.

'Hello, I'm Donald,' the six-year-old announced carefully in a low tone. 'My brother Harry is three and my sister is almost one and we're going to have a party. Who are you?'

'Good, good,' he said with bemusement, and without looking at the child. 'Babs?' he said, grasping both her hands in his. 'What are you doing here? How did you know about Uncle Richard?'

'Why doesn't he answer me?' the boy asked.

'Why don't you answer him, Jonathan?' Babs said, pushing the little boy closer.

'I – er, yes, I'm pleased to meet you, er—'

'Donald . . .' the boy coaxed, nodding encouragement, and Jonathan repeated the name after him.

'Donald. Yes. Look, I have to go and help Mother. But perhaps we can talk later?'

'Me and Donald and Harry and Tracy,' said Babs, and there was a smile on her lips he couldn't define.

He asked, 'Are they yours?'

'Yes, all of them,' she said, still with the enigmatic smile. 'Six-year-old Donald, and the other two.'

Edmund Preese arrived then. He came up to Jonathan and made his parents' apologies. 'Remember me? We met at Toad Hall when I thought you and your . . . girlfriend were trespassing.'

'I remember. Are you the trespasser now? Did you know my uncle?' Jonathan was so confused by the unexpected meeting with Babs, he hardly knew what he was saying. 'Sorry, I – you'll have to excuse me, I have to get back to my mother.'

'Mum and Dad are so sorry they can't be here,' Edmund said as he followed him through the last-minute arrivals down the aisle. 'They've known your uncle for many years and would have loved to pay their respects, but it was impossible, so I'm here instead.'

The vicar stood and conversations died as the service began.

Jonathan heard little of the service. His mind was on the six-year-old boy standing beside Babs, who could be heard talking occasionally and being gently hushed by her. Six years ago, when they had parted, Babs had been expecting a child, his child. Donald must be his. Her intention, her promise, to have an abortion had been a lie.

He looked for her when they were outside the church,

standing shaking the hands of the mourners as they left, but although he waited until the doors were closed behind the last one, he didn't see her.

He had to talk to her. But where would he find her? Her name would have changed now she was married, and her parents no longer lived in the same area. Pictures of her standing with the three children filled his mind. He was dazed by the wild thoughts that crossed it.

'Jonathan. Wake up and help, dear,' Caroline said. 'You're coming back to the house in the car with me, aren't you?'

Caroline had arranged for caterers to provide the spread and two young women to act as waitresses, so she was free to talk with the friends. Lottie sat in the kitchen wondering whether to leave, or wait in the hope of a word with Jonathan. She had watched him in the church and was aware of how upset he was. He needed someone to listen while he got it out of his system. Who better than herself?

The hum of conversation and the occasional burst of laughter from the other room made her feel cut off from the occasion but she stayed, chatting to the caterers as they dashed in and out with trays of food and drinks. Jonathan or Caroline would come to find her soon.

It was Jonathan who came into the kitchen. He was looking for a dustpan and brush to deal with some broken glass. He stopped and demanded, 'What are you doing here? I thought you left after the service.'

'Hello, Lottie, dear,' Caroline called from behind him. 'I was looking for you. Come out and meet some of Richard's friends.' Giving her son a fierce glare, she took Lottie's arm and led her out, handed her a drink and introduced her to several people – including a couple who lived in a flat next to Jonathan's.

'Hello,' the wife said with a smile, 'Aren't you Jonathan's friend? We've seen you coming and going, haven't we, James?'

'My friend too,' cooed Caroline, 'dear girl that she is. My brother Richard adored her.'

'She's an employee of mine,' Jonathan added firmly.

Edmund stayed, talking to Loraine about toads.

'There's a toad crossing outside the property,' he told her, 'where the toads cross on their way to water to spawn. Hundreds get run over, so every year a group of volunteers stand at the side of the road and help the toads across, carrying them in buckets to avoid them being killed by traffic. Fewer now than when the toad-watch started, but well worth our time.'

'How do they know when it's time? Do they travel every night?'

'During the season, around February and March, they're on the move when the weather is moist. Drizzling rain, wet underfoot, those seem to be the conditions they need to persuade them to travel. The volunteers go out at dusk and wait for them.' He smiled at her. 'If you're really interested, why don't you come one evening and see for yourself. Bring Ancret too if she's free. I'll provide the transport and there's hot coffee in Toad Hall afterwards,' he promised encouragingly.

Loraine smiled back and promised to try. She knew both she and Ancret would enjoy the experience.

When most of the guests had gone and there was an opportunity to talk, Caroline said to Lottie, 'Don't worry about Jonathan, dear. He's very upset. And I've been thinking – perhaps he doesn't feel happy at starting a relationship with you while you're working beside him. If you leave, maybe he'll feel more able to relax.' She opened her handbag and showed Lottie a long, narrow envelope. 'He'll be a rich man once probate is granted. Richard has left everything, including this house, between us. Of course, Jonathan will want to sell and allow houses to be built over the grounds, but I want it to stay as it is. I want to live here and being on my own isn't a worry. I'm comfortable with the place. I never liked the flat. I enjoy wandering into the garden, the feeling of space and freedom. But my son has already started trying to persuade me to give it up. Who d'you think will win?' she asked with a chuckle. 'Jonathan is very strong-willed, but I'm quietly determined.'

'Why did he leave the property between you? Surely he could see there might be problems? Disagreements even?'

'He knew that if we sell I'd be able to use the money to travel, or to buy a really nice property. There'd be enough

111

money for me to live wherever I want to, and that's a luxury when you think about it; to choose your location isn't something everyone can do.'

'No, you're right, it is a luxury. But if I could choose I'd live here.'

'Also,' Caroline went on with a conspiratorial wink, 'I might want to remarry. Whatever I do, with Jonathan owning a good business and financially secure, I won't have the uncomfortable feeling that he's thinking about what he'll do with the money when I'm dead.'

'Caroline! As if Jonathan would think anything so heartless.'

'I'm joking, of course. But I have to admit that, like a lot of parents, especially as they grow older, the thought does cross my mind on occasions, particularly when Jonathan is talking of expansion, opening a second office. If he does that, money will be tight for a while, even with what Richard has left him. The pressure for me to agree to sell will be enormous, but I hope I can stay.'

'He won't try to persuade you to leave, I'm sure he won't. He has enough for his needs, and the business is doing well.'

'The money left to him will make him a wealthy man, but what the property would be worth to developers is something completely different. Enormous sums would be bandied about. Enough to turn the most sober of heads. Who knows how many houses these acres would hold?'

'But if you don't want to sell?'

'I want to live here for the rest of my life. It's where I was born and where I lived until I married. It would be a neat way to end it.'

'I think I'll go now. I'll be at the office at eight thirty tomorrow and just see how it goes. I don't want to leave. I love working beside Jonathan, we make a good team.'

The caterers were leaving with the day's debris, but some guests still remained. Loraine was talking to Jonathan and Edmund and one or two others near the open door with the house lights and those in the garden blazing. A few small groups stood around, wanting to leave but hanging on to the last vestiges of conversation as though afraid to break up the occasion and leave Caroline alone.

112

Caroline asked Lottie to take Jonathan a cup of coffee before she left. 'To encourage the last few to go,' she explained in a whisper. 'And give him a chance for another word with you.' She cast a furtive glance around, and slipped something into Lottie's handbag. 'Take this, dear. I have the feeling he'll be needing support just now.'

Lottie walked through the huddle of people around the doorway and handed the coffee to Jonathan, who was standing next to Loraine and Edmund. As he took it, she stretched up and touched his cheek with her lips. Loraine watched her walk back to where Caroline stood smiling, then turned to Jonathan. 'That girl is trouble,' she said.

Jonathan marched across to his mother and slammed the coffee cup down on the hall table. 'Mother, I don't want you to invite Lottie here again. My business connection with her is over and I want it to end right now.'

'Jonathan—' Lottie wailed, looking from him to Caroline and back again. There were several people standing near enough to hear. Caroline gestured towards them and glared at Jonathan.

'Please, Jonathan. This isn't the time! Can't you see the child is upset?'

'What child?! This isn't open for discussion. The business decisions are mine and I want her to go now, immediately. Lucinda will bring anything you've left in the office, and she'll post your forms and any money due to you, so there's no need to return.'

In his mind he saw, not Lottie, but Babs and her children, half smiling at him. *I'm Donald*, he heard the little boy say. *Who are you?* And Ancret's beautiful face appeared, staring at him, her sad expression showing her rejection of him so clearly, then fading away, bringing him back to Lottie who was a nuisance and his mother who encouraged her.

'Get her out of here!' he said, pushing his way to the stairs and running up, chased by his demons.

Lottie was drenched in humiliation. Tears came. Her legs trembled and threatened to let her down. 'All I've done is love you and help you,' she shouted between sobs. How could he say these things in front of Richard's friends and

Caroline? And, worst of all, Ancret's mother? How Ancret would laugh.

Over the murmur of embarrassed talk, as people tried to cover up the difficult moment with chatter, the air around her seemed to be filled with derisive laughter. It glowed in the eyes of everyone there, these witnesses to her cruel dismissal.

Jonathan came back down, pale-faced, dutifully preparing to shake hands with the departing guests. Lottie looked at him, just inside the door, turned away from her, his shoulders bowed; and something in her snapped. How dare he treat her like this? Why was she standing here as though waiting for a second helping?

She went to the hall cupboard and collected her coat. Ignoring Jonathan, she kissed Caroline and went to the door without a word. Then she stopped and looked at him. 'You'll have to phone for a taxi, I had a lift with Lucinda.'

The last of the mourners hovered, talking in desultory whispers before quietly moving away, leaving the three of them with nothing to say. When the taxi arrived, he stood and watched her get in. It started to move away, then stopped and Lottie got out.

'Now what is it?' Jonathan demanded.

'I'm staying. I promised Caroline I'd sleep here for a few nights so she won't feel bereft.'

'My mother is my concern. Just go. I don't want to see you here again.' The words were loud enough for the remaining guests to hear. Lottie's expression was cold.

'Never see me again? Oh, I can't promise that,' she replied enigmatically.

'Hey,' he called, running out and waving as the taxi moved off empty. 'Now what have you done?'

He bustled her out of the door to where his car stood. 'Get in. I'll fetch my keys. Mother, I won't be long. I'll take Lottie home and be back soon. And that will be an end to it,' he added firmly.

Caroline went to the passenger door and said, 'I'm sorry, dear. It was the funeral. I never dreamed he'd be so upset.' She frowned, wondering whether it was seeing Babs again that had upset him so badly. Or the absence of Ancret, selfish

114

woman that she was. 'Don't worry, dear. I'll talk to him when he's calmed down.'

'He's been very lucky, hasn't he?' Lottie said, her voice brittle with anger. 'First you selling your home to give him a start, then my uncle being killed and leaving him his half of the business, now your poor dear brother leaving him money and property – with more to come after your time.'

'Yes,' Caroline said, frowning as she wondered what Lottie meant by the remark. 'Jonathan is very lucky.'

'And some people make their own luck,' Lottie said enigmatically, as Jonathan slid in beside her and turned the ignition key.

When he left her outside her home, she didn't go inside. The walk to the taxi rank wasn't far and it was still early. Reaching into her handbag, her fingers found the key to Jonathan's flat that Caroline slipped her, and she smiled.

Jonathan put Lottie from his mind. All his thoughts were of Babs and her children. A feeling of dread drenched him in cold sweat. *I'm Donald, who are you?* the boy had asked. *Who are you? Who are you?*

Jonathan answered aloud, 'I think I'm your father.'

When the pains began, Ancret refused to believe they were labour pains. It was too soon, not even the end of February. When the pains continued, gentle but persistent, she wanted reassurance, she wanted to talk to her mother. But Loraine wouldn't be back from the funeral yet, and she daren't phone her when she might be with Jonathan.

The afternoon moved into evening. She pulled the curtains across and turned on the lights. The day had ended early and at three thirty she felt as though it were the middle of the night, a night when she would be alone and uncertain what would happen next. She had read all the information she'd been given, but now it was actually happening, she felt as uninformed as a primitive woman in an isolated cave.

At five o'clock she phoned the shop and spoke to Angela. Casually, she asked when her mother was expected back.

'She didn't say, but I imagine she'll be home by six. The funeral was at midday and she wouldn't know anyone to talk to who would delay her.'

115

'I'll leave it until seven and phone then.'

'Are you well?' Angela asked politely, and Ancret was about to tell her she was fine when she remembered one of her many lies.

'I've had the most awful cold, and I didn't think it wise to go among a crowd and give it to others. Besides, I didn't really feel well enough to make the journey. Headache and tiredness, you know what I mean. I'm sure Jonathan will understand.' A slow, spreading pain took her in its grasp then and she ended the call. How long before she could talk to her mother? Another hour? Two?

She reminded herself that the situation was of her own choosing. She had made the decision to deal with this herself and that was exactly what she would do. When her mother phoned, it was almost eleven thirty. She had been with Edmund and a group of volunteers, wearing borrowed wellingtons and waterproofs, collecting toads in buckets and carrying them to safety across the road. After listening to the story of the toads of Toad Hall, she asked about the funeral. Loraine told her about Lottie being there, and Jonathan's outburst.

'And what about you, daughter? Is everything all right with you?'

'I've been busy,' Ancret said, saying nothing of the pains. 'I've spent the day cleaning, sorting out cupboards, washing and ironing, and throwing away some clutter.'

'It's too soon, or I'd say you were nesting,' her mother said. 'You are all right?'

Hiding the slowly developing pains and relaxing whenever they eased, Ancret talked briefly to her before excusing herself, saying she was tired. They both promised to phone again soon.

The pains subsided and although she didn't go to bed, she slept.

A sharp pain woke her and she looked at the time. It was three o'clock in the morning, the time Loraine was always woken by her terrifying dream. Was it an omen? Had the dreams been a warning? Would her son be born and then die? She tried to shake the superstitious nonsense from her, but visions of her mother distraught, nursing a

116

child and crying, pleading for someone to help, wouldn't go away.

Strange that she had always been certain it would be a son. She had refused confirmation when she went for a scan; she didn't want anyone to spoil the moment when she looked into her son's face and knew she had been right, that there had been communication between them before his birth. She lay back and thought about the moment when she would hold him in her arms. The pains continued, gentle as yet but growing increasingly strong. She went with the pain and lay watching the hands of the clock go round. Too soon to phone the midwife. She would know when the moment came.

With her key, Lottie went into Jonathan's flat. Everything was tidy and the rooms had the abandoned look of a place rarely used and uncared for. Although the heating was on low, it was like walking into a freezer. She pulled her coat more tightly around her and began to search.

She didn't know what she was looking for. She wandered, vaguely looking into cupboards and drawers, then tried the desk. One compartment was locked; the rest held only household accounts and bills, both paid and unpaid, in separate folders, neatly labelled. Abandoning the living room she went into Jonathan's bedroom. Here she emptied every drawer and cupboard, replacing the contents as carefully as she could. In a bedside cupboard, carelessly thrown in with books and a torch and a few pairs of socks, she found a watch. It was one she recognized as having once belonged to her uncle, Jeff Talbot, Jonathan's one-time partner.

Putting it back exactly as she had found it, she decided to talk to the police. Luck was something some people attracted, but the convenient death of two people might be something more. And the way he had treated her, humiliated her, had convinced her he was capable of anything to get what he wanted.

At six o'clock in the morning, after talking to the midwife, Ancret called for a taxi and went into hospital. The slow labour went on and she began to wonder if she had been too hasty. She could have sewn the brim on a couple more hats

117

instead of sitting here waiting for a baby who was in no hurry to be born.

The baby was finally born early the following morning after a slow, relatively easy labour. Only at the end did Ancret begin to think she couldn't cope any longer, and by that time she was in the capable hands of the nurses and being told what to do.

Although they talked her through the final stages of labour, she was unaware of their words. Everything was a blur of pain, fear, excitement and amid it all, joyous anticipation. She uttered only a few muffled cries towards the end and the nurses praised her restraint. Finally one of them held up the baby for her to see, assuring her that everything was fine before taking it away for the standard medical checks. She saw it held up and whisked away without any feeling of reality. 'It's my son who deserves the praise,' she panted. 'He's made it as easy as he could for me.'

There was a bigger surprise when the nurse handed the child to her, wrapped in a clean white blanket, and said, 'Here she is. Welcome your beautiful daughter.'

'My daughter? I have a daughter?'

She was quite unprepared for the overwhelming surge of joy that flowed over her when she took the child in her arms. She held her tucked against her breast and it was as though the space there had been waiting all her life for her daughter to fill it.

In the flat above Moments, Loraine was unable to sleep. She walked around from room to room, starting jobs then putting them aside, stopping on occasions to part the curtains and stare out into the dark, silent street. Ancret was calling for her, but there was nothing she could do about it.

# Seven

Ancret felt no disappointment at being told she had a daughter rather than the son she expected. She laughed excitedly. 'She's a wonderful surprise. I'm so thrilled!' Moments later she couldn't imagine ever wanting the child to be a son.

The nurse moved away. She had been watching in case there had been serious distress, as sometimes happened when a mother desperately desired a child of a particular gender. Having talked to Ancret and made sure there was no problem, she went to get her a cup of tea.

Surreptitiously, Ancret loosened the blanket and examined the baby's left hand. There was no sign of an extra finger; yet that too was no disappointment. Her baby was perfect, and wouldn't have to face the simple operation necessary to remove it.

As soon as she was able, she telephoned Loraine and told her the news. 'I'm on my way,' her mother told her.

Still holding her baby, she stared at the telephone, frustrated in her happiness by having no one else to tell. Jonathan? Caroline? They should have been involved in this wonderful event. But there was no one else. Then, unbidden, a picture of Edmund entered her mind. Would he have been pleased to have a daughter? She thought about him, while enjoying the warmth of the baby against her. She couldn't imagine him reacting in such an alarming manner as Jonathan to the announcement that he was to have a child.

She wondered idly what he was doing, then, remembering the early hour, realized he would be asleep. Was he alone? Or did he have a partner? She knew so little about him, apart from the fact that he ran a hotel with his parents. A previous marriage had failed but that didn't mean he had remained single.

She was still thinking about Edmund when her mother arrived, breathless with excitement, and then all her thoughts were for the baby.

Lottie was wide awake, going over in her mind her interview at the police station earlier that evening. She relived the anxiety of trying to convince a cynical policeman that she was not vengeful, just worried, explaining that if her uncle had died unnecessarily she and her aunt needed to know. There was no great enthusiasm, but she was assured that, together with the final questions about Richard's death, they would go over the circumstances of her uncle's.

'My uncle's watch is in Jonathan's possession, and I don't think he would have given it to anyone but my father – his brother,' was her final shot as she left.

'Probably put there by her,' one of the officers muttered. 'A woman scorned and all that.' But the suspicion was noted and questions prepared.

Although it was a long way from dawn, she rose and made herself a hot drink. Had she made a terrible mistake? In the dark hours, it seemed a stupid thing to have done. What if Jonathan was accused not of stealing but of Uncle Jeff's death? For a moment or two it had even seemed possible that Jonathan was indeed guilty of the death of his partner. The night hours emphasized worries, exaggerated them, made everything feasible, she knew that – it was something about the loneliness, the isolation, the inaccessibility of answers and the impossibility of finding someone with whom to talk out your anxieties.

When Ancret's mother looked down at the baby she found it hard to hold back tears. 'She's so beautiful,' she murmured as she took it into her arms. 'D'you know, since you told me she had arrived, my arms have been physically aching to hold her.'

'D'you think she looks like Jonathan, Mummy?' Ancret asked.

'Daughter, you could convince anyone that such a small baby is the image of them. It isn't easy to persuade a doubtful father that a child is his.'

'Mummy! What d'you mean?'

'A newly born child is an unpainted canvas. Expressions, mannerisms, likenesses, they all come later.'

Ancret was puzzled by her mother's odd remarks. What put such thoughts into her mind, she wondered. 'So she's like Jonathan?' she asked.

Loraine pursed her lips and nodded.

Ancret laughed. 'Not that there's any competition for the title of Natalie's father. I've only ever loved Jonathan.'

'Natalie?' Loraine stared at the sleeping child. 'Yes, I like that.'

Besides gifts for mother and baby, Loraine had also brought news of an exhibition which was to take place in Cardiff the following autumn.

'It's going to be a grand affair by the look of the details planned so far. You're invited to display up to six models on a stand. According to the diagram it's in a good position, halfway around the circle of displays. It's near the dais where Mrs Dorothy Piper-Davies will open the proceedings,' she said with a wry smile.

'Oh dear. Mrs Piper-Davies and I aren't exactly friends.'

Telling Mr and Mrs Flowers that the child they would be fostering was a girl was a happy experience. They were the only other people Ancret was able to tell and she laughed joyfully at Marguerite's excitement.

'With two boys of our own, both at school, it will be lovely to have a little girl to enjoy.'

'For a while,' Ancret reminded her.

'Of course we understand that. She's yours and we'll never allow her to think otherwise, however long she stays with us.'

Marguerite Flowers came to the hospital to be introduced to her new foster child and she was as loving as Ancret could have hoped. She discussed the child's needs with the nursing staff before coming back to talk to Ancret at length about what Natalie would require, making arrangements for the purchase and delivery of all that was needed. Ancret looked thoughtfully at the extensive list, considering her remaining bank balance.

'The money we put aside to help us through the quiet periods of the year will soon be gone,' she told her mother on the phone later. 'I hadn't dreamed that a child would cost so much. And there's the monthly payment for her care.'

'We'll manage,' Loraine assured her with more confidence than she felt.


Jonathan was concerned about the renewed interest of the police. When they began asking questions about the death of his partner two years previously, he became alarmed. His answers were defensive and he felt like running away from their ill-concealed suspicions.

'Do you have in your possession anything belonging to Jeff Talbot?' he was asked.

'No, of course not. It's all such a long time ago. Anything in the office – like a jacket, I seem to remember, and a few pens – was returned to his widow. Why d'you ask?'

'No reason, Mr Power.'

When he went to see his mother and was told they had been to see her too, asking about how he began his business, Jonathan began to feel hunted. He went to the police station, spoke to an inspector and demanded to be told the reason for the endless questions.

'We're just completing our enquiries, sir, nothing to worry about.'

'Completing your enquiries? My business partner Jeff Talbot died in an accident two years ago.'

'We need to check on everything after a sudden death, you have to understand that, sir. Even if it means looking back on previous events that might or might not be connected.'

'But my uncle was seriously ill. He'd had a heart attack that might have killed him if he'd been unable to seek help. The condition the illness had left him in meant his death wasn't unexpected. The doctor explained to us he'd have to be very careful. I think it was a warning to my mother, preparing her for the inevitable. Besides all that, how can his death relate to Jeff Talbot's accident?'

'That's what we need to find out, sir.'

'It wasn't to my advantage to kill Jeff. In fact it put me

in a desperate situation for a while. I needed him to help me cope with the growing business. It was new and there was no money available to hire extra staff. We worked for practically nothing. Because of the nil return on our investment, we'd both agreed to leave our fifty per cent to the other if something happened. There would have been nothing to share: the business would have had to close down if the little we had was divided.'

'And how long would this arrangement have lasted?'

'Three years only, while the investment was worth so little. After that the arrangements would have been reorganized.'

'And how long did the agreement have to run?' The question was asked casually but the answer seemed damning.

'A few more months.'

'So, although his death was . . . inconvenient, there was a certain advantage in the timing of it?'

'No, it wasn't like that. Ask his wife. In fact, I paid for the funeral, an unnecessary gesture offered out of my regrets and long friendship. It was all I could manage at the time. I'd have been better off in many ways if Jeff had lived.'

'But you'd have owned only fifty per cent of Pen-Marr Estate Agency?' He didn't wait for Jonathan's reply; he just nodded and walked out of the office.

Jonathan watched from the window as the policeman walked back to his car. Where had all this come from? There had been no such difficulties at the time of Jeff's death. The car that had hit him had never been found, no one had been charged. Presumably the case had remained open. But at the time, his alibi had been strong, unshakeable. He had been in West Wales, having taken his mother to where she was giving a demonstration on skin care and make-up.

He remembered the day well. With so much to do he had resented having to drive her to Tenby and hang around while she gave her talk and demonstration. He spent the three hours sitting in cafés, walking to the beach, watching the busy little harbour and sitting in yet more cafés as the time slowly passed.

It was a fascinating town, charming and full of history, but on that day, when he needed to be somewhere else, he was frustrated at the waste of his time and saw none of its many attractions. He had simply waited for the time to pass, wishing he could sometimes say no to his demanding mother.

So what had changed to make the police suspicious? Did they believe they had missed a possible motive? If only someone had been charged and found guilty of careless driving, this nightmare wouldn't be happening.

It was as he was walking back to his car that he began to think about a possible explanation. Jeff Talbot might be dead, but his niece wasn't. Could Lottie have something to do with this? Come on, he told himself, let's not get paranoid. She was only nineteen. How could he believe she would do something so devious and evil? But then, paranoia was not such a distant stranger as he might have believed. Because here he was, a rational man, prosaic even, experienced in business, good at understanding people, reasonably honest, starting to think that one of his assistants, who just happened to have had a crush on him, was capable of telling the police he might have murdered his partner and his uncle.

He wished Ancret were there to talk him out of his fears. She would laugh, tell him he was too vain if he believed a girl like Lottie would care that much. And, he told himself as his worries increased, Lottie would have had to care for him quite a lot, for love to turn to such hatred. He thought back to the way he had dealt with her infatuation. Although much of the trouble could be placed at his mother's feet, there was no doubt he, personally, had handled it badly.

Lucinda knew Jonathan was more worried by the continuing interest of the police than he pretended. He had made light of it to her and said nothing at all to his mother; he had told Lucinda that he didn't want Caroline worried while her grief for Richard was so acute. He had no one apart from herself with whom to talk about his fears. And although she had worked for him for several years, they had never been able to share confidences.

Making an excuse of needing to do some urgent shopping, she left for an early lunch and went to Moments. The salon was empty at first, then Angela came in and explained she had been in the fitting room, helping Loraine with a client.

'I'm sorry you had to wait. Would you like to make an appointment?'

'I'd like a brief word with Loraine,' Lucinda replied. 'It's very important.'

'I'm sorry, but Loraine will be with her client for a while yet,' Angela told her. 'We allow at least an hour. Can I ask her to give you a ring?'

'No. I have to see her, now.'

Angela looked at her watch. 'I should think she'll be another half an hour at least. A bridal gown isn't a five-minute purchase,' she explained politely, 'and we never rush them into making a decision.'

'You don't know when Ancret is coming back, do you?' Lucinda asked.

'I haven't asked, but didn't she say March? It's almost the end of February, so it won't be long. Sorry I can't be more helpful. She'll be back when the college term ends, I imagine. Isn't that at Easter? Is it anything I can help you with?'

Lucinda hesitated for a moment, then decided to take the girl into her confidence.

'Please don't tell Loraine I've discussed it with you, but it's Jonathan. He's a bit upset by his uncle's death and – well, I thought if I had definite news of when Ancret is coming home it might cheer him.' She said nothing about the police and their questions. The least said now, the sooner the rumours would end. And there were rumours; the regular visits to the police and overheard snatches of conversation were enough to set tongues wagging.

'I'm sorry, but I understood their relationship had ended. But perhaps I'm wrong. I try not to become involved, you see. Ancret and her mother work together and talk about private things sometimes. I've learned to shut myself off from it. It's best, don't you think?'

When Loraine came into the salon she was ushering before her a smiling, rosy-cheeked young woman. Behind them was an older woman, probably the mother of the bride-to-be, Lucinda guessed.

'Miss Bishop is taking model number 77464, Angela, the Lady Emmeline,' she said as she guided the young woman to the counter. 'I thought the Lady Angelique at first, but

125

when she put on Lady Emmeline, we all knew it was the perfect gown for her.' She chattered happily, unaware that Lucinda was standing near the door.

'What a perfect choice,' Angela agreed. 'I'm so pleased to have seen you wearing it. I wish you every happiness for your special day.' Angela's voice was warm and genuine. After preparing the credit card machine and receipt book for her, she stepped aside and allowed Loraine and the mother to deal with the sale, while she led Lucinda to the furthest side of the room out of their hearing.

When the two women had gone, Lucinda was already late returning to work. 'Can you spare a moment, Mrs—' She realized that she didn't know Ancret's surname and smiled. 'I'd better call you Loraine,' she said, half apologetically.

'It's Carter, but of course call me Loraine. It's my business name, after all. Now, how can I help?'

'It's Jonathan,' she began when Loraine had taken her through to the workroom at the back of the shop. 'He's having a difficult time and, well . . . He has no one close to talk to and I wondered if you have a date for Ancret's return. It would cheer him, I think.'

'Ancret and Jonathan are no longer close, I thought you would know that.'

'I do know, of course I know. But you see, the police are asking difficult questions about his uncle's death. Oh, he hasn't done anything wrong,' she added hastily as Loraine took a step backwards. 'Something, or someone, has made them hesitate to close the case.'

'I'm sorry, my dear. It's kind of you to be so concerned for your employer, but I don't yet know when Ancret will be back. When she does come home she'll be very busy. There's a lot of catching up to do, with orders coming in for summer events. And she's been asked to exhibit some of her designs in an important charity do here in Cardiff.'

'I'm sorry to have bothered you. I just thought he'd feel better if he could talk to her.'

'I'll tell her when I next speak to her and explain about Jonathan's need for a confidante.'

'You won't tell Jonathan I've talked to you?'

'Of course not, but I often wonder why we're so ashamed

of showing that we care,' Loraine said as she showed her out.

'Will Ancret be home soon?' asked Angela when they were alone.

'In another two or three weeks, hopefully. Even though she's done what she can while she's been away, the work is piling up.'

'I knew Jonathan wasn't what he seemed,' Loraine said when she spoke to Ancret later. 'Haven't I always said he was hiding his true self?'

'You can't really believe he's a murderer. That's ridiculous.'

'Someone always says that when a murderer is caught. "I'd never have believed it of him."'

'Mummy, that's nonsense.'

'Is it?'

'Of course it is!'

'Yes . . . I suppose it is,' admitted Loraine reluctantly.

'But is he really in trouble?'

'If he's innocent, then no. He'll have to be patient through the final questioning and that will be that.'

'Natalie is going to her temporary home at the weekend and I'm coming home.'

'Thank goodness for that. You will be all right, won't you? It isn't an easy thing to do what you've decided.'

'It will be hard. She found a place in my heart that will be a constant pain when I leave her. But it has to be this way.'

'We'll have to face a few weeks warding off questions and being careful with our answers, then this deception will become easier.'

'Hardly. We have to continue lying about our beautiful baby until we can bring her home and tell everyone she's adopted. More lies.'

'For how long, Ancret?'

'I don't know. I've painted myself into a corner, haven't I?'

'Both of us will get sticky feet before this is over.'

'I should have told Jonathan, not walked away and grieved

127

for his unreliability and lack of compassion where a child is concerned.'

'You would never have coped with the pressure. I can see that. Imagine being hounded by Jonathan begging you to have an abortion and Caroline supporting him, as I'm sure she would. She admitted once that she never wanted grandchildren. Maybe it was vanity or maybe there's another reason; either way you're best out of it. No, we have to go with it and see where it takes us.'

'Away from Cardiff one day? To another place where we can start again?'

'Maybe.'

'Oh, Mummy, I'll miss little Natalie so much. It will be like leaving behind a part of myself.'

'You'll see her often. And you can get used to anything, in time, believe me.'

Ancret wondered if her mother was thinking about the child in her dream, but she said nothing to encourage her to explain.

'I've arranged to visit Natalie every other Sunday,' she told her instead. 'I want her to know me and love me as I love her.'

'I believe Mr and Mrs Flowers will support you as you wish. There's only one thing, I hope I can visit her with you. Not every time, but on occasions. I want her to know me too.' As she said this, she knew she was lying and that she would never go to visit Mr and Mrs Flowers. That would ruin everything.

'Of course you will.'

It was harder than Ancret had imagined saying goodbye to her daughter. It had sounded so simple until she had held her, bathed and fed her, had looked down on her sweet, peaceful face during naps, had watched as she stretched and awoke from sleep. She took enough photographs to fill a first album. She left films for the Flowers to take more. 'It's all I'll have for the first months of her life,' she said sadly.

'No, there'll be visits, and letters from us, and we'll email when something interesting occurs. Who knows, it might be you who discovers her first tooth and witnesses her first steps.'

Their final word was to promise that everything of importance would be reported. There was nothing more she could do. When she left the house, where Marguerite and Simon Flowers stood holding her child and waving goodbye, she turned back only once. Then she got into the taxi and forced herself to look ahead at the tasks waiting for her in the room behind Moments.

After looking through the appointment book and glancing through the daily log, which her mother had kept all the time she'd been away, Ancret tried to rest. Every time she closed her eyes she saw her daughter's face, and that desperate ache in the crook of her arm, where Natalie had spent so much time since her birth, wouldn't go away. She knew she wouldn't sleep.

When her mother went to bed, after they had talked a while, she went back downstairs and into the workroom. She fiddled with design ideas, scribbling on her sketch pad aimlessly, then began to picture a small hat that would go with one of the new bridal gowns in the showroom. She saw in her mind's eye a young woman wearing the slim-fitting cream creation and started working. Her nimble fingers began to make the hat from a small, elongated oval base, which she slowly, painstakingly covered with individually made roses in cream and apricot. It was a delightful hat, a hat around which to spin dreams, and when she had finished it she knew it was perfect. It had already served one purpose; It was five thirty a.m. and her first night without Natalie was over.

Jonathan was sitting with a glass of wine at his elbow watching the early evening news in the silent flat. He had so desperately wished for solitude when his mother had shared it, wanting the opportunity to live his life the way he chose, invite Ancret without having to make devious plans to steal a few private moments, not having to make allowances for her, be at her beck and call, be her chauffeur. But now, with so much on his mind, he would have welcomed her company.

The loud knocking on the door and the simultaneous ringing of the doorbell made him jump. The impatient demands didn't sound like his mother; anyway, she had her own key. It was almost as though the place was on fire, he thought with amusement as he went to answer. Perhaps by some miracle it was Ancret. He was smiling as he opened the door. But the smile froze as he recognized the policemen who had questioned him before.

'Do come in, before you alarm all the neighbours,' he said with sarcastic politeness.

'Thank you, sir.'

He followed them into the lounge and pointed questioningly to the bottle of wine. Both men shook their heads. He sat and looked at them, trying to appear nonchalant, even amused by their visit. The questions, which went over the same ground as before, sobered him, and he wondered when it would end.

'Would you have any objection to us looking around?' he was asked. He spread his arms wide and said, 'Do help yourselves. Nothing is locked, you are welcome to look where you will.'

'A cup of coffee would be nice, if you wouldn't mind,' one of them asked. But Jonathan shook his head. 'You want me out of the way while you search? No, I don't think so. I'm coming with you.'

Inexperienced as he was, he could see that the search was cursory until they came to his bedroom. They opened the wardrobe doors and investigated the pockets of his suits, then one of them approached the bedside cupboard and was joined by the other. Jonathan frowned. What could they want in there?

They opened the drawer and shuffled the handkerchiefs and gloves about, then knelt down and opened the door of the cupboard below. Books were lifted out and placed on the floor, followed by a box which they opened. Inside were a watch, several pens, a pocket-sized Filofax and a desk diary.

'Are these items yours, Mr Power?'

'No, they belonged to my deceased partner, Jeff Talbot.'

'Can you explain why they're here and not with his wife? You see, you told us—' He thumbed through his notebook and went on, 'You said you had nothing belonging to your ex-partner.'

'I'd forgotten these. I told Mrs Talbot they were in the office, but at the time she didn't want to see them. When I

130

returned his coat and a few of his collection of pens she asked me not to take the rest as she was too upset to handle them. I took her at her word and they've been here ever since. The watch might be worth something and I didn't want it to get lost.'

'Mrs Talbot will be able to verify what you're saying?'

'Of course.'

When they made a phone call, he knew someone would go to talk to Mrs Talbot without giving him time to speak to her himself. He felt sweat trickle down his body. This was serious. Everything he said seemed to make it worse. Who had done this? If it wasn't Lottie, could it have been Mrs Talbot? Surely not. She had remained friendly and even grateful for his support at the time of Jeff's death. But if she had been harbouring resentment and suspicion, she might deny knowledge of the watch and pens. It would be another step taking him towards a full investigation.

Ancret began her plans for the exhibition, thinking about a suitable theme for her display. Then, once her ideas were on paper, she concentrated on hats for summer weddings and the gratifyingly long list required for Ladies' Day at Royal Ascot in June. A client phoned for an appointment and spoke to Loraine. 'Oh, good afternoon, Mrs Piper-Davies,' Ancret heard her say loudly. 'Of course – yes – I understand perfectly. You will bring your outfit so my daughter can see exactly what style and colour you will need, won't you? – She will give you a hat to enjoy – At two fifteen? – We'll be expecting you.' She put down the phone and smiled at her daughter. 'As you heard, that was Mrs Piper-Davies wanting what she called a "consultation".'

'Wedding? Christening? Garden party?'

'Her son's wedding.'

'I'll give her a joyful hat for a joyful occasion,' Ancret smiled.

Money was tight with the extra expenses for baby Natalie, but Ancret knew she had to try and rent extra space to store hats if she were not to have to refuse orders because of lack of room.

'The irritating thing is, if I were still close to Jonathan

he'd have been able to help. I'm sure he'd know of a place we could rent. It only has to be secure and clean.'

'Why not ask him? You haven't parted swearing never to set eyes on each other again, have you?'

'I haven't contacted him since I got back.'

'Put another way, he hasn't contacted you. His mother probably forbids it,' she added with a grim smile.

'I could ask, couldn't I,' Ancret mused. 'Perhaps I will.'

When she went to the estate agent's office, it was closed. She expected there would be a notice explaining why, but there was nothing. As she was turning away, a police car drove up. With idle curiosity she watched as the driver got out and opened the rear door to allow a man to step out.

'Jonathan?' she said aloud. She made to move forward but then stopped. This was not a good time to talk to him. He looked harassed and not a little angry. What her mother had said, that he was being questioned about the two deaths, must be correct. She began to walk away. Better let some time pass rather than intrude at this inconvenient moment.

Then she heard his name being called. Looking back, she saw Lottie running towards him. 'Is everything all right now?' she called. 'Are the police satisfied? My aunt assured me she told them everything they wanted to know.' Ancret came closer, wanting to intrude, offer her own good wishes, push this irritating girl out of the way.

'I'm glad you're pleased. I thought you were the one making them suspicious,' Jonathan said. 'I'm glad I was wrong.'

'You thought I'd do such a terrible thing? Oh, Jonathan, how could you think that? I'd never do anything to hurt you. You were unkind when I showed you I cared a little, and you dismissed me from a job I loved, but I'm too fond of you to want revenge. I understood your state of mind.' Her eyes filled up and she stared at him with a pleading, hurt expression.

A movement at the edge of his vision made him turn, and he and Ancret stared at each other. In a moment of madness, a childish instinct he immediately regretted, he hugged Lottie and told her he was sorry.

Ancret didn't move. She stood and watched as he walked

132

into the office, unlocking the door while still holding Lottie close with an arm around her shoulders, and disappeared inside.

She went back to the workshop and with a few strokes of her pen created a bold and beautiful hat. It would be a large model, with a huge brim and shallow, puffed crown in gaudy fuschia pink that would turn heads whenever the wearer passed by. The wide brim would curl under and she could see in her mind the flowers she would make of the same material, fastened beneath the brim on one side, with stems popping out, so that from every angle the hat offered surprises. It would be a hat for someone oozing confidence, someone who loved to be both noticed and remembered.

Hours later, as she ironed the brim of another model under layers of wet cloth, she was laughing at the joy of the beautiful fuschia creation, and crying tears for – she knew not what. Loneliness? A need to hold her child? A need for someone to hold her? Jonathan?

She was lonely, she admitted it. For a moment she regretted parting from Jonathan and all he had promised. Then, as she looked again at the perfectly shaped hat, lifting it off its stand and putting it on her own head, using mirrors to see every side, she felt the warmth of success flow through her. This was a joyous hat; it promised wonderful times for whoever bought it. She held it up in front of a mirror so she could continue to admire it, and sighed contentedly. This was who she was: Ancret, a designer of beautiful things, a woman who sold dreams.

When she looked at the time, she realized with a shock that she had been there for seven hours. As her mother hadn't appeared to offer at least a cup of coffee, she must think she was still out, talking to Jonathan.

'Mummy?' she called, walking past the silent, dark salon with its models eerily displaying dresses shrouded in night covers. 'I'm starving. Is there any hope of some food?'

'Where have you been?' Loraine asked.

'Come and see.' Ancret smiled and led her mother to the workroom where, on a plastic head, in front of the spotlit triple mirror, the hat was displayed. Loraine gasped with delight. She looked at it wordlessly for a while, then said,

'It's a wonderful hat. Ancret, I'm so proud of you.' She continued looking at it from all sides, picked it up and examined the neat stitching at the join in the headband, where the label had been sewn in. Then, with a smile, she said, 'I hope we have a client who deserves it. It's far too good for Mrs Piper-Davies.'

'Do we have any spare cash?' Ancret asked.

'No, none that we don't need twice over.'

'Who cares. Let's eat out tonight.'


Jonathan spent some time trying to trace Babs, but he was unsuccessful. The last time he'd heard of her, she was married to an older man who, she had told his mother bitterly, didn't have his way to make. But, with no idea of her married name, he was frustrated. He had called at her mother's address, to be told she had moved away and none of the neighbours knew where to find her. Still thinking of Babs and her children, particularly Donald, he arrived at his mother's house one Sunday morning, intending to do some gardening, only to be startled out of his reverie. The house was full of people.

He stepped into the lounge and the first person he saw was Lottie.

'Caroline, Jonathan's here,' she called, taking his hand and leading him to where his mother sat on a couch between two other women. He recognized one of them, having given her lifts to several of his mother's talks and demonstrations.

'What's going on, Mother?' he asked, bending to kiss her cheek.

'A surprise party, dear,' Caroline said. 'They arrived with everything for lunch and I was told nothing about it. Wasn't that clever of them?'

'Not if you'd been out,' he said with a laugh.

'No chance of that. I made sure she'd be here,' Lottie said, touching Caroline's cheek affectionately.

He looked around at the smartly dressed guests, half expecting, hoping, to see Babs there. But apart from Lottie, who shone like a bright star dressed in a pink, sequinned top and tight velvet trousers more suitable for evening wear, the rest were of his mother's age and older. Babs didn't belong with them. But neither did Lottie, he thought, as he watched her mingle and offer food and drink. He wondered, half amused, whether her clothes had been chosen by his mother.

Whoever had come up with the idea of this luncheon party had obviously contacted Lottie to make the arrangements. Why hadn't it been he they had turned to for help? Looking around, he recognized many of them; they had either been neighbours or were people connected with his mother's business. 'What's the occasion?' he asked. 'It isn't your birthday.'

'She needed a day of fun,' one of them explained. 'After the shock of her brother Richard's death, and the worry of you being questioned by the police and everything.'

'But there was nothing worrying about my being questioned,' he said at once. 'Come on, I was only helping them to save my mother getting any more upset.' He turned to Lottie and spoke a little sharply. 'I hope you haven't been exaggerating, making it seem more than that?'

'Helping with enquiries,' another said, 'isn't that what they call it? Your poor dear mother was desperately frightened for you, wasn't she?' she asked of the room in general. There was a chorus of agreement.

'I was with Uncle Richard when he died, so of course they had to find out exactly what had happened.' He tried to smile but his face stiffened and anger was growing. 'I'll get myself a drink,' he said. 'Then, if you'll excuse me, I'll start clearing the garden before the light goes.'

'Oh, not today, Jonathan,' Caroline pleaded. 'Not after all this has been arranged.'

'Who did arrange it?' he asked, when they were alone. He became further irritated when she gave the expected reply.

'Lottie, of course. Isn't she a darling?'

'She's persistent, I'll give you that,' he muttered.

Determined as he was not to give Lottie an opportunity to treat him as a close friend, he was pleased with the idea of this surprise. Caroline was certainly enjoying it, and he had to thank the girl for that – albeit with caution. He didn't work on the garden – but, before the party began to break up and Lottie could suggest he stayed or asked for a lift home, he left.

*   *   *

135

A rather more subdued Dorothy Piper-Davies came on time to keep her appointment, and when she saw the hat Ancret had created on the night after her parting from Natalie, she wanted it. The suit she had brought did not match, but she insisted that she would buy another one that did.

She returned a few hours later, ignoring the repeated request to make a new appointment, and showed Ancret the dress she had bought. It was a perfect choice. Rather reluctantly, Ancret let her have the beautiful hat. 'I'll be able to wear it to Ascot as well as the local charity lunch,' Dorothy explained, without balking at the exceptionally high price. 'It's too beautiful to wear once and put away in a box. It's a wonderful hat and it deserves to be seen.'

Flattered at the generous compliment, Ancret promised that she would make Mrs Piper-Davies's future needs a priority. 'But of course you will,' Dorothy said in surprise. 'I'm a very important person.'

The first visit to Natalie was difficult for Ancret. Holding the baby in her arms, coaxing her to take the milk Mrs Flowers had prepared, changing her nappy, afraid of handling the tiny helpless body was bitter-sweet. She was emotional when it was time to leave; saying goodbye that second time was one of the most difficult moments of her life.

Darkness had fallen when Marguerite Flowers walked her to the bus stop. There was a fire up on the hill.

'The gypsies are back,' Marguerite said. 'They no longer live there through the winter like they did when we were children, but they return sometimes for a celebration. A wedding party or a birthday. The farmer allows them to keep an old vardo there and they paint it and make sure it's properly cared for.'

'Perhaps they'd allow me to visit them one day?' Ancret said, raising an arm to stop the bus as it came into sight.

'You'd be welcome.'

Late that evening, when she and her mother were about to go to bed, Ancret checked her email and found a message telling her that after her visit, Natalie had settled peacefully and was sleeping contentedly. She hid her tears and told Loraine that she was happy with her choice of foster parents.

'I don't think I could have found anyone better.'

'And next time, can I come?'

'Next time, of course. I had to go alone today. I was afraid that if you'd been there, filled with love for her and sympathy for me, I might have succumbed to my longing and brought her home. And that would never do, would it?'

'It won't get easier, I can tell you that. But you'll learn to cope.'

Once again Loraine's words were strange, hinting at something unexplained. Was this to do with the child she held in her dreams and for whom she pleaded so desperately? Ancret wondered if she would ever know. Surely if there had been a child lost in the past, now would be the time to be told about it, now she was a mother herself?

Loraine had the dream again that night, clinging to a child and pleading for help. But although Ancret held her until she woke, trying to make sense of what was being said, she learned nothing further about the reason behind her mother's great sadness.

# Eight

Jonathan ate out most evenings and reached the flat about nine thirty, then worked until he was tired enough to sleep. He missed Ancret and wished things could have been different. He often sat and wondered whether he had been wrong to tell her about Babs and the loss of her two children. There was no doubt Ancret had been shocked by his unfeeling behaviour. But it had been the right thing at the time; they had been too young and he had his way to make, unencumbered by the responsibilities of a family. And apart from that there were the risks about which his mother had urgently warned him. It wasn't the deed that had been the mistake, but telling Ancret about it. Hadn't it?

Thinking more deeply, he began to imagine the possible outcome if he had married Babs. There would probably be no business, no Pen-Marr agency, no smart flat, no expensive car. Yet, looking around this soulless room where he sat alone, with only the now blank screen of the television for spurious company, he wondered if he had made a terrible mistake. Had he been wrong to force Babs to give up their children? He *had* forced her, talking to her endlessly and with scarcely veiled threats, cruelly using her love for him to get his own way.

She had done what he asked, but she had cried pitifully as he argued, persisted and even shouted until she relented and gave in. He remembered swearing to love her for ever, but when it happened a second time and he accused her of deliberately becoming pregnant, everything had ended.

She had seemed less distressed at the loss of her second child, hiding her true feelings from him, accepting the cruel loss not with regret or bitterness but almost with indifference, drained and weary. Prepared for long, drawn out

138

arguments and pleading and tears, with his mother joining him in the persuasions with gentler words, he had been faced with Babs's cold, calm acceptance. He should have known then that he was killing not only a child but her love for him.

Now, having seen the little boy called Donald, he realized why she had shown no remorse. She had left the clinic without undergoing the operation. His demands had been ignored and now the child was there to taunt him, making him face the situation his mother had predicted. *My name is Donald. Who are you?* the voice in his head had asked in that deep monotone. The chances of the boy not being his were remote. The dates were right and the look on Babs's face, defiant, satisfied, left him in no doubt.

Anger filled him like a foul poison. How could she have been so dishonest? She knew how he felt about having a child, especially after the first one, even if he hadn't fully explained the reason. She must know now that his fears were justified.

There had been no great emotional goodbye; the engagement had ended with hardly a whimper. His pleas for a return to their closeness, his promises of love and commitment, had faded. When Babs moved away, he didn't know until weeks had passed.

It was as though everything that happened at that time had been stored on film. He sat there reliving it, but with previously unimagined insight into Babs's despair. Now he was beginning to understand just a little of how she must have suffered. She had gone to the clinic on the second occasion with his words ringing in her ears, repeated accusations that the pregnancy had been a deliberate ploy on her behalf so he would marry her and give up on his ambition. Had she been hoping, even at the last minute, that he would change his mind? In those moments of clarity he likened her situation to that of a condemned criminal, but Babs had been guilty only of loving him.

After the first shock of telling her she had to get rid of it, his determined refusal to accept a child into his life, she had said very little, but her indifference had been a cover for her true feelings. Disguised by her subdued acceptance, had she decided then to leave him? He and his mother had failed to persuade her to give up the child: seeing the little six-year-old boy called Donald had made that clear.

All his concerns were for himself until that point. He saw in his head the group standing in the church, Babs and the little girl and the younger boy, and the one with Down's syndrome called Donald. His mother had been right to warn him.

Then he heard more persistently the child's voice, with its slow, carefully spoken demand. *I'm Donald. Who are you?* He answered in his mind, *I'm the man who wanted you killed.* And the shocking truth frightened him more than anything else in his whole life. Having seen the little boy standing there, a part of a family, interested in the proceedings, happy and loved, brought it home. He had wanted this little person dead.

Guilt swamped him like a gigantic wave of icy air. Ancret was right; he had been completely forceful and unfeeling. He listened to the silence, knowing that if he had behaved differently he wouldn't be sitting here alone.

As he finished his drink and prepared for sleep that he knew would be a long time coming, he wondered whether there was any point in calling to talk to Ancret. He was already blaming his mother, easing his own conscience by telling it as she had explained it to him. Perhaps if he were totally honest about what had happened, told Ancret the full story, shed his shame and guilt in front of her, she might forgive and allow them to begin again.

Babs was asleep when the sound of one of the children crying woke her. She went into the bedroom where Tracy and Donald slept and saw Tracy on the floor, sleepily rubbing her eyes. Donald was sitting up in bed. It was he who had called his mother.

'Dream,' he said, pointing to his sister. 'Bad dream.'

'That's right, Donald. Good boy for waking me.'

'Good boy,' he repeated with a smile.

Babs remade the bed, gave them both a small drink of water, sang to them softly and waited until they had returned to sleep. Life on her own with three children was not easy.

Her husband had left when Donald arrived; that had been a dreadful shock, but she had never regretted having him. Like most children with Down's syndrome, he was loving and so straightforward, bringing his own special joy. How could she regret having him?

Adopting him after Harry and Tracy had been deliberate. He was to replace the little boy she had lost. He too would have been a Down's child, but he'd had so many other problems as well that he couldn't have survived.

She often wondered if that had been the reason for Jonathan not wanting a child, the fear of having a less than perfect baby. If so, that nonsensical attitude had been encouraged by Caroline; looking back, she had told Jonathan what to think in most situations. He was a weak man, like her husband. Maybe they both needed a strong woman – something she was not, she thought sadly.

She made a cup of tea and sat thinking about Jonathan. Would her life have been happier if she had stayed with him? Marriage to Jonathan wouldn't have been perfect. It would have meant sharing her life with Caroline. His mother would never have been content to stay uninvolved. Whatever Jonathan did, Caroline had to be a part of it, wearing him down if he disagreed with what she thought best, and that would never have changed.

Jonathan had one final visit from the police. They told him that there would be no more questioning, that the case would most probably be closed.

'Cautious as ever,' he said with a smile, silently thankful to Lottie for persuading her aunt to accept his innocence. 'You never really give up, do you?'

'Miss Lottie Talbot came into the station,' the policeman began. Presuming he knew what was about to be said, Jonathan started to interrupt. Then, as the words continued, he stopped. 'Miss Talbot regrets her accusations and believes they were unfounded. Her aunt hadn't wanted her to drag it all up and they both assure us that the allegations were false.'

Jonathan stared at the man. *Miss* Talbot? 'Don't you mean *Mrs* Talbot, Jeff's wife?'

'Lottie Talbot. Miss,' the man replied, checking his

notebook. 'But don't worry, Mr Power, everything has been sorted out and we're satisfied.'

The second man explained, 'It seems that the death of your uncle upset her, brought back memories of her grief when she lost her own uncle.'

So it had been Lottie who had started the enquiry and not her aunt. He thanked the constable for informing him and went to find Lottie.

She was in the office browsing through a magazine, a packet of sandwiches on the desk beside her. She had begun to call occasionally on the pretext of visiting Lucinda or asking about Caroline. 'Lucinda's gone to the printers to collect some leaflets,' she said. 'I promised to stay and watch the shop until she gets back.'

He told her what he had learned and for a while she insisted that a mistake had been made. Then she smiled and tilted her head on one side. 'Jonathan, why are you so angry with me? You should be flattered.'

'Flattered?' he repeated. Then he sighed deeply. 'Tell me how you work that out, please, I'd love to hear your explanation of this.'

'I'd do anything to attract your attention, you must know that by now. I love you, Jonathan, and you must know that too.'

'So you try to get me arrested?'

'I was hurt. You humiliated me in front of all Uncle Richard's friends. I wanted to make you feel hurt too. There was no danger of you being arrested. I knew my aunt wouldn't go along with it. She considers you a friend and often tells me about how generous you were, with time and money, when Uncle Jeff died.'

He shivered visibly at the thought of how easily he might have ended up in prison.

'I wanted an excuse to be with you, put you in a mess then help you.'

'By telling dangerous lies?'

He stood to leave but she slipped around in front of him and leaned against the door. 'Forgive me?'

'Get out of my way. You're either dangerous or stupid, I'm not sure which. I *am* sure I don't want to see even your shadow ever again. D'you understand? Stay away from me and my mother.'

Lottie walked away from the office, slowly but with no sign of regret. Jonathan would come round, she was sure of it. Flattery was a woman's best weapon.

As soon as Lucinda returned from her errand, Jonathan went to a wine bar and dwelt more on the loss of Ancret and of Babs, wishing he could go back and relive it all, do everything differently. But how different would he make it? He would still not have wanted the children: at the time he and Babs had broken up, he'd had a long way to go, the business to build. But, given the chance of reliving more recent months, he wouldn't have pressured Ancret. If he'd accepted her need for a career they would have been happy. It seemed that happiness would elude him for the rest of his life. And most of the problems were due to his own stupidity.

He spoke to his mother on most days, and although he didn't talk to her about his sad reminiscences she picked up on his mood today. A voice on the telephone can be very revealing to someone who knows you well. Caroline's concerned questions resulted in no answers, but she knew he was unhappy. And she was determined he would turn in his loneliness to Lottie and not Ancret.

The following evening he went straight back to the flat after closing the office. Sitting on the floor outside the door was Lottie, beside her a carrier bag from the local supermarket.

'What are you doing here?' he asked ungraciously.

'Your mother sent me,' she said, pulling herself up. 'She's worried and I promised to call.'

'My mother sent you,' he repeated disbelievingly. 'I'm a grown man, why should I believe she asked you to call?'

'Because it's true. Well? Are you going to let me in?'

He unlocked the door and she went ahead of him into the kitchen. She lifted the carrier bag and proceeded to spill the contents out on to the work surface.

'Dinner,' she explained succinctly.

'I'm eating later.'

'Twenty minutes, tops,' she said unconcerned. She washed salmon fillets and put them under the grill, then prepared a

143

salad. A baguette was broken into several pieces and a tub of Welsh butter, rich and salty, which she knew he loved, placed beside it.

'Aren't you even going to wash your hands?' she asked, as he stood watching her. And then he laughed.

'You've spent so much time with my mother you're beginning to sound like her.'

The meal was simple but fresh and enjoyable. Lottie talked very little, answering his questions but not expanding her answers as she would normally have done.

'I should have opened some wine,' he said, but Lottie shook her head.

'I don't want to be blamed for your hangover tomorrow morning.'

'I said a bottle, not a box.' He looked at her, wanting to share a smile, but she refused to raise her eyes from her plate, concentrating on adding a recalcitrant piece of beetroot to her fork.

'I'll clear the dishes, then I'll go,' she said as she removed two portions of fresh fruit salad from their plastic dishes.

He didn't reply. He was confused. One part of him wanted her to stay, another warned him of the consequences. His heart ached for company, but Lottie was persistent, his head warned him: the well-worn saying about being given an inch and taking a yard was certainly true of Lottie Talbot. The strongest voice was telling him to let her stay, as a barrier against another lonely evening. Yet another part of his over-active brain was reminding him that it was she who had reported suspicions about her uncle's death to the police.

'I have to go out in fifteen minutes,' he said rather abruptly, having made up his mind how he would end their cosy tête-a-tête.

'You go and get ready while I clear this away. Then I'll phone your mother if that's all right with you, then go home.'

'That's fine. Well, thanks for a surprise meal. Tell Mother I enjoyed it.' He felt ill at ease and he knew it showed. He hesitated to leave the room. How could he shower knowing she was in the flat? The lock on the shower-room door had been broken for weeks and he'd meant to get it fixed, but had decided there was no need as he so rarely invited anyone in. But how would she know? And besides, she'd hardly walk in and accost him, would she? What was the matter with him?

Aware of his discomfort, although not understanding the reason, Lottie said with a half smile, 'Don't worry, I have the car and I'm sure it'll start first time. Go and have your shower, and I'll be out of your way in a few minutes.'

Just a few words and she made him feel like a petulant ten-year-old. He almost decided not to shower. Why should he? Again she had spoken to him like his mother. Time to shower, make sure you clean your teeth, fresh socks in the drawer marked 'Socks' . . .

He closed the bedroom door and stripped off, throwing his clothes towards the linen basket. The shower was running so he didn't hear her enter, but when he went to pick up a clean towel she was standing behind the door, leaning back, watching him, her eyes moving up and down his body in a deliberate way.

'Lottie! Please go away!'

'You're lonely, I'm lonely. Why should I have to leave?' She moved sinuously towards him and began stroking his arms, his shoulders, then slowly downward. When she knew he was unable to resist, she kissed him.

'This isn't fair,' he murmured.

'No, not fair. You're at a disadvantage, aren't you?' She pulled her sweater over her head and began removing the rest of her clothes.

Common sense fought against desire and won. He picked up a towel, wrapped it around him and pushed her gently away. 'You have to go. You can't do this.'

'Why not? We both want it and no one else will be hurt.'

'There's no future for us, and you're too young to waste yourself on a casual one night stand. And that's all it would be.' He handed her the sweater she had abandoned and led her out of the bedroom. 'I'll talk to you tomorrow.'

He waited behind his bedroom door until he heard the door close and her footsteps fade. He was trembling and angry. His anger was against Lottie, not himself. Still wearing only the towel, and with the shower raining down without him, he picked up the phone.

'Mother, I do not want to see Lottie here again. D'you understand? She's becoming a perilous nuisance. Will you please not invite her to call on me and make sure I've eaten all my greens and washed behind my ears? It's a game to her, perhaps to you too, but it could land me in serious trouble.'

'What are you talking about, dear? I haven't seen her for a week, and I certainly didn't ask her to call.'

Ancret was dressing the window on Sunday morning. It was the week she didn't visit her daughter and she was too restless to work on her hats. She dressed a model in a slim-fitting bridal gown with an ivory skirt and a pale cream bodice, placing an artificial bouquet in the stiff hands. At one side was a sparkling dress with an ivory base. Multi-coloured, figure-hugging, this lovely material was becoming more and more popular for bridesmaids. A van pulled up and a man got out. He tapped the window and waved.

'I thought it was you,' he mouthed. She opened the shop door and invited him inside. 'Hello, Edmund. I'm just stopping for a cup of coffee, would you join us? Mummy is just making it.'

'Thank you, I'd love to. Will the van be all right there? I hate paying parking fines.'

She finished fixing a posy in the hand of the second model and pulled down the sun blind while he watched.

'Are you the designer?'

'Just the hats. Mummy and I make hats. Hats by Ancret.' She gestured into the workroom before switching off the light and leading him up the stairs.

'How fascinating. And how dull my life is by comparison. I'm the gofer in my parents' hotel. I take the visitors out on various trips. In fact, I'm going to Oxwich on Gower for tea. D'you fancy coming? Your mother too, of course?'

Ancret was tempted, but declined. 'Mummy isn't well,' she explained in a whisper. 'Best I stay home.'

'Otherwise you'd come?'

'Ask me again.'

Loraine felt dizzy and weak when she woke. As she began to rise, sickness threatened.

'Mummy, I'll telephone the doctor.' Anxiously Ancret began to dial, but stopped when her mother begged her not to make the call.

'I don't want the doctor, I don't need anything except an aspirin. Bring me a drink then I'll go back to sleep. I'll be fine when I wake up. I slept heavily, that's all.'

Doubtfully, Ancret agreed.

On the following Sunday, Loraine didn't visit Natalie as planned. She made the excuse of being tired after another restless night. Uneasy, wishing she didn't have to leave her mother for so long, Ancret went alone. She was a little surprised at her mother's decision. Loraine hadn't seen Natalie since her visit to the hospital.

Marguerite Flowers had been baking when Ancret arrived and she was offered a slice of chocolate cake with her cup of tea. The two boys were doing homework on the computer, and the baby was sleeping in her play-pen.

'I hope you don't mind my putting her in the play-pen, Ancret? Perhaps I should have asked you first? I want to get her used to going in there before she's mobile. It'll be so useful when there's a knock at the door, or I have to leave her for a minute, to be able to pop her in there where she'll be safe. If she's like my boys, she'll complain, but she'll be safe.'

'It seems a sensible precaution to me,' Ancret smiled. 'And no, you don't have to ask before doing what you think best.'

'Thank you.'

When Natalie woke, Ancret changed her and played with her for a while. At four thirty she stood to leave. 'I'd better catch the next bus,' she said. 'Otherwise I'll have a long wait before getting my connection.'

'Simon's out with his brother,' Marguerite said. 'They sometimes like to go for a long walk on Sundays. Fishing too sometimes, but they'd hoped to be back before you leave.'

'I'll see him next time.' She handed the boys some chocolates she had brought for them and gave Marguerite a hand-knitted coat for the baby made by her mother. Then, as she was closing the gate, she saw two men approaching, waving and hastening their steps. A glance at her watch made her

147

anxious. She didn't want to be late home with her mother unwell, and the bus was due in about ten minutes.

She waited while Simon introduced his younger brother, Jason, whose eyes smiled in obvious admiration.

'Do you have to go straight away?' Simon asked. 'Isn't there another bus later?'

'Yes, there's another bus. But I don't want to leave my mother too long, she wasn't well yesterday and she had a very restless night. Perhaps next time?'

Jason was tall and fair, very like his brother. His figure, disguised by corduroy trousers and bulky anorak, was hardly visible, but she knew that under the shapeless clothes he would be slim and well proportioned. His face was lean and strong. He looked the kind of man one could rely on in any situation. She stopped herself there. Her life was filled with complications and another man was something it would be impossible to take on board. It was a pity though. There was something about Jason Flowers that strongly appealed.

She felt Jason's eyes on her as she walked her slow, swaying walk to where a few people stood waiting for the bus. Although she wasn't looking for romance, couldn't even find room for someone else in her life at that time, the incident was warming, reminding her she was an unattached and attractive young woman. She was smiling when she found a seat, using the brief but pleasing memory of Jason to ease the pain of parting from Natalie.

When she got home, Loraine was in the workshop making a feathered trim for a hat on which Ancret was working.

'Mummy, I thought you'd stay in bed!'

'Nonsense, daughter. Look, what d'you think of these?' She lifted a sheet of paper to reveal a baker-boy hat in blue velvet with a huge covered button in the centre of the crown, under which there was a large appliqué flower in purple. Beside it was a baseball cap with an extra long brim which, as shown on the sketch pad close by, was designed to point sideways between eye and ear. This one was yellow, with brighter yellow dandelion flowers upright on one side and neatly hand-stitched leaves in lime-coloured leather lying across it. The stems were covered wire, and at once Ancret bent them twice so the flowers drooped over the edge, their heads tilted up like naughty faces.

They laughed at the effect and Ancret hugged her mother. 'They're both wonderful ideas. What if we make about five or more and make a display for April Fools' Day? Just for fun. Although I think they'll sell too. For every serious hat wearer there are a dozen who'll enjoy the entertainment.'

Ignoring their growing hunger, they sat and sketched until they had worked out seven or eight designs to try, talking about the changes already noticeable in Natalie.

'Oh, Mummy, I wish there were more hours in a day and days in a week.'

'If you were given an extra day how would you spend it?' Loraine asked.

'With Natalie.'

'I'll come next time. I feel deprived too. I haven't seen her since she was a couple of hours old and I've never met her foster parents at all.'

'I met Simon Flowers's brother today. Jason. He seems very nice. I think Natalie's safe and secure within the family. I hate leaving her, each time is worse than the last, but at least I don't have worries about her well-being.'

On the following Sunday, Ancret had arranged to see her daughter again, The Flowers family were going away for Easter and it would be too long between visits if she didn't go that week.

Unfortunately Loraine was still unwell. She sat at the table making up some of the designs for the fun hats they planned, but as soon as she stood up and began moving around she began to feel breathless. A cough bothered her, while she was troubled with exhaustion if she tried anything strenuous. She felt weak and unable to make the journey, even when Ancret suggested a taxi for most of it.

'You go, and make sure you take lots of photographs,' said Loraine. 'I don't want to pass this cold on to a tiny baby, do I?'

'It's more than a cold, Mummy. I'll go without you only if you promise to see the doctor tomorrow.'

Loraine nodded, but the look in her dark eyes made Ancret doubt the honesty of her intention.

'I'll go earlier and be back before evening.'

Loraine went to a cupboard and brought out a large card-board box. 'Take this to her. It isn't a play toy, just an orna-ment for her room.'

Inside Ancret found a beautifully made gypsy doll, with a tray of tiny pegs and wooden flowers, just the way they were depicted in magazines and story books. 'It's wonderful, Mummy! Perfect! When did you find time to make it? I haven't seen any of it.'

'In odd moments. Sometimes when I couldn't sleep I'd creep down and spend a little time making some of the small pieces, things I could quickly hide if you heard me and came down.'

Ancret stared at the doll, with its plaintive expression, the beautifully sewn dress and hand-knitted shawl, the leather boots and the long, dark hair. There was a bird in a wooden cage, and of course the woman was wearing a hat, a shape-less one-piece hood, ancient looking as though distorted by the weather. It had been fashioned and aged by her mother's skilled hands. She picked up some of the items from the tray, amazed at the tiny handkerchiefs, admiring the chrysanthemum-like flowers and the pegs, each an exact, tiny replica of the pegs made to sell door to door in past times and now rarely seen outside museums.

'Why a gypsy? What gave you the idea?'

'It's a figure we no longer see on our roads. Once they were so common a sight people rarely remarked on them, but now most of them are gone. A memory of my childhood perhaps.'

'The pieces are so tiny, yet everything, every stitch, is perfect. You, Mummy, are a very clever lady. I won't take it to the Flowers's though. I'd be so afraid of losing it or finding it broken. I'll keep this safe and treasure it until Natalie is grown up.'

She showed the doll to Helena when her friend called one day, without telling her for whom it had been intended. She longed to be able to talk to Helena about Natalie, show her photographs. It was becoming more and more difficult not to talk about her daughter. Every week there was something different to see as the little girl changed from helpless infant

150

to a child who recognized her with a smile, and struggled to turn from front to back, then back to front as she began the battle for mobility. Smiles were genuine and Ancret knew her daughter recognized her when she appeared.

When Helena saw the fun hats Loraine had started, their novelty appealed. 'Ancret, they're beautiful.'

'Mostly made by Mummy,' she said proudly. 'We aren't selling them for a week, we thought we'd advertise them in a display in the hope that we'll attract viewers who'll return as customers.'

'The stitching is perfect and the designs are wonderful. Fun hats, but made by an artist.'

'Mummy is so clever. And a good teacher. The two don't necessarily go together but in her case it did. I wish she didn't work so hard though. I think she's tired, but she won't see a doctor.'

'Give it a week or so, then go and see him yourself. Perhaps if he called she'd have to tell him what's wrong?'

The window display caught people's attention. Although the hats themselves were not suitable for weddings and other grand occasions, they brought casual passers-by to stare; and also, thanks mainly to Dorothy Piper-Davies, the other kind of client, the kind of customers Ancret wanted, wealthy people with taste, who were prepared to pay for top quality.

'Such fun, dear, don't you think?' she overheard Dorothy remark. 'I do think a sense of humour is important, whatever your business.'

Ancret began to face the fact she had been trying to ignore, that to attract so many new clients must eventually mean she would need a trained assistant. With the exception of every other Sunday, when she never failed to visit her daughter, her time was filled.

Caroline seemed surprised by Dorothy's interest in Ancret and shook her head when her friend extolled her talent. 'Nonsense, Dorothy, it's her mother who's the designer. When she goes Ancret will fall flat on her face. Yes, she convinces many people. But I know her, you see, dear. There'll be nothing left once her mother stops designing, mark my words.'

*   *   *

151

Jason was there when Ancret arrived one Sunday afternoon to see Natalie. He didn't intrude on her time with her daughter, but sat, pretending to read the paper, exchanging an occasional word with her, with the boys or with Marguerite and Simon. He left his chair once to help the boys with something they were unable to fathom on the Internet but most of the time he was there, a comfortable presence, part of Natalie's foster family; someone, Ancret knew, who would always be a favourite uncle.

He walked to the bus stop with her when she left, asked about her mother and suggested they meet sometime during the week. She smiled but shook her head, her long dark hair flowing around her, picked up by the wind which teased her long skirts and had them fluttering around her legs.

'You look as though you're about to fly away,' Jason said with a laugh. He was nervous, wanting her to say yes, hoping the slow head-shake would miraculously change from negation to assent.

'I am. I'm flying away until next week. I'm sorry, Jason, but I truly don't have a moment to spare during the week. I have clients to see, hats to design and make and besides all that I run a gown shop. I'm not exaggerating my importance, I really am a very busy person.'

'You don't have help?'

'Of course, but the nature of my business means that I'm the pivotal head. I can't sell designs that aren't completely my own, or my mother's. When a client comes for a consultation she expects to buy a hat that's mine, and will be uniquely hers.'

The bus rumbled into view and the people waiting began to shuffle forward. Jason offered a hand. 'If you ever find yourself free, please phone me.' He took her hand and kissed it. 'Oh, you'll need my phone number.' He took a scrap of paper from his pocket and wrote down two numbers. She took it as she stood on the platform, before the door closed and the bus moved away.

Jonathan was depressed. He did what was required of him in the office and it was only there that the gloom lifted, as he dealt with clients and advised people about their needs.

He had always enjoyed partnering people to houses and believed his knowledge amounted to a skill. Sometimes a client would request a property in one area and he would take them somewhere entirely different. His suggestions frequently paid off, as the client was shown a part of the city they had never considered or even visited. He had information on schools and doctors and bus routes and parks, so he could answer many of their questions with ease. It was only after the office closed that his spirits fell.

One evening, after a particularly quiet day, he sat in the corner of a bar whose sign had offered 'Pub-Grub'. The place was already busy and soon filled up as more people came to eat. Before his meal had arrived, a man approached and asked if he could share his table.

They both sat for a while glancing around the room, rereading the menu as people do to fill time when they are with strangers and want to avoid a conversation. When both meals arrived together, they smiled as they offered each other condiments, and soon began to exchange pleasantries.

'The place is filled with families,' the stranger remarked, as a child was heard crying. 'How pubs have changed, eh?'

'Everything has changed. Women's attitude more than anything else.'

'Oh. Trouble with the girlfriend?'

'Two actually.'

'Lucky fellow.'

'One won't marry me and the other won't take no for an answer.' Jonathan began eating, turning away, angry with himself, aware that he had said too much to a complete stranger.

'Women are stronger today. We've all had to adjust, haven't we?' his companion said, calling a waitress to order more drinks. 'Same again?'

'I dislike strong women. My mother was strong,' Jonathan responded, after nodding agreement. It would be safe to talk about his mother; he was unlikely to meet this fellow again. 'She worked all through my childhood and I suffered because of it.'

'Really? My ex-wife lost her mother when she was quite young. That must have been worse. Yet I don't think she's suffered terribly, apart from the initial abandonment, and that must have been hard for a small child. Yes, she and her sister coped, they've both grown into well-adjusted and capable women.'

'Then why is she your ex?'

'Good point.' He chewed and looked thoughtful before answering. 'I suppose we grew apart and one day we both realized there were no good reasons for staying together. We didn't have children, there was no one to get hurt, so we divorced. It was all very amicable. I don't think her growing up without a mother was responsible. Or whether my mother did or didn't work. It isn't what life throws at you, it's how you deal with it, don't you think?'

'I can't let this woman go,' Jonathan said. He was careful not to mention names. A name like Ancret was too unusual to be easily forgotten. 'I know it's over. She and I can't agree about what our life will be. We envisage a completely different future. She wants something I can't accept. But until I can forget her, leave it all behind, I can't move on.'

'Persevere a bit longer. Perhaps it'll come right.'

'I don't think so. She's a strong woman and I've had enough of women who stubbornly go their own way and demand that the rest of us follow.'

'Then it's the persistent little miss.' His companion smiled inwardly as he stood to leave. Whoever she was, the ex-girlfriend deserved more than this man offered. He silently wished her luck in keeping clear of him and his plaintive need for a submissive woman.

Jonathan watched him go, resentfully thinking about the man's lack of sympathy. He could have agreed with some of what I said, he thought with mild irritation. That was the usual situation when you discussed a problem with a stranger; you were given sympathy and some support. Not left with the feeling that you deserved all you got!

Lottie was waiting when he entered the office the following morning. She was sitting on the corner of his desk, one leg swinging provocatively. She was smartly dressed in a mid-blue suit and a white blouse, her legs, in high heeled shoes, clad in sheer tights and visible almost to the top of her thighs.

'Hello, Lottie,' he said with a sigh. 'What can I do for you today?'

'You can meet me for dinner tonight.'

'Now why would I do that?'

'Because you want to?' She smiled, staring at him disconcertingly. 'And I want to?'

'I have other arrangements.'

'It's a celebration,' she told him, her smile widening.

'What are you celebrating?'

'I went for an interview today, with Hartley and Jenkins.'

Jonathan nodded. The firm was a rather old-fashioned estate agency in another part of the city.

'I told them their advertising sign needs updating as it's dull and boring, too many words in too small a space so the telephone number is hard to read. I criticized the way their properties for sale were shown and said the photographs were too small and boring. I also said their offices need fresh paint in a cheerful colour, as there's nothing to entice clients over the threshold or persuade them to have confidence in their ability to sell houses.'

'You said all that? Hardly the way to beat off competition. You obviously didn't want the job. So are you celebrating not getting a job you didn't want in the first place?'

'Oh, I got it. I start next week!'

She shouted the last words and threw her arms in the air. He hugged her, laughing as she held him tight. 'What confidence! What cheek!' he said as they both laughed uncontrollably. 'Tell them from me they're lucky to have you,' he added as laughter subsided and she still held him. As he released her she kissed his cheek, then, as he turned, his lips. This time he didn't try to move away.

Loraine still hadn't visited her granddaughter. The cold – or many of the symptoms – still bothered her and the tiredness that saw her going to bed before ten o'clock every night was getting worse rather than better. The doctor had treated her for a chest infection, but the generally vague feeling of being unwell lingered on.

Ancret, meanwhile, went every other Sunday, working before and after her visit. On occasions she took Natalie for

155

a walk. Sometimes Marguerite and Simon and the boys went with her, other times it was Jason who shared the hour in the park where they fed ducks and did all the things other families were seen to do.

On arriving home there were no more surprises. Her mother hadn't been busy during her absence; the making of the wonderful hats was never repeated. Ancret didn't question her. But she suspected her mother spent much of the time she was away sleeping, or at least resting.

Lottie excelled herself in the first few months with her new employers, selling properties as well as attracting an increasing number of new clients. She scoured the papers for private vendors and approached them with the promise of a good deal. She had leaflets printed for pushing through letterboxes, inviting the occupants to consider having their property valued with a view to moving to a completely new area. Some she interviewed; by reading their needs and aspir-ations, she coaxed them with the promise of extra cash if they moved to a cheaper area, or flattered them into believing they deserved a better address.

She met Jonathan several times a week. Although he had not yet taken her to bed, she knew that one day he would. Keeping regular contact with his mother made it easier to become a part of his life and the three of them would often meet on a Sunday to go for a drive. They would choose a place where they could have lunch, then leave Caroline sitting in the sun or at a pleasant pub, and go for a walk. On these walks they talked.

The conversations were frequently about the business they shared, and she made him laugh at the audacity she displayed when clients needed encouragement to buy. He realized he had lost a very efficient and highly motivated assistant and often told her so.

'Why don't you open a second branch?' she suggested one day. 'I'll manage it, and between us we'll make it a fantastic success.'

Something made him hesitate, even though it was an idea he was already considering. He was attracted to the idea of working with her again. It hadn't been hard to admit to becoming fond of Lottie with her bright, happy companionship, but would they work as a partnership? To marry her was tempting. It would certainly please his mother, and that was definitely a plus. She would be an asset to the firm and certainly be a loving wife. Yet the shadow of Ancret remained.

There was also the memory of her involvement in the accusations about his uncle's death. Would he be wise to trust her?

One lunchtime he had arranged to meet Lottie in a pub. As he waited for her he met the man to whom he had once opened up and, rather foolishly, told of his love life.

'Hello again. Fancy a drink? I owe you one, I believe,' Jonathan said.

'You sound more cheerful,' his companion said, when they had a glass in front of them. 'Shall we toast to your freedom?'

'To freedom, yes. Women can bring an end to loneliness sometimes, but they also tangle everything so you can't see or think logically, do what you want, do what you know is right.' He raised his glass again. 'To freedom. You can't beat it.'

They clinked glasses. 'So what happened to the one you can't leave behind?'

'Gone!' Jonathan said cheerfully.

'And the persistent miss?'

'Too persistent! The name's Jonathan, by the way.'

His companion responded, 'And I'm Jason.'

Then Lottie entered and he excused himself and went to greet her. He turned and waved as they left together. Jason was left wondering.

Loraine didn't get out of bed one day. Alarmed, Ancret phoned for a doctor.

Helena couldn't come to help, so Angela, who had arranged to take a weekend off, came to work in the salon while Ancret looked after her mother, fetched medicine and made her comfortable.

'Don't worry, I can stay all day if necessary,' Angela offered. Ancret gratefully accepted. It was a Saturday, and besides worries about her mother, she was frantic at the thought of not being able to visit Natalie the following day.

She almost told her friend the truth. It would be so helpful to be able to confide in someone, have them available for the occasional emergency, but she held back. Once a secret was allowed to escape there would be no stopping it. She recited the magpie rhyme in her head. *Seven for a secret never to be told.*

News of Loraine's illness proved her point. Jonathan arrived as the shop was closing. He and Lottie had been going to the cinema when Lottie mentioned having heard that Loraine was ill. 'I'll just call on the way, see if I can do anything,' he said, turning the car and retracing his route.

'No, Jonathan,' Lottie wailed. 'We'll miss the beginning and you know I can never catch up.'

'Come on, there'll be fifteen minutes of advertisements and trailers first. There's plenty of time.'

'Someone told me Loraine is ill. Can I do anything?' he asked, when Ancret opened the door. The sight of her warmed him, filled him with a happiness he couldn't have described with a thousand words, so his face showed excitement rather than sympathy. 'I'm sorry, Ancret. I can imagine how worried you must be.'

She glanced across to Lottie, waiting in his car.

'Still being flattered by the tiresome teenager?' she said.

'She needed a lift,' he lied.

'Then she needs you more than my mother does,' she replied, stepping inside and closing the door.

He stood for a while staring at the glass door with its blind pulled down just a few inches from his face, and wondered whether she was standing the other side of it, aware of his need of her.

# Nine

Ancret stood inside the shop door waiting for Jonathan's footsteps to retreat. When they did not, she moved the door blind a little and looked out. He was standing with his back to her, while at the kerb, she could see Lottie beckoning rather impatiently for him to come. He sensed rather than saw the movement of the blind and turned swiftly. He knocked loudly on the door. Unsure why, she opened it.

'Let me come in, Ancret. I want to help,' he said. 'Can I get you anything?'

'I can cope,' she replied. 'My friends are doing everything they can. Helena is managing the shop with Angela.' She began to widen the gap in the door. 'You'd better go, your girlfriend is calling you.' The word resounded with jealousy, and she was ashamed and more than a little confused. She didn't love Jonathan, she certainly didn't want to marry him, so why was she upset at the thought of him with Lottie?

He stood there, hesitantly moving from one foot to the other. The couple each avoided the other's eyes. A loud crash from upstairs startled them and they ran to the stairs and hurried up. Jonathan was at her mother's bedroom first and he went in. Loraine was lying on the floor, her legs tangled in bedding that held them angled upwards, her feet still resting on the bed.

'Loraine,' he called, kneeling down beside her. Then, turning to Ancret, 'Phone for an ambulance, quickly.' After a brief look at her mother and an anxious glance at Jonathan, she used the phone beside her bed and made the call. Jonathan was cradling Loraine's dark head on his arm and talking in low whispers. Ancret threw herself down beside the semi-conscious woman. 'Mummy. What happened? Did you fall?' She looked at Jonathan, who shook his head.

159

'It might be more serious than a fall. Look at her face.' Loraine's face looked distorted, distressingly unfamiliar. Ancret choked back panic, unable to speak, afraid of upsetting her mother further by revealing in her voice her own fear.

Pulling herself together, reminding herself that her mother was depending on her as never before, she softly coaxed her to relax. 'Help is on the way, Mummy, you'll soon be all right.' She tried to make Loraine more comfortable, her manner reassuring now she had control.

'While we wait, I'll go over to Lottie, tell her to take a taxi home,' Jonathan said. 'I'll phone for one from here before I go.'

'There's no need for you to stay. I'll manage. You take Lottie home, or wherever you were going.' Still that childish jealousy, even at a time like this. In a flash of revelation she asked herself whether it was her dislike of the girl rather than love for the man. The thought was a relief in the middle of the alarm and anxiety and she wondered that the human mind could come up with such notions, when all her concentration should have been on her mother.

Jonathan had ignored her remark. Having arranged the taxi, he went out to explain to Lottie what had happened.

Ancret was moistening her mother's lips as Loraine came round and tried to talk. 'Hush, Mummy, just lie still until help comes. We'll get you into hospital and soon have you back on your feet.'

'No . . . how . . . hospital . . .' The words were slurred and difficult to understand at first. But Loraine repeated them anxiously until Ancret understood.

'Hospital is the best place for you to get help, Mummy, please don't refuse to go. It won't be for long, a day, perhaps two.'

'You . . . alone,' Loraine uttered slowly.

'She isn't alone, Loraine,' Jonathan said as he came back into the room. 'I'm here to do anything I can, and Helena will help her. Don't worry, we'll all make sure she has time to look after you.'

Tearfully, Ancret thanked him. 'You can go as soon as the ambulance arrives,' she said, rubbing away her tears with the back of her hands like a child.

'You'll go with your mother and I'll follow in the car so I can bring you home.'

They had made Loraine as comfortable as they could. Jonathan said, 'Why don't you get a few of your mother's clothes together, and toilet things she might need. You might not have to stay, Loraine,' he added reassuringly, 'but it's best to be prepared.'

A small overnight case had been filled before the knock on the door announced the arrival of the ambulance men.

It was frightening to be sitting beside her pale and sick mother as the ambulance drove them through the busy streets. A sobering reminder of her mother's mortality and how suddenly life could change. Within seconds and with no warning, she might have found herself facing life without her.

Lottie waited in Jonathan's car until the taxi arrived. It was some time before she gave her address and was driven away. She looked back to see the ambulance arrive. If she were to persuade Jonathan that his future was with her, it would need a lot of effort on her part to prize him away from Ancret. Although they had ended their relationship, with its talk of marriage and the abortive attempt to buy Toad Hall, he was still there the moment she needed him.

Frustration at the ease with which Ancret received Jonathan's help whenever she needed it made her more determined to end their relationship for good. He still loved Ancret. Somehow she had to change that and persuade him that his life would be happier with her. If she were to hold on to Jonathan, she had to do something quickly. But what?

He still hadn't succumbed to her charms apart from some rather passionate kisses. She thought of some of the romantic stories she had read, in which cars broke down and the couple had to spend a night on a lonely mountainside while thunder and lightning raged around them, trees creaked eerily and strange sounds made it necessary to cuddle up close. She could hardly arrange all that, and she was doubtful it would work. But . . . she still had a key to the flat.

Instead of going inside when the taxi deposited her outside her parents' house, she went to the bus stop, catching a bus that would drop her close to Jonathan's flat. She had nothing with her except a small handbag, but for what she planned there was little she would need.

She took a leisurely bath, washed her hair and wrapped one of Jonathan's huge white towels around her. The soaps were on the television, and she sat and watched them for a while. Then, choosing a book from the shelves, she discarded the towel and settled into his king-sized bed to read.

Loraine was sleeping when Ancret and Jonathan left the hospital. It was almost midnight, and the nurses had assured them that she would sleep through the night and there was nothing they could do until the following day. Jonathan looked at Ancret and hugged her. She looked so tired, her beautiful eyes heavy and filled with sorrow. He didn't want to leave her alone just yet. She needed company for a while, or she'd never sleep.

'Come on, darling, let's go and find some food. I'm starving.'

'I couldn't face food at the moment,' she said.

'Not preparing it, no, but if I put a plate of delicious stir-fry in front of you I'm sure you'd eat it.'

'It'll have to be a sandwich or bacon and eggs. I don't have the ingredients for anything more exciting.'

'I do. I bought it today, intending to indulge myself after the cinema. And yes, that was where I was taking Lottie. There's nothing going on,' he added as she gave him a slow, half amused look. 'I think she'd like there to be, but on my part it's nothing more than a young woman with the same occupation as myself.' He leaned over and touched her cheek. 'She was all dressed up in her best, but she didn't look as lovely as you look now. You are a beautiful woman, Ancret.'

Ancret moved as far from him as she could in the confines of the car. Breaking the mood that was beginning to wind itself around him, filled with hope and memories and regrets, he told her about Lottie's suggestion that he should open a second office and give it to Lottie to manage.

'It seems a good idea. Does she intend you to open near Hartley and Jenkins?'

'Are you following her progress?' he said teasingly.

'People tell me things. They assume I'm still interested.'

They drove to the flat. He left the car some distance away rather than put it in the garage, explaining that it would make it easier to drive off when he took her home after they had eaten. 'Unless you want to stay?' he offered. 'Mother's bedroom, of course.'

It was tempting not to go back to the shop and face a night alone, but she shook her head. 'I need to be there in case the hospital calls.'

They went in. Jonathan disappeared into the stark, modern kitchen with its stainless steel fittings and utensils, and began preparing their meal. Ancret looked around, feeling like a stranger in the flat where she had once spent so much time. She touched his magazines and a carelessly folded newspaper, wondering if they might one day return to being friends. Never anything more, she reminded herself. Forgiveness would never come. She could never forget his callous attitude to unborn babies. Nevertheless she experienced a comfortable sense of coming home.

She wandered around the room, looking at the photographs left by his mother. Most were of Caroline herself, taken at various places, on holidays and during talks she had given over the years. None of these showed her with her son. There were several glamorous studio close-ups, while others showed her addressing an audience and receiving endless bouquets of flowers. The few pictures of Jonathan as a baby and growing up were gone; removed, she guessed, by Jonathan himself.

She picked up a property magazine and sat near the radio, which was playing softly. Before she had taken off her long shawl, the wok could be heard hissing on the heat and she could hear vegetables being chopped.

When she went into the bathroom she frowned. A couple of wet towels were on the floor, the room still warm with that soapy smell of a recently run bath. Some woman's clothes were hanging half in, half out of the linen basket. She felt momentarily the shock of betrayal, before reminding herself it was none of her concern. Jonathan was a single man and he could do what he pleased. It was a reminder of how difficult it was to let go when a long, loving affair ended. The sense of belonging had stayed with her, even though she told herself it was over and would never be revived. Yet she couldn't resist mentioning the mess.

'There aren't any clean towels in the bathroom, Jonathan. Where will I find them?'

He came out of the kitchen and nodded with his head in the direction of the bedroom. 'Same place. The cupboard in my room.'

He removed the wok from the heat and waited as she opened the bedroom door, as though expecting her not to know where the cupboard was. When he saw her take a deep breath, open-mouthed, and utter a deep-throated 'Oh!', he came to stand beside her. Lottie was lying in his bed, the duvet only half covering her, staring at them with an unconcerned expression on her face.

'Jonathan. You're very late. Where have you been?'

'What are you doing here?'

'Waiting for you,' she said, as though the question were a silly one.

'I'd better leave,' Ancret said. Her heart was racing with renewed shock. She couldn't cope with this, she really couldn't.

'No,' Jonathan almost shouted. 'You stay. It's Lottie who's leaving.' He turned to face Lottie. 'Get dressed and get out of here. And before you go, I want my key.'

'I can't go now, Jonathan, it's the middle of the night.'

He threw some notes at her and pointed to the phone beside the bed. 'A taxi,' he demanded. 'Now, this minute. Or I'll call the police and report an illegal entry. It's about time I paid you back for accusing me of murder, isn't it?'

'I don't want to hear this,' Ancret said. Her embarrassment was more for Lottie than herself. Whatever she had done, it wasn't right for Jonathan to send her out alone so late at night. Besides, he must have done something to encourage her. Even in the twenty-first century, it wasn't usual for a girl to get into a man's bed without having an invitation – unless she had been there before.

She reached for her shawl, opened the door and hurried away through the dark streets. She had her purse with her, fortunately; at a phone box she would order a taxi for herself.

She heard footsteps and hid until Jonathan had given up and returned to the flat. She felt a little sick, ashamed of becoming involved in Jonathan's love life – if that was what it was. But she was human enough to be curious about what would happen next, although she thought it unlikely she would ever find out.

She had to wait ten minutes for her taxi, shivering in the cold darkness, but she didn't see Lottie leave.

Loraine was in hospital for two weeks. Ancret was told she had suffered a stroke. The nursing staff talked to Ancret on two occasions about her mother's nightmares. 'She becomes very upset and we wondered if you knew the reason for them, so we can perhaps reassure her if it happens again.'

'I can't help,' Ancret told them. 'I have no idea of the cause. But I think it's something in her past, rather than just an overactive imagination set off by a half-remembered television drama or something she's overheard. They're always the same. Someone seems to be trying to take her baby.'

'I didn't have that impression,' one of the nurses said.

'Then they must be different from the ones she has at home. She's clutching a child and pleading for help. She grips the imaginary baby so tightly it's certain that someone is trying to take her.'

'Isn't she asking for help with the child? That's what I imagined, not that she's begging to be allowed to keep it.'

'That's an interesting thought.' Ancret frowned. 'It certainly opens up other possibilities. But what help could she be asking for? Financial help?' She thought of the bank book with its monthly payments that ended on her eighteenth birthday. Perhaps that was what the dream was about. Yet that problem had presumably been solved. She thanked the nurses for their attempts to help and went back to her mother. If only she could persuade her to talk. The illness had reminded her that time was passing. Even tomorrow could be too late.

Throughout the time Loraine was in hospital, Jonathan kept in touch, and it was he who went with Ancret to bring her mother home. After the shop had closed, Helena had stayed to welcome them back and report briefly on the day's business. Knowing that Loraine needed plenty of rest, Jonathan had arranged for a meal to be delivered from a local restaurant, and he stayed to share it with them.

When he left, Ancret went to the door with him to thank him. He leaned towards her and kissed her, reminding her, 'I'm always here for you. Please remember that.'

Almost tearful with guilt, she watched him drive off. She had deprived him of the choice of whether or not he wanted to know his child. Her situation was more difficult with every passing day. It had all seemed so simple at the beginning. She had engineered a quarrel and sworn she'd never love him again. Now he was slipping back into her life and she seemed powerless to stop him. Even reminding herself of his callousness towards Babs didn't help.

She ought to have moved right away, made certain they would never meet, but that had been an impossibility. With a newly acquired business there was no money to spare for a move and besides, the business needed the stability of a permanent address.

She had thought she could hide the baby and then, when she and Jonathan no longer saw each other, when there were no regrets and even the most beautiful memories had faded, she could introduce Natalie to everyone and use the prepared story of an adoption. Now the lies and the deceit were crippling her. There was no peace. I'll soon be suffering dreadful dreams like those of my mother, she thought as she tossed and turned during the night.

She couldn't sleep and soon gave up trying. Besides the disturbing thoughts about what she now considered her betrayal of Jonathan, she was aware her mother was sleeping in the next room, ill, and maybe in need of her. She wrapped herself in her duvet and settled into the chair next to Loraine's bed. The light was low and, despite herself, she began thinking about designs for the exhibition in August. Tiptoeing down the stairs without using a light, she found her sketch pad and began to draw.

Although her eyes were closed and she rarely moved, Loraine wasn't asleep. She was aware of Ancret moving about. She too was wondering about telling her daughter the truth. How much should she tell? How should she tell it? Could she say just enough to satisfy her, then persuade her not to investigate any further, or would a few words open up a Pandora's box that would never again be closed? Time was short and there were so many decisions to make.

She was tired, achingly so. The thought of the revelations, and the conversation that would surely follow, seemed too much for her to cope with. Perhaps it was better to leave it to the fates and her daughter's intelligence. She moved slowly and steadily to the edge of the bed so she could reach the locked drawer. Sitting up with difficulty, she extracted birth and marriage certificates from an envelope at the back and tried to tear them up, using her teeth and her stronger hand. She failed, but managed to put them back in the drawer before falling back against her pillows, utterly exhausted, lacking even the energy to lock the drawer again. She had left enough confusion to ensure that Ancret would never find her father. Although she now began to regret leading her daughter to the Flowers – that had made the discovery a little more likely. But she offered up a prayer that if it happened it would be a long way in the future.

Connecting one slim, frail thread, and leaving it in the lap of the gods to decide whether or not it would lead to the answers to Ancret's questions, had been an impulse. Now she hoped against hope that the truth wouldn't be revealed before the man's death. And her own.

Whether it was the unearthly hour or the anxiety about her mother's health, Ancret's designs were nothing like her usual elegant, light-hearted, happy hats. One drawing showed an undisguised pair of gloves. Single-sided only, one glove swept down from a tiny saucer of a crown across the wearer's cheek while the other almost covered the crown and crossed the wearer's head towards the forehead. Weird, Ancret thought, putting it aside. Another was shaped like a fez but had on its side a series of crossed feathers, each falling down towards the shoulders at the back and on the sides, with a slightly shorter section on the front as though the wearer was trying to hide from view. She played with the design for a long time, opening the area near the eyes and bringing the

167

feathers across one cheek, before that too was put aside.

Dawn showed through the half-open curtains and she stood to look out at the sky. The sun wasn't yet above the horizon, but hazy stripes in every shade of pink and orange, apricot and purple made her gasp with pleasure at the wonderful display. She watched for a while, then picked up her pad again.

This time the mood of her work was lighter. Tall feathers decorated an irregularly shaped crown; each feather had been partially stripped of its barbs with the vane cut away in swooping curves and dipped in colours, so that the quills showed starkly white. The hat would be of multicoloured chiffon on a lightweight base, and she scribbled beside her drawing every hue she had seen in the sky that morning, fixing the beauty of the early dawn sky on her memory. Another quick sketch showed a hat with the crown covered in layers of frothy, downy feathers; a blue hat, the feathers white. This was better, she scolded herself.

Loraine woke soon afterwards. Ancret made tea and was pleased to see her mother was awake. She put the kettle on, and kissed her before helping her to sit up.

'Do you feel rested?' she asked as she straightened her mother's pillow.

'Yes, but I don't think you do.'

'I'm fine.'

'You've been in your workroom almost all night.'

'Mummy, how could you know that? You've been asleep.'

'No one sleeps without a bit of awareness, my daughter.' She held out a hand. 'Let me see your drawings while you go down and bring me a cup of tea.'

'No, they aren't anything that will see the light of day, just idle scribblings,' Ancret replied. Loraine moved her hand insistently. Reluctantly she gave her sketch pad to her mother.

When she came back, her mother was studying the pages of work.

'I hope the glove hat won't be in sombre colours,' she said. 'It'll look like something from a horror film unless it's in pastels.'

Ancret was thoughtful as she poured tea and handed her mother a cup. 'I was thinking sombre thoughts I suppose, worried about you, guilty about what I did to Jonathan.'

'Your hands create beauty, fantasy, joyful dreams. You should never work unless you're feeling happy. Your emotions show so clearly in your work.'

'You like the feather idea?'

'Not as much as the gloves. It's reminiscent of so many others, a cliché of a hat. To me, who knows you so well, it looks like an attempt to deny your mood. You were looking at something you didn't want to see. The other one, the glove design, needs something light, that's all. Thin, supple material, delicate colours, and your talented touch.'

Ancret smiled, marvelling at her mother's perspicacity.

Lottie saw little of Jonathan. She had phoned the office and had been told by Lucinda that he was out and was not expected back. She had called there, to be told the same thing by a new girl who had been appointed to take her place. She had even waited in her car outside the flat; whether he had seen her and driven away, she didn't know, but he hadn't appeared on the occasions when she had been there. Even Caroline seemed less friendly than before. She had overstepped the mark by getting into his bed. That had been a stupid mistake. Men like to make most of the running, even these days.

She gave her notice at Hartley and Jenkins. Even though they pleaded with her to stay, she left and began looking for something different. Something that would keep her away from Jonathan. But not for long. She hadn't given up on her ambition to persuade him that she was his future. That ambition was stronger than ever.

An office with a building company selling new houses was tempting, but there again she and Jonathan might have met. A meeting would have to be carefully arranged; she didn't want to bump into him by accident, not yet.

It was at a photographer's that she eventually accepted a job. It was on the far side of Cardiff, where she was unlikely to bump into Jonathan. She had been there two weeks and she hadn't seen him – but she did see Ancret. And she was pushing a baby in a pushchair. She didn't approach her. This was too good to waste. How wise she had been to keep in touch with Caroline.

At home that evening she spoke to Jonathan's mother and then waited. Jonathan was certain to be curious. Would his curiosity be strong enough for him to phone her and ask for details? Hope flooded through her like a warm tide.

As August approached, Ancret was kept even busier than usual preparing her exhibits for the charity show. Mrs Piper-Davies called several times and, besides choosing a hat to wear, she spoke to Ancret in a way that was almost an apology.

'You and I got off on the wrong foot, didn't we?' she said one day when she called to introduce a friend who needed an outfit, complete with hat, for a daughter's wedding.

'I think we were both to blame.'

'Perhaps, but I didn't think such wonderful work could come out of such . . .'

'Lowly surroundings?' Ancret laughed. 'It wasn't an unsuccessful gown shop, you know. It's always attracted high-class customers. My friend Helena had a good business long before I came in and flooded it with hats.'

'Better now though,' Mrs Piper-Davies said in a whisper. 'And call me Dorothy.'

Being on the committee, she had the final say about which exhibitors went where. She arranged for Ancret to have a prominent position, with the added advantage that there was extra space around it. She met Ancret in the hall a few days before the event, so she could visualize the area she had been allocated. Ancret thanked her, but Dorothy brushed away the words with an impatient wave of her beringed hands.

'Jonathan, dear,' his mother said when she telephoned him at the office, 'I saw Lottie today and she told me something very surprising.'

She sounded upset but he was determined not to listen to any gossip that came from Lottie. 'I don't want to hear this Mother. I don't want you to encourage her, she's trouble.'

'Did you know Ancret has a child? It's about six months old according to Lottie so,' she stopped and the choking in her voice gave him an image of her tearful face. She took an audible breath and went on, – 'It's about eight months ago that she left you, isn't it? And until then, you and she were – oh Jonathan, it could be yours! My grandchild!'

'Where did she see Ancret and a child?'

'Walking along a street north of Cathays Park she said. She was pushing the pram, and bending down to talk to the baby, smiling, laughing.'

'And you know Ancret was the mother because she was seen pushing a baby in a pram? What nonsense.'

'She did go away for a while, dear. And I've never really been convinced about her helping out a college friend, have you?'

'She was away for a few weeks, not nine months!'

'But it's possible, Lottie was convinced it was Ancret, and from the way she behaved, that the baby was hers.'

'How can you believe such a story? If Ancret had been pregnant I'd have known and it would have been dealt with, as with Babs. She joked about it once and I told her how I felt about it. There's no way she would have done that to me. She knew how important it was. And have you thought she might have been with a baby belonging to a friend? Or holding the pram while someone went into a shop? There are a dozen reasons for her being seen with a child and the most *un*likely of them would be what Lottie suggested.'

'She didn't suggest it, dear, Lottie wouldn't be so unkind. It was I who thought it might be your child.'

'Forget it, Mother and please, keep away from Lottie.'

He didn't put the phone down, he wanted to ask if the child was all right, or had showed signs of a problem but he dared not. Firstly because Lottie was wrong, it couldn't be Ancret's baby, Secondly, if it were a child of his and it was disabled in some way, then he wanted to deny it. His mother knew this, she of all people would understand his unspoken concern.

'She didn't say anything about it being – ill – or anything.'

'Then that proves it, doesn't it? It can't be mine!' First Babs and now Ancret. It was too many coincidences for one lifetime. They couldn't both had given birth to a child without telling him. He had to find Babs, asks her outright if the little boy called Donald belonged to him. As for Ancret, that was utter nonsense, an example of Lottie trying to create trouble and his mother enjoying it.

He went into a pub for a snack and a pint for a late lunch, and wondered if Jason would be there. They had met several times, although none of their meetings had been arranged. They just seemed to frequent the same pubs and both had erratic lunchtimes. He was trying to take his mind off the disturbing thoughts his mother had planted, and the repetitious going over dates and ages and all the imponderables of having a situation being presented with none of the facts.

Taking out a notebook, he began to work out the possibilities of opening a second office in a different area of Cardiff. He knew it was impossible but he played with costs and predictions to keep his mind away from Ancret.

'Can I join you?' Jason asked politely. Smiling, Jonathan moved his newspaper and empty plate to make room at the small table.

'You're just in time to tell me I'm being stupid,' he said when Jason had settled with his drink and a sandwich.

'You're being stupid,' Jason said. 'Now tell me why.'

'I had an idea that I could afford to open a second branch, but common sense tells me I can't. Yet I'm still playing with the idea. I need someone to talk me out of it because expanding a young business too soon or too far is a recipe for disaster.'

'I have to agree with that,' Jason said. 'That's what happened to me. I had a small shoe shop and foolishly I bought the property next door and expanded the shop to include handbags and accessories, helped by my wife. Overheads doubled, the sales remained almost the same as before and I lost the business and, incidentally, my wife. She was going to the wholesalers time and again to plead for extra credit and it wasn't credit she was after. She ran off with him when he promised a better future than I could. He offered sympathy and all she got from me was worries and moans about what she was spending.'

'I'm sorry,' Jonathan said. 'I had no idea.'

'It's all right, don't be upset. How could you have known?' Jason said with a forced smile. 'It's a few years ago now and I'm able to talk about it without collapsing into a heap. But take it as a warning. Be sure you're financially secure before jumping into something that could destroy what you have.'

'Even if I sold the flat and lived over the shop – and that's bad for the image – there still wouldn't be sufficient to buy a place, pay for refitting and advertising and employ staff to run it. No, you've confirmed what I already knew. Thanks.'

'What happened about the women in your life? Wasn't there a significant someone? The ex-lover? The precocious miss?'

'My thoughts are with a third woman at the moment. An ex-fiancée who I need to catch up with.'

'What a fascinating life you lead. When do you start writing your autobiography?'

'There have been three women and they've all let me down. Mother warned me each time.'

'Perhaps your mother is the problem? They can be very possessive of sons.'

'Mother wouldn't interfere in my private affairs.'

'Of course she wouldn't.' Jason spoke apologetically. 'What do I know?'

'There still is someone special, but it's over and I don't think our relationship will ever be revived. I'm quite enjoying the idea of being a single, thirty-something, and free to go out on the town.'

'I like that too.' Jason stood up to leave. 'What say we meet for a drink and dalliance one evening. Friday?'

'Why not,' Jonathan agreed. 'In here about seven?'

The exhibition that August was an enormous success. Ancret had more enquiries than she knew how to handle. Loraine was still unable to do very much, and Helena had stayed in the shop with Angela to deal with customers and ensure that Loraine was comfortable. So Ancret was on her own.

A young woman stopped to talk to her and explained that she had just finished her degree at art college. 'Would you be willing to look at my stuff?' she asked. 'I have a particular interest in hat design. From what I can see of your work, I think you might like what I do.'

Ancret agreed, handing her a card that bore her Moments address and phone number. 'Although you must understand that I'm not in a position to offer you a job,' she told her apologetically. 'My business is still new and I don't have an opening for anyone at present.'

A group of people approached the stand, and she excused herself as she recognized Edmund.

'Don't tell me you're interested in hat design,' she teased.

'No, but these young ladies are.'

'Who are they, more students?'

'Yes, they're mostly photography students. They're from London, staying at the hotel as part of a sightseeing tour, picture-snapping around Wales. They go back tomorrow, and will I be glad! I don't like the way they remind me of my age. I've been up till all hours waiting to bring them home from the nightclubs. Then they're up bright-eyed each morning for me to drive them to some beauty spot for photographs.'

He stayed with her, talking easily about the work on display, stepping back when someone wanted to talk to her, until his group returned to him. She waved as he was ushered out of the door in a gaggle of excited youngsters, and nodded as he called back, 'See you soon – if I survive—'

At the end of the day the girl returned with her portfolio, struggling in with the ungainly folder as the viewers drifted away. 'I know this isn't the right thing to do,' she said apologetically. 'But I only live around the corner, so if you could have a quick glance to see whether they interest you . . . Then, if you'd like a more detailed look, we can arrange a proper meeting.' She hesitated as Ancret frowned. 'Sorry, I shouldn't be so impulsive. I'll go away and phone you in a day or so.'

Ancret held out her hands and took the heavy folder, which bore the name *Annie Harper*. Putting it on the floor, she knelt down and opened the pages. The owner of the work knelt beside her. Ancret looked at page after page, while curious people hovered around them before moving on, and other exhibitors began to pack their work into boxes. From time to time she nodded approval and uttered compliments.

'Come and see me tomorrow,' she said. 'We'll talk. But even though I think you have something special, there isn't a chance of asking you to join me. Which is a pity, as I desperately need help. It's just that I can't afford anyone as talented as you. And,' she added, 'my business can't afford to take on anyone with less ability. The best or nothing at all. What a sad situation, eh?' They arranged a time for the following day, and Ancret watched her walk away with regret.

As the stands were being dismantled Caroline walked in. 'Ancret, dear. I just heard that you're helping here. Good display, isn't it?'

'Hardly, not any more. It finished about half an hour ago. Most of the exhibitors have taken their stuff and left. And I wasn't helping,' she pointed out politely, 'I was an exhibitor.' She waved a hand to her five hats, still on their stands.

'Oh, very nice.' She hesitated and Ancret guessed she had something more to say.

'Was there something you have to tell me, Caroline?' she asked.

'No. Although I am a little curious to know whose baby you were taking out last week. A friend's, was it? A career girl like you, I can't imagine you looking after a small child.'

Ancret's insides curled up into a tangle of panic. She turned away from the bright, still pretty, face of Jonathan's mother and touched one of her creations to give herself time to recover. How could she respond to a question about the woman's grandchild with lies? But she didn't have a choice. When she spoke her voice sounded calm. 'It's the daughter of a friend,' she said. 'Someone from college.'

The sickness that always came at such times threatened to overwhelm her. She excused herself and began to dismantle her display. Boxes were there ready to receive the hats and when they were packed ready for the taxi that was due in a few minutes, she looked up. Caroline was gone.

The feelings caused by her increasing guilt had faded by the time she reached home. She forced herself into a bright, cheerful mood and went in to tell her mother all that had happened.

'There was a girl there called Annie Harper, a student. She showed me some of her designs and she's very good. I wish I could employ her. I need help if I'm to take advantage of the interest shown during the exhibition, but it isn't possible.'

'You have plenty of orders?'

'I handed out cards to lots of interested women, besides making appointments for most of the next two weeks, Mummy. I really think we're going to be working every hour I can stay awake.'

'Have a careful look at the girl's work, see what her handwork is like. She needs to be good at more than design. If you really think she's good, take her on.'

'I can't afford to.'

'Seems to me you can't afford not to. First you have to make sure the commissions are really coming in, see if all the promises develop into actual sales. Then you either lose most of them or take an assistant.'

'I'll think about it,' Ancret said, but secretly she had no idea whether she could acquire enough work to be able to afford someone like Annie Harper.

Loraine was interested in everything Ancret told her, but after an hour Ancret realized her mother had fallen asleep. She was sleeping much of the day and night now, waking and wondering what time it was.

Whatever time she awoke, particularly during the night, her first words were usually, 'What time is it?' Ancret wondered why this was so when her mother no longer had anywhere to go. Persuading Loraine to allow the doctor to call was no longer a problem. Loraine welcomed the young woman – who spent more time than she should talking to her patient – and obviously enjoyed her visits.

Ancret spent much of each night sitting near her mother's bed sewing or sketching. That night she sat sewing the headband into a turban and wondering how Caroline had managed to find out about the baby. How much longer could she manage to keep Natalie a secret?

Annie Harper called the day following the close of the exhibition, and the two women got on well from the first moment. They compared ideas and discussed future collections, and Ancret knew that somehow she had to take this bright, young, talented woman into the business or she'd regret it for ever.

Annie was tall and slender and had a way of walking that was not dissimilar to Ancret's long slow steps, and a shared fondness for long, flowing garments. They could have been sisters, Ancret thought, with a stab of sadness at the reminder of her lonely state.

Two weeks later she and the accountant had come to an agreement with Annie, and she started work on the first of September. The wages were minimal, but Annie had agreed to work for such a small amount of money on the promise that it would be reviewed after three months and her appointment placed on a proper footing. Ancret was relieved when, during the weeks following the exhibition, their combined efforts showed a huge increase in business, and also that she and Annie worked in perfect harmony. Bouncing ideas from one to the other added a fresh excitement to her work and gave Ancret hope for the future.

With her mother unable to help as she had in the past, and the time approaching when she would bring Natalie home, she was aware of her good fortune in finding Annie at such an opportune moment.

'I honestly don't know how I'd have managed without you these past weeks,' she said at the end of the month, when business was showing no sign, as yet, of easing off for the autumn and winter doldrums.

'Don't worry about work slowing down, as it will,' Annie said, aware of the problems of the quiet months ahead. 'We'll manage to keep busy, I have a few ideas. I've enquired about teaching a few evening classes and as a peripatetic art teacher at a couple of schools. We can take it in turns to work and stay with Loraine. It won't be for more than a couple of terms, then it will be Easter and the rush will be on again.'

'That brings us into March,' Ancret said thoughtfully. February, when Natalie would be a year old, was when she had agreed to bring her home. It was time to prepare her story, practise a new set of lies.

# Ten

September had been a busy month. There were weddings and christenings and, with the approach of autumn, occasional requests for a special hat for a charity event.

Mrs Piper-Davies came into the salon one day and asked to see Ancret. Angela politely explained that she was not free, but that her assistant, Annie Harper, would be able to see her. Dorothy complained loudly that as an important client she needed to see Ancret herself.

'Will you please tell her I'm here,' she demanded.

'Perhaps if I made an appointment?' Angela reached for the diary but Dorothy slapped her hand down on it to stop her opening it.

'No, I think not. Please inform her that I'm waiting. Dorothy Piper-Davies, if you didn't already know. Please hurry, I have appointments to keep.'

Angela didn't know quite how to handle this. Dorothy showed no sign of agreeing to see Annie or leaving the premises. Ancret heard her voice, loud and authoritative, and came out of the workroom with a smile of welcome. 'Please come through, Dorothy. I have a break in my appointments now, if you wish?' She popped back and apologized to Angela, explaining that over-ruling her instruction was the simplest option with someone like Mrs Piper-Davies.

'Thank you, Ancret. I do need an urgent word.' Dorothy bustled in, laden with bags of clothes shopping, and handed one of them to Ancret. 'Lunch,' she announced. 'At the mayor's parlour. This is the outfit, what d'you think?'

They discussed the possibilities for a while. Then, as Mrs Piper-Davies was leaving, she said. 'This celebrity lunch. I believe you know one of the guest speakers. Mrs Pen-Marr? She told me her son is a friend of yours.'

'Goodness, is she a celebrity?'

'She's quite well known for her talks on fashion and make-up and she does an excellent one on "Accessories to Impress". Quite a character but rather sweet.'

When her client had gone Ancret thought about Jonathan's mother. On impulse she telephoned her. She knew it was a mistake as she tapped in the digits, but in this instant she knew she could help.

'Caroline? It's Ancret.'

'Oh, hello, dear. How are you? Are you well? And your mother? I hope she's improving, such a shock.' The automatic politenesses came out and Ancret smiled, realizing they were giving the woman a chance to recover from her surprise.

'I was talking to Dorothy Piper-Davies a moment ago and she told me you are one of the speakers at a very prestigious lunch. I was wondering, would you like me to make your hat?'

'Oh yes, the luncheon,' she said, correcting her politely. Ancret smiled at the image of Caroline daring to correct the forthright Dorothy. 'Yes, it should be a grand affair. You want me to advertise for you?'

'No, Caroline. I thought you might like to wear one of my hats, one specially made for you, that's all. I obviously made a mistake asking.' She was about to say goodbye when Caroline said quickly, 'I'm sorry that sounded so rude. I've no excuse, I was being bitchy and that isn't like me at all. I suppose it's embarrassment, seeing Jonathan so happy and you being lonely and – well . . . I'm sorry, dear. I'd love you to design a hat specially for me.'

'Good,' Ancret said, swallowing the angry retort that had been ready to explode from her. 'Of course there'll be no charge.'

When her mother heard the offer she frowned. 'For someone trying to leave a man behind, you're being unnecessarily kind to his mother.'

'I know, and I can't understand why I did it. Perhaps because Dorothy can afford anything she fancies and Caroline can't or won't spend so extravagantly. Just this once I thought it would be nice for her to wear something really special.'

179

Loraine was improving slowly after her stroke. A physio-therapist called regularly as Loraine couldn't attend hospital, but found her to be an uncooperative patient. Apart from when Ancret, or Angela, or the willing Annie Harper helped her, she was unable to rise from her bed. Today she was sitting in the armchair in her room, the willow basket beside her filled with bunches of antirrhinums placed in the two jam jars which Loraine had always insisted on using as vases. She slept a lot, which Ancret assumed was due to her medication.

Ancret went up several times during the day as she and Annie worked in the room behind the shop. Angela and Annie also popped up for a brief 'hello' when the opportunity offered.

Angela now ran the salon with the occasional help of a new Saturday girl, dealing expertly with bridal gowns and outfits for mothers and guests. Although they stocked other clothes, the business seemed to cater more and more for weddings, and they had begun sending clients to a local business where suits could be made or hired. This earned them a small commission, which Ancret gave to Angela.

Angela couldn't help with the model hats but she gave invaluable assistance, when the shop was quiet, by keeping the various books up to date. When the shop closed she often stayed on to write letters, send payments and submit orders. The three women rarely had to be told what was needed. Ancret had found herself a perfect team. She never failed to thank the girls for their expertise and generosity with their time.

She was on her own when Caroline called to discuss the hat she would wear to the lunch. Annie had requested a day off to help a friend to move house, and as the business still usually closed on Mondays, Angela too was absent. Ancret was waiting when Jonathan's car pulled up, and watched as he got out and went around to the passenger door to help his mother alight. She opened the shop door to welcome Caroline but didn't go out. Jonathan hesitated, then drove off with a wave.

When she saw the outfit Caroline had chosen, a layered pink, frothy number with a sprinkle of glittering sequins around the bottom of each frill, her first thought was that the style was rather dated and too young for the woman proudly holding it against her. But her second was that Caroline would be utterly happy wearing it and would carry it off with aplomb.

She knew immediately what was needed. She remembered the cheerful chiffon she had sketched in an attempt to drive away sombre thoughts on the night when she had sat beside her mother drawing solemn hats.

She brought out a couple of sketchbooks and added several drawings, colouring some, leaving others plain. Then she opened the page showing the rainbow-hued chiffon. Caroline agreed at once when Ancret added to her drawing, colouring it to match her dress.

'Could you add a few sequins?' Caroline asked. 'I do love a bit of sparkle.'

Ancret drew a small shower of dots rising up from several of the folds. 'Perfect,' Caroline breathed happily. Measurements didn't take long. When she had finished, Ancret invited Caroline upstairs to see Loraine.

She saw Caroline hesitate and remarked casually, 'Mummy's improving, she's sitting out in her chair and able to talk. She'll enjoy a bit of company. You can tell her about the celebrity lunch-*eon*.' She emphasized the second half of the word and noticed Caroline's approval.

'I can't stay long, dear.'

'A few minutes would be fine.'

She left them alone while she made tea and cut some cake, then took the tray to her mother's room. The two women were talking. And, to her horror, she heard Caroline say, 'We did get a surprise when Lottie told me about seeing Ancret with a baby. For a moment we wondered if that had been the reason for her absence.'

Not giving her mother the chance to reply, Ancret went in with the tray, talking as she entered. 'Mummy, you should see the lovely hat Caroline's chosen. She looked through my sketchbook and I drew a dozen ideas, but she knew straight away what she wanted and it will look lovely on her. I'm going to call it Rainbow.' She put down the tray, moving the willow basket to one side, then went on, 'Show Mummy what you'll be wearing, Caroline. It's so charming.'

\*　　\*　　\*

Jonathan was missing Lottie. Not for the promise of a relationship, but in the office. She had been good and after a number of attempts, he had failed to find anyone to replace her. The girls who had applied had looked bored even before he told them what the work entailed, and many shook their heads and declined before he had offered them the position. He had tried three and none had shown an interest in the work.

If an enquirer asked about a house that had been sold, there had been no attempt to offer them something else or even ask for a name and address in case something suitable came on to their books at a later date. Questions were answered vaguely, wrong information was frequently given. Several times, when he or Lucinda had belatedly heard of these carelessly treated prospects and telephoned, they were told the client had tired of waiting and had chosen another agency.

'What are we going to do?' he asked Lucinda, when a client complained he had made four phone calls asking for details of a property to be sent to him and was still waiting. 'I can't be in two places at a time and we need someone to man the phone.'

'Swallow our pride and ask Lottie to come back?'

'No. I couldn't face that again.'

Lucinda placed the half-yearly accounts in front of him. 'Business is already suffering because we aren't on top of everything,' she said, her red fingernail tapping the totals in the profit column. 'It isn't serious yet, but once we allow it to slide it's so easy for everything to slip away.'

Jonathan knew she was right. He also knew he was mostly to blame. It was all right to blame inefficient and uninterested assistants, but he had spent too much time dreaming about what might have been, and too little concentrating on his business. That had to change, and quickly.

He worked all day and late into the night for three days, sitting at the office desk, listing people to contact, planning an advertising campaign and preparing a leaflet drop in a few likely places. He went through the diary and the book beside the telephone and noted the chances they had missed, angry with himself. He hadn't been on top of things. He hadn't been dealing with the minute-by-minute affairs that kept the business afloat. Immediacy had always been his watchword, but he hadn't lived up to it himself.

The business missed Lottie, but he was missing Ancret. If only he could accept they were finished, then perhaps he could give all of his mind to work instead of only a part of it. If he could talk to her he might see that there was nothing left of the love they had shared. A dead love affair sometimes needed a final goodbye before it ended.

With Ancret designing and making a hat for his mother he had an excuse to call on her. It would be acceptable to go to the shop to thank her, and his appreciation would be genuine. Ancret's offer was something that had delighted his mother, even though she had pretended it was she doing the favour by accepting it.

Perhaps if he could see her, talk to her, it would bring to an end his regrets, his futile searching for new hope. He needed to put her out of his mind. It wasn't Ancret he needed, he told himself, she was just a symptom of his loneliness. His mother was still living in the house left to her by her brother and the flat was cold and unwelcoming, echoing to even the smallest sound he made as if abandoned and haunted. But that vestige of hope remained. If he called when the shop was closed, she might possibly invite him inside. Hope doesn't die to order, he thought foolishly.

'I've called to thank you for your kindness to Mother,' he said when she opened the door to him that evening. He made to step inside, but she didn't move.

'I'm glad she's pleased. Excuse me for not inviting you in, Jonathan, but I have something to finish before we eat and I don't want to leave Mummy any longer than I can help. She's on her own so many hours of the day.'

'Can I see her?' he asked.

She shook her head. Then a lie occurred to her. 'The truth is, I have someone coming to see me in an hour and I need to get ready.'

'A man?' he asked.

Again she nodded. 'Someone very special.'

He walked away telling himself he was pleased, that now it really had ended and he could move on. He wondered

183

what Jason would say. That he hadn't persisted strongly enough? Or that it was a satisfactory ending? He had to admit that it seemed anything but satisfactory.

Ancret watched him go with mixed feelings, the strongest of which was regret.


Jonathan was waiting outside when Lottie finished work the following day. He opened the car door and called to her. Without preamble he said, 'If you'd like your job back it can be arranged.'

'Jonathan! You missed me!'

His heart sank at her flippant tone. 'Yes, but only at the office,' he said firmly, already regretting his decision. 'I don't want you to think there's any other reason other than you're very good at your job and the business needs you.'

'And you don't?'

'I don't,' he said, shaking his head, his lips a tight line of emphasis. 'If you can't accept that, then forget it. But if you do want to come back we'll discuss salary tomorrow lunchtime. Come to the office, right?'

'Why not now?'

The thought of a return to the empty flat and another lonely meal decided him. 'Just a drink then,' he said.

'Jonathan,' she said teasingly, 'I think you're afraid of me.'

'No,' he said firmly. 'Just tired of your silly games.' He stood and looked at her, one hand on his car door, waiting for her reply. 'I want this to be a professional appointment that ends when the office door closes. Well? Is it yes or no?' He relaxed then and said, 'Come on, Lottie, you're young and very attractive. Please don't waste time flirting with me. You'll miss opportunities for something really special. You deserve someone who'll appreciate you. Someone younger, kinder. It all got very silly, didn't it?'

'Yes, I was having fun at your expense and I went too far. I'm sorry.'

'Let's forget it ever happened.'

'About that drink, let's make it tomorrow, shall we? I'm meeting someone later on and I want to get ready.'

Driving home Jonathan laughed. Two brush-offs in twenty-four hours. That was something to celebrate. He garaged the car and walked to the pub.

Jason was there talking to a couple of people. Jonathan nodded and went to the bar. He ordered and paid for a meal, bought a drink and found a table some distance away, not wanting to intrude.

He glanced up once or twice to see that Jason and the couple with him were looking at him. He turned away. Meeting people was something he usually enjoyed, and adding to his acquaintances was good for business, but tonight he wasn't feeling either businesslike or sociable. When it seemed that the three were planning to come over, he went to the bar, apologized, cancelled the meal and left.

That night he lay in bed thinking about the women who had passed through his life. He wondered again where Babs had gone. He thought again of the child they might have had, trying to imagine a different conclusion. But deep in his heart he knew that, if he were given that time to live over again, he would have made the same decision – even though, besides losing Babs, that same act had been the reason Ancret had left him too.

Was he going to be one of those men who drifted into late middle age, looking after an ageing mother and being thought of as a wonderful son? He didn't want to be a wonderful son, he wanted to be a husband with a loving wife always there for him. Unwillingly at first, he allowed his thoughts to drift to Lottie. Her stupidity had been irritating but all she had done was attempt to make him notice her. There must be many worse beginnings to a love affair.

Caroline's hat was a success. In spite of her early sarcastic comments about advertising Ancret's work, she proudly told several people the designer's name. And she added in hushed whispers that Ancret was in love with her son, who had ended the affair leaving her broken-hearted.

For Ancret it meant an increase in business at a time of year when it usually began to wane. Annie and she were kept busy; the business was still growing, justifying her decision to take on her talented assistant. The bank and her accountants were pleased with its success.

She spent every evening either in the workshop or sitting sewing beside her mother. She discussed the progress of the loans and explained to Loraine how she hoped their borrowings might be repaid much sooner than they had predicted. 'Thanks to Dorothy Piper-Davies and Caroline, and finding darling Annie of course,' she said, looking at her mother.

'You're an artist. You'd have succeeded no matter what had happened,' Loraine said. 'I'm pleased that it's working out so well, daughter. I can rest happily now I know you're safely established.'

'Rest?' Ancret retorted with a laugh to cover her alarm. 'As soon as you're recovered, I expect you back in the workshop! We have next season's designs to prepare. Besides, it's only October. There's the winter months to survive, remember.'

'October's a sad month,' her mother said.

'Was it a month when something awful happened to you?' Ancret still held the constant hope that her mother would open up and talk about her past. 'Mummy, can't you understand how much I need to know why we are here without any family connections? There has to be someone out there. Please, won't you talk about it?'

There was no reply; whether it was Loraine's stubborn determination not to talk, or whether she had genuinely fallen asleep, the result was the same. With a sigh, she went to prepare supper.

The dream her mother suffered that night was more distressing than usual and Ancret cried as she tried to comfort her, ashamed of worrying her when she was obviously so ill. It began as always with Loraine clinging on to an imaginary baby, pleading for help. Then she began shouting, staring at someone only she could see. 'I've tried to tell her. I have.' There were a lot of tearful, garbled mutterings of which Ancret only understood a few words, mostly *please*. Then, 'I promised myself I'd talk to her when she was twelve, and then eighteen, and twenty-one, but I can't.' More confused mumbling, and Loraine began thrashing around on the bed. Ancret talked to her soothingly, trying to wake her as gently as she could, even though she usually allowed the dreams to come to their end unaided. 'I'd ruin everything.'

The words were clear, then after more confusion, 'With a few words I'd take away what she is, and what would I put in her place?' She began to groan and the sound was heart-rending.

'Please Mummy, wake up,' Ancret pleaded. 'I'll never ask you again, I promise.'

'My girls,' Loraine sobbed. 'So precious.'

*Girls?* Hope engulfed Ancret. Did she have sisters somewhere? A father and sisters? Maybe nieces and nephews? Forgetting her former guilt, she shook Loraine softly, her hand on her mother's shoulders. 'Mummy, wake up. What were their names? My sisters. Where are they?'

'Please help me—' Loraine begged. 'Please.' Clutching the bedclothes she had gathered into a shape like the baby she was imagining, she called out, as though after someone walking away, 'Please!'

It was the last word she spoke. Ancret sat with her as she fell into a troubled sleep. As the dream ended and her mother's face relaxed, she knew something was seriously wrong. She called an ambulance, which took Loraine to hospital. All the next day Ancret didn't leave her mother's side. At three the following morning, a doctor gently confirmed her mother's death.

It was Helena who came first to offer sympathy and help. She and Angela dealt with the few clients who had appointments for fittings, and made no further bookings. The shop closed for a day then, following Helena's advice, it reopened. They offered sympathy, promised support and got on with the business in the shop. Unable to do anything to help apart from working, Annie finished the few hats they had been making and began on others.

Ancret moved like a marionette with broken strings as she dealt with the authorities and prepared for her mother's funeral. She was shivering all the time, and thought she would never be warm again. The shawl she held tightly around her had no effect and she wrapped herself in her mother's coat at night, imagining she was in the warmth of Loraine's loving arms.

Jonathan visited the evening following her mother's death.

She wanted to run into *his* arms, to be comforted by *his* warmth. Protection from the icy coldness that had engulfed her was what she wanted more than anything else. She felt desire too, and with it shame. It would be so easy to allow him to comfort her but so wrong to use him in such a way.

She pulled away from his attempts to hold her and reminded herself there was no going back. She was in need of him at this time, but he was still the man she could never love enough to marry. To use him would have been cruel, knowing she would turn away again once her grief had subsided.

'Do you need any help?' he asked, standing as near as she would allow. 'You'll need certificates and all that stuff. I can do some of it for you.'

She remembered the drawer her mother kept locked. 'I'll have to find Mummy's keys first, won't I?' she said sadly.

'That's right. No more secrets. Are you ready to deal with it all?'

She turned towards the stairs and he followed her. Then she stopped. This was hers to deal with. 'No, Jonathan. I must face this on my own.'

She walked into her mother's room, opened the drawer and found, neatly labelled in her mother's handwriting, an envelope marked *Birth Certificates etc.* And there her confidence left her. She wasn't ready for this. Placing the envelope, unexamined, ready for the undertaker the following morning, she reached for one of her thickest shawls and went for a walk.

She went towards the busy shopping centre. She needed people around her, but anonymous faces, no one to whom she needed to talk. She wasn't ready to talk yet.

Then, in a small wooden café that had been there seemingly for ever, surrounded by the modern buildings, she saw Edmund sitting nursing a cup of coffee. Thoughts of avoiding familiar faces were banished. It was such a relief that she sighed out loud before calling to him. Edmund was exactly what she needed, a kind, friendly man who would listen.

His reaction was all she could have wished. He received her news with immediate warmth, placing a kind hand over hers and offering a sympathetic ear. 'Would you like a coffee or would you prefer to walk?'

'Walk,' she replied.

'Talk about it?'

'How long have you got?'

'Till ten o'clock or thereabouts, then I have to go back to set breakfast tables and see to night-time drinks and all that. This week's party are theatre enthusiasts and they've just been swept off to go backstage at the Sherman and then to tea, followed by a play at the New Theatre, and supper somewhere on Cardiff Bay. Turkish cuisine I believe. What exciting lives we lead these days.'

'Come back with me, will you? I need to go through my mother's things and I can't face it alone.'

The first shock was that her mother's name wasn't Loraine Carter. She had been born Connie Sullivan. Her father's address was a farm north of Cardiff. There was no sign of a marriage certificate in either name. On her own birth certificate was the greatest shock of all. She was Ancret, but the surname shown there was not Carter either. She hadn't been christened Ancret Carter; her mother was named as Connie Sullivan. Father unknown.

Edmund said nothing. He just nodded and shook his head where appropriate and made tea, persuaded her to eat a little and offered his arms. It was so tempting, but she declined. When he was leaving she wanted so badly for him to stay. But this was a test, proof of how she would cope or otherwise alone. She closed the door behind him and was locked in with the silence.

The telephone rang, startling her. She picked up to hear Edmund say, 'I'm hungry, will you eat with me? Welsh, Chinese, Thai, Greek – Cardiff has them all. Turkish if you like,' he added, trying to make her smile.

'Welsh,' she said.

Ancret hadn't intended to talk too much about her mother's death, but after a meal and a bottle of wine it all came out. Edmund said very little, just a few words to coax her when she needed it. He asked few questions, offered no advice.

'The night before she died the dream was more lucid, her words were clearer than before. I – I think I might have sisters, or half-sisters maybe.' She glanced at him as she added, 'There's no sign of a marriage certificate.'

'That might explain why she didn't talk about it. People can still be edgy about these things.'

When he left it was after midnight. He had telephoned his parents to apologize for not getting back to deal with the late-night chores. Ancret heard him laugh at something and he explained. 'My father wanted to know if she was "nice". His way of asking whether he and Mum would like you. I said you are absolutely beautiful.'

Although the house was as silent as before once he had gone, it no longer seemed so empty.

The days before the funeral were filled with office visits, writing to various places for forms, filling them in, going to see the funeral directors, accepting condolences via letter and phone. There was so much to do that Ancret was usually unaware of the empty building. Edmund phoned every evening and she began to look forward to his call, disappointed when she picked up the phone and the voice was not his. Each night, by the time she was ready for bed she was exhausted. Sleep came quickly, obliterating the pain of her loss and giving her no time to brood about the future.

Jonathan came every day and helped with any queries. Sometimes he came alone, once with his mother, who brought flowers, and twice with Lucinda. Even Lottie sent a card. Ancret showed it to Jonathan. 'Is she working for you again?'

'Yes. But I don't think there'll be any more trouble. Lucinda will make sure of that. She knows everything that happened.' He saw her looking at him curiously. 'She's good at her job and we need her.'

'Of course.'

It wasn't until after the funeral that the reality of her situation finally hit Ancret. Going back into the rambling premises of the shop and workroom and the flat above, she stood in the living room, glancing across at the open door of her mother's bedroom, and saw a future stretching before her of many evenings like this – alone, with only her work to comfort her. There would be Natalie, but no adult with whom to share laughter or tears, no one with whom to exchange ideas.

During the days there would be Annie and Angela, sometimes Helena, plus their customers and clients to fill her time and make her feel important and needed, but once the door closed everyone else would be on the outside, in the busy world where anything was possible, while she would be locked in with a million memories of the past and few hopes for the future. At twenty-five she was too young to live on memories.

Edmund took her out several times. Work still occupied most of her days, not always from necessity but to obliterate the emptiness. No further revelations came to light and now she thought they never would. Edmund knew about her lack of a family, but she hadn't told him about Natalie. She wouldn't be able to make him understand and she couldn't bear to lose his friendship. What a mesh of lies. How would she ever extricate herself without losing every friend she had? Only with Marguerite Flowers could she discuss the future, and Marguerite's advice had always been to face the situation square on and tell Jonathan about his child. That was something she couldn't do; it was far too late for truth.

She began visiting Natalie more often, taking her out for half days and full days, initially with Marguerite Flowers and then on her own. It was October, only four more months before she had agreed to bring her home. Would the little girl feel lonely too? Natalie was part of a large family at present. To bring her here, to the flat where everything fell devastatingly silent at five thirty, was bound to be strange to the child. She'd be used to quieter days that livened up at that time. She had imagined her mother there, being able to take her out for walks and introducing her to other children, but now she was alone and she was completely unprepared. The reminder that Loraine hadn't seen Natalie since that first day in hospital brought tears; with no one to witness them, she allowed them to fall until she was exhausted.

Needing reassurance, even though it would be weeks before she brought Natalie home, she wrote to Marguerite and Simon Flowers explaining how she felt and asking if they would still call and see Natalie sometimes. It wasn't something she could do on the telephone. They would need time to discuss it, to decide whether their break from the little girl should be sudden or whether they could cope with staying friends after having her for a year as their own. Their answer was to write straight back telling her they would never want to lose touch. And they invited her to stay with them for a weekend.

'It will be a start to her acceptance of you as an important part of her life. Later on perhaps we can come to stay with you and fill the flat with some of her toys, so she won't feel strange,' Marguerite suggested wisely.

Making sure she had no appointments that next weekend was simple and Helena willingly agreed to help in the salon. Ancret began to gather a few things to take, including gifts for Marguerite's family.

She wondered how she would cope, after a weekend as a temporary part of a real family, walking back into the empty flat. It would be the first time she had left the flat for more than a few hours since her mother had died. It would also be the first time, she realized with overwhelming dismay, that she had stayed in a normal household with a normal family. Even at college she had shared a flat with another girl. Since college she had been on holidays in the artificial environment of a hotel, and had spent a few weeks in a couple of rooms while waiting for Natalie's birth. By devoting themselves utterly to her work, she and her mother had isolated themselves from everything other people took for granted. In a bleak moment, she wondered if it had been worth it.

Edmund was becoming a friend. Making no demands on her, he seemed to sense when she needed him and would appear as the shop closed. He was usually in the large Transit, having deposited that week's hotel guests somewhere of interest. On one occasion a group of visitors filled the vehicle and she was invited to join them for some sightseeing. Once or twice he invited himself for a meal – which he usually brought with him – and these were the evenings she enjoyed best. Echoes of his presence filled the flat for hours after he'd gone, banishing the silence, bringing light to the shadows.

One of the best surprises was when he brought a picnic. Insisting that October was not too late for eating out, he drove her to a park where he set out food and drink. There was romance in the air as he took out blankets, putting one on the moist grass and another around her shoulders.

Her heart beat faster. The food seemed an irrelevant part of the evening, Edmund's company was enough. He was relaxed and attentive, their chatter the easy conversation of friends. Apart from an affectionate kiss as they packed up to leave, he didn't touch her. But the way he looked at her, the obvious admiration – and maybe something else besides – offered promise. Ancret knew this was one evening she would never forget. If she and Edmund had a future, this would be a turning point.

Jonathan was restless. He told himself there was no chance of a reconciliation with Ancret, so what was stopping him from taking Lottie out for a meal? She was clearly still interested in him, even though there had been no repeat of her earlier foolish behaviour. She occasionally suggested a meal or a drink after work. She was young, attractive and good company. He couldn't deny that her interest was flattering. Weeks had passed since Loraine's funeral and there was nothing in Ancret's manner to give him hope of a return to their loving relationship. There was nothing to lose, so he invited Lottie out for dinner. 'Cinema as well, if you like,' he offered. 'You deserve it after the way you've worked since you came back.'

'Not the cinema, Jonathan, I'd prefer a meal after a drink in some quiet pub.'

It was as he was waiting for her to appear that Jonathan met Jason again.

'Can I join you? Or are you waiting for someone?'

'The "Persistent young thing" will be along in a while,' Jonathan explained with a wry grin.

'Good on you.' Jason glanced at the doorway. 'Look, I don't know whether you fancy it, but my family are having a sort of party in a couple of weeks time. My ex-father-in-law is seventy. D'you fancy coming along?'

'I can't butt into a family gathering,' Jonathan protested.

'It's more than family.' He scribbled an address on a beer mat and handed it to Jonathan. 'Half the street will be there. I'd be glad of a friendly face. I'm not keen on this sort of thing since my wife – you know. If you're there we can slope off and find a pub.'

Jonathan agreed, then stood up to greet Lottie. She was dressed in leggings and a skimpy top with what looked like a man's shirt over it. Jason turned to his friend and gave a low whistle. 'Of course, if you're otherwise occupied I quite understand.'

'I'll be there,' Jonathan said.

Because of Jason's obvious admiration, he welcomed Lottie with more affection than he intended, putting an arm around her shoulders and kissing her lightly on the cheek. She turned and found his lips with her own; exaggeratedly tiptoeing, Jason waved and left.

With the intention of weaning Natalie out of their lives and into Ancret's, Marguerite and Ancret began to meet more often. Marguerite knew that the extra involvement was helping fill in some of the gaps in Ancret's life and willingly took Natalie to spend extra time with her.

As their friendship ripened, Ancret let slip a few confidences. She told Marguerite of her mother's secretiveness and her unexplained change of name.

'I believe my mother's maiden name was Sullivan, although Dad refuses to talk about her,' Marguerite surprised her by saying. 'No relation though. All my family are accounted for. My mother was a Howells and she died when I was fifteen and Sophie was eleven.'

'Shall I see you as usual on Sunday?' Ancret asked as they parted one evening, after she had bathed Natalie and put her to bed. There was a momentary hesitation before she added, 'Please, don't worry if you can't manage it. You and your family have been wonderful, specially these past few weeks. Shall I phone on Monday to see if you're free during the week?'

'Of *course* come Sunday. The reason for my hesitation was deciding when would be the best time. It's my father's seventieth birthday, you see, and we're inviting a few friends.'

'In that case I won't come. I wouldn't want to intrude on a family affair.' But she wanted to. The name Sullivan wasn't that common. If there was the slightest chance of Marguerite's father knowing someone of that name she wanted to take it.

'You must come. After all, Natalie is one of Dad's friends and he'd love to meet you. Get here early, in good time for lunch.'

Jonathan arrived at Jason's home at eleven and they walked together to the party. The house was already full. They struggled through the hallway between groups of chattering people, all holding glasses, and pushed their way through to the kitchen. It was a surprisingly mild November morning and the back door stood open. Through the conservatory glass, several people could be seen in the garden beyond.

Since helping his mother with the grounds of his uncle's property, and studying the way the regular gardener dealt with it, Jonathan had become interested. He asked, 'When you've grabbed a couple of beers, can we go and look at the garden?'

'Fine by me. I have an abysmally small plot myself, but I enjoy pottering.'

Pouring beer into two glasses and handing one to his friend, Jason led him out through the conservatory and around the corner to where a large vegetable plot had recently been dug. A slow spiral of smoke corkscrewed up from a bonfire, filling the air with smells evocative of other days: Guy Fawkes and fireworks, ghost stories told with verve and fearful realism, hide and seek played in the friendly darkness. Even the sun failed to dissipate the memories of those far-off times, memories teased by the wonderful scent of bonfire smoke.

A young woman at the far end of the garden held a child in her arms. She turned, then froze as he recognized her. 'Ancret?' he said in disbelief.

'Oh, d'you know each other?' Jason asked, walking with arms outstretched to take the child. 'Then you must also know Natalie. Isn't she a gem?'

Oblivious now of everything except the woman walking her swaying walk towards Jason, handing him the child, Jonathan stood and watched as she waved, then took the child back from Jason and started to approach him.

'What are you doing here? How d'you know Jason?' he asked.

'She's a friend of my brother and my sister-in-law, Marguerite,' Jason explained.

Shyly, the little girl had buried her face in Ancret's shoulder. 'Whose baby is she?' he asked. 'Marguerite's?'

Just then, Marguerite came out, calling that lunch was served. 'Have you been having a lovely walk with your mummy, darling?' she asked, reaching for the child. 'Shall we put her in her high chair so she can join us?' she asked Ancret. 'Or are you brave enough to hold her on your lap?'

'What does she mean, "Mummy"?' Jonathan asked. 'Why is she calling you her mummy?'

'Because that's who I am. Her mother.' Ancret suddenly felt cold, as she had during the hours after her mother's death. Dampness from the ground crept up and seemed to encase her in ice. 'Natalie is my child.'

'Who's the father?' he demanded, while Jason eased past him, took the child from her arms and went into the house.

'She was born in February.' All her carefully thought-out lies faded from her mind and she told the truth.

'I don't understand.'

'I tried to tell you I was pregnant. You must remember how it upset you? In reply you said that on no account would you have a child. That if I became pregnant I'd have to have an abortion, give up my baby. Now d'you understand?' Her voice was bitter.

'So that was why you went away. You were having my child.' He pushed roughly past her and hurried into the house.

Marguerite was marshalling the guests towards the laden tables. A hurried discussion had explained to her what had happened and she saw Jonathan forcing his way through the crowd of the lively guests, heading for the door. She said, 'Would you like to see Natalie?' She still had the child in her arms and offered her towards him. He turned away angrily, not even looking at her. He couldn't look at her, she would be like Donald. His mother had warned him, and Donald was proof she had been right.

'No. I want nothing to do with her.' He hurried from the house and didn't look back.

# Eleven

Jason took the child from Ancret and said urgently, 'Go after him.'

She ran, but almost gave up as he reached his car and opened the door. She got there as he inserted the key in the starter. The driver's window was open and she grabbed his arm.

'Jonathan, please listen to me.'

'She's yours?' he asked rhetorically, staring at her with cold eyes, narrow with hatred.

'Yes, she's mine – the child you'd have made me destroy!'

'Get out of my sight! I have to get away from here!'

'Come back and look at her.'

'I can't!'

'Please!' she shouted as he pushed her hand away and started the engine. 'Please – help me.' The words out of her mother's dream reverberated in the air around her. *Please – help me.* She didn't know why she said them. They had issued forth without thought or intention, an echo of her mother's agony.

He said something as he wound up the window and began to move off. But she didn't hear, wasn't even aware of him speaking. She was frozen with shock, listening to her own words in counterpoint to her mother's voice. She was in a different scene in a different time, listening to the pleading, begging call for help with a child, unable to take in his final, bitter remarks – or to hear Marguerite's voice calling her from the doorway.

'Please, help me . . .' she whispered again. She was bereft, completely alone, nothing but angry faces all around her, she and her mother surrounded by disapproval and a demand to be gone. This was how it must have been for her mother, she thought as reality slowly returned. Loraine had felt as she did now as she had pleaded for help for her child. Had 'Father Unknown' walked away with hate in his eyes as Jonathan had done, while her mother had called out 'Please, help me'?

Ancret knew she had been even younger than Natalie was now when her mother had been abandoned by 'Father Unknown'. The label that so often put blame on the mother for being too casual with her sexual favours was rarely seen as the action of a man who refused to acknowledge a child he had helped to create.

Shivering with misery and shame, fear and anxiety, and a dozen emotions she would have been unable to name, she turned and walked slowly back to where Marguerite and the others were waiting. Jason held Natalie, who was crying, upset by the shouting and confusion, and Simon stood beside his wife. There was sympathy, not anger, on every face. She opened her arms and took her daughter, wondering what would happen now the secret was out. Like her mother before her, she knew she could expect nothing from her child's father.

Jason took off his jacket and wrapped it around her and the baby, while Marguerite led her inside. There was silence where there had been lively conversation and laughter. As they went in, voices jerked into life, but the guests avoided looking at them. Ancret wanted to run away, but she couldn't. Her daughter lived here and Natalie needed a return to the security, the calmness that had been broken the moment Jonathan had arrived and had seen her and known she was his.

She deliberately walked into the room and helped herself to a glass of punch, introducing herself with her full name and occupation, engaging a stranger in conversation. Others soon joined in and although she felt as though claws were tearing at her insides, and her head was so tightly packed it might explode, Ancret coped. Before long Marguerite warned them that the guest of honour was approaching. Everything went quiet and the room breathed slowly. Thank goodness. Now the attention would be on someone else.

*    *    *

Jonathan drove fast and furiously, with no thought or care for himself or anyone else. Swinging the car too fast around corners, overtaking at dangerous moments, he eventually stopped and turned off the ignition. He didn't get out; he sat there imagining the face of a small child.

*I'm Donald. Who are you?* the voice in his head asked. Could he have coped? People did, after all. And Babs seemed more than content; she seemed relaxed and happy. Momentarily he was convinced. Then his mind returned to Ancret. How could she? To deliberately deceive him in this way was unbelievable. To lie about some college appointment, to hide away until the child had been born and never give a hint of what was happening. It was unforgivable.

He was very distressed. Any slight weakening and he knew he would cry. His life was in shreds. Ancret, whom he loved so much. He didn't know her at all. He wondered, how could she have become pregnant? He'd been so careful. Perhaps the child wasn't his? Where had she been on the days she was too busy to see him? If she could lie about a child, was there anything she was incapable of?

His hands made fists and he clenched them until they hurt. Jealousy was a weapon and he needed to use it. He wondered how he would have handled this if he had been told. Why had it happened a second time? It was so unfair. He could never have children, he knew that, so why was he tormented in this way? As he sat in the car, with no sound except the engine ticking as it cooled, he gradually became aware of his whereabouts. He was outside Lottie's house, actually in her parents' drive. What had brought him here? A need for sympathy perhaps. But how could he tell her that Ancret, whom he had loved, had cheated on him in such a terrible way?

He couldn't tell his mother either. He was alone with the problem and it was one that wouldn't go away. He looked up at the house. On this winter afternoon, lights showed and he imagined being in there with a family: arguing, talking, sharing news, laughing. Normal communication – something he was denied. He wondered whether Lottie was at home. He wanted to see her, desperately needing someone who cared, who would listen to his news, even though the most important item of all would remain unspoken.

He pressed the horn several times, disturbing the Sunday quiet. After several bursts, someone looked out. Then the front door opened and Lottie appeared, dragging a coat around her shoulders as she ran towards him.

'What's happened?' she asked, immediately seeing from his taut face that something was wrong. 'You look awful, Jonathan. You shouldn't have driven in this state.'

'I know. But I wanted to see you.' He leaned over and opened the door. She slid inside, taking his hand in hers.

'Tell me what's made you so upset.'

'Don't ask me to explain. It's something I can't face.'

'Ancret?' she coaxed, stroking his hand, leaning closer and kissing his cheek. 'Tell me, Jonathan. I can help, but only if I know what's wrong.'

'Ancret has a child. A daughter.'

Shock registered on her face. 'Then it *was* her child she was with that day.' She looked at him, careful not to say anything derogatory. She didn't know how he felt about either Ancret or her child. 'Is she beautiful?'

Jonathan turned his head sharply. 'I don't know. I couldn't look at her.'

He was silent for a while. Lottie waited for him to say something more, but as the silence remained unbroken, she asked whether his mother knew. He shook his head slowly.

'I'm presuming the baby is yours,' she said. Still no reaction, so she added, 'I'm pleased for Ancret, if that's what she wants.'

'Is it wrong not to want children?' he said suddenly, staring at her in the gloomy light inside the car. 'She knew I didn't want a child, not ever.'

Guessing his mood and hoping she was making the right response, she answered at first with a question to herself. 'Do I think it's wrong? Well, my answer is that it's wrong to have a child unless you're really sure and are prepared for the differences it will make for the rest of your days. I never want a child, I'd resent the way my life was taken over. The responsibility for another human being is terrifying, something I'd hate.'

'I did want children,' Jonathan said sorrowfully, 'but I

know that any child of mine would be handicapped and I couldn't face that. So I can never have a child.'

'I understand,' she said, although she did not. 'Anyone who marries you would have to accept being childless. And if they loved you, really loved you, they'd agree without question.'

'Marry me, Lottie. Marry me and let's live for each other and share every moment. I love you, you know. I've tried so hard not to because of our age difference, but I love you.' He pulled her into his arms and kissed her. 'My anger towards you was because you disturbed me. I found you so attractive, funny, bold, clever, and so desirable, and I hated myself for it. I considered it my weakness. I thought—'

'Oh shut up, Jonathan,' she whispered against his lips, 'and take me home.'

He released her and drove shakily to the flat.

An hour later, passion spent, calmly aware that his words of love were not true, coldly understanding that he was proposing and declaring his love because of Ancret's betrayal, Lottie accepted. She wanted Jonathan under any terms. Love on the rebound was better than no love at all.

Ancret stood back as Marguerite's father walked in. Cheers rang out and he looked startled, then pleased, as the guests sang 'Happy Birthday'. When everyone had greeted him and he was at last sitting alone Ancret approached him, uttering the conventional politenesses. She was still shaking from her encounter with Jonathan, but she had to find out if there was anything this man could tell her.

'So you're the mother of little Natalie. How d'you do,' he said formally when she introduced herself. 'Quite the nicest of the little brats Marguerite has looked after. Glad to see them go, most of them. Noisy little characters. My daughters were probably as bad as the worst of them, but one forgets.'

They talked about Natalie for a while, and other children that Marguerite and Simon had fostered. From time to time people came to hug him and shake his hand, say their goodbyes and leave. Determined to ask her questions, Ancret stayed beside him, hoping he wouldn't be coaxed away before she could talk to him about her mother.

As the clock moved towards the time when she would have to leave, she said, 'I'm trying to find some of my family, and when my mother died recently, I learned from the birth certificates that my name wasn't Howells. Mummy changed it. On her birth certificate she was called Sullivan. There's no sign of a marriage certificate,' she said hesitantly.

Marguerite's father stared at her, jerking away from her as though he'd been shot. 'Sullivan?'

'You know someone with that name?' she asked as hope surged.

'It isn't uncommon,' he said, recovering his composure. 'Several families called Sullivan in the town.' He gestured with a thumb towards the hill in front of the house. 'Up on the hill, those gypsies. Some of them were Sullivans. A common enough name. I don't know anyone called Ancret or Loraine. Waste of time worrying about who you are, young lady. Best let it go. It's who you are now that counts. Here and now, and into the future. Don't look back. I never do.'

'Mummy's first name was Connie.'

He turned his head and looked at her slowly, as though seeing her for the first time. 'Connie Sullivan? You're her daughter?' He stood up, went to the window and looked up at the hill, his mind drifting back over the years in spite of his words to the contrary.

Hope swept over her as she asked, 'You know something about her?'

'Nothing. Nothing at all.' He pushed his way through the now diminishing crowd to the kitchen. He went outside, where light rain was falling, and stood in the gradually darkening garden, looking up at the barely visible hill.

When she collected her coat to leave, the old man had disappeared.

Marguerite walked with her to the bus stop and Ancret told her of his reaction. 'Marguerite, are you sure you don't know anyone called Sullivan? I'm sure your father remembered something. Why won't he help me?'

Marguerite's voice was casual as she replied, 'There are several families with that name. It's just coincidence, nothing more. Possibly it's the name of someone he's quarrelled with.

202

He's a bit of a bully sometimes, likes his own way. Stubborn if I'm honest.'

'I need to know who I am. You can understand, can't you? I want to know what genes I'm passing on to my daughter.'

'I'll talk to him tomorrow, I promise. But don't get too hopeful.' Marguerite smiled, but the smile failed to reach her eyes. 'Perhaps you've disturbed some unhappy memories for him. As I say, he can be a bit prickly sometimes. I can't imagine they're anything to do with your mother, not really. Can you?'

'Hardly likely. I suppose many families have secrets they want to keep. You're right, I must have touched the edge of one of his.'

She didn't go straight home but instead went to a cinema, grateful for the anonymity of the darkness. She sat through the film without understanding or caring what it was about, then walked home slowly, through the late evening crowds, delaying the moment when she had to step inside the empty house. There she would be alone with her thoughts on all that had happened on that confusing day.

Since the death of her mother, living alone, there were occasions when the rambling building was eerie, too silent. Models stood elegantly dressed, unmoving, staring sightlessly into corners. Shadows changed throughout the day and night, natural and artificial light making familiar things unrecognizable.

Sometimes she stood in the darkness and imagined she could hear breathing, then she would run up the staircase after flooding the place with light and switch on the radio to smother the silence. She missed her mother terribly and never more than now, after a day when she'd had to face so much.

She had used the shop entrance to go inside; she didn't like using the back lane entrance after dark. Standing behind the shop door after turning on the lights, she felt very cold and weary, emotionally drained. She stood there and went over the moment Jonathan had learned about the baby, reliving the hurt of his strong reaction to the revelation, his refusal to look at the child. Then, as if that weren't enough, there had been the odd behaviour of Marguerite's father. Her mind was in turmoil, thoughts of her mother's secrets vying with her own, more recent ones. The way she had deceived a man and hidden from him the birth of his child. Whatever his feelings, however he had behaved when she had tried to tell him, there was no excuse for her own behaviour.

Her sympathies were with Jonathan. What she had done was really beyond explanation, even if he had given her an opportunity. She had been wrong. Surely she was strong enough to have defied him openly instead of behaving the way she had? Running away from trouble was all very well in small matters, but when something as important as a child was involved, her behaviour had been inexcusable.

She went upstairs determined to write it all down, to explain to Jonathan how she felt at the time, the reasons for her decisions, to excuse herself by claiming she had been emotionally confused. Hormones, her mother had said, she should use the excuse of her wildly erratic hormones. She doubted that Jonathan would understand, but it was worth a try. She had to settle things between them. He had the right to know his daughter, she thought, adding the rider, *if he wanted to*. There was strong doubt about that.

When she had made three attempts at explaining her actions and failed, she gave up. She went downstairs to check unnecessarily on the door bolts and window locks. On the mat beneath the shop door she saw an envelope. Not Jonathan's writing, so who? Ripping the envelope impatiently she read the brief note. 'Jonathan and I are getting married,' it said. It was signed 'Yours happily, Lottie'.

Unrepentantly aware of her sarcasm, she wrote a reply wishing them the happiness they deserved. She addressed it to them both at Jonathan's flat.


The Flowers and Natalie were on holiday, spending a week in a friend's bothy in mid-Wales. There was no excuse to visit them before or after they went and Ancret waited impatiently for the third Sunday to come round. Fortunately the time was filled with increasing numbers of appointments, and any spare hours were occupied in making hats for the approach of spring with its abundance of weddings. Many of her designs were small and intricate, taking hours of careful, concentrated handiwork. She was thankful for the overflowing order book and the ability to immerse herself in what she was doing to the exclusion of everything else.

Lottie and her mother flicked their way through dozens of catalogues and browsed the department stores in search of a suitable wedding dress. Jonathan had suggested a short engagement, and although Lottie had imagined a big wedding, herself in white and a group of bridesmaids, a choir, an organ and all the trimmings, she agreed. She wanted to marry him and she was afraid that, if he had too much time to consider, he might change his mind. Ancret was still a threat.

Caroline had other ideas. A society wedding was what she had long dreamed of. As usual, she had her way.

'You can't marry in a register office as though there was something shameful about it all,' she complained. 'For a man in your position in the city it has to be a proper white wedding with at least two hundred guests. You owe it to me, for one thing. Don't I deserve to see you off in style?' She glanced at Lottie and saw her agreement in the shining eyes and wide smile. 'I'm a beauty consultant, and Lottie will make such a lovely bride. You owe it to her, too.'

'Pity we can't go to Moments for our clothes,' Lottie's mother said as they abandoned yet another shop's offerings. 'Ancret and her staff have a reputation for providing the very best.'

'I'd rather go naked!'

'Don't do that, Mrs Pen-Marr would have a fit. Although in this day and age it might start a fashion!' her mother said with a loud laugh, as she imagined Caroline's face.

The wedding was booked for January. It was not the bride or her mother but Caroline who came to be advised by Angela. She chose her outfit and selected a hat made by Ancret, paid for them and was about to leave when Ancret came into the salon, having heard her voice.

'Have you found what you want for Jonathan's wedding?' she asked politely. She was wary, wondering what Caroline's reaction would be to the news about her granddaughter. To her surprise Caroline didn't mention Natalie. Ancret knew that she had to bring the subject up, have done with the outburst that was sure to come.

Her heart racing with anticipation of a row, she watched the heavily made up woman with growing curiosity. Surely she wasn't going to pretend it hadn't happened? She couldn't be that indifferent to her son's child?

Caroline discussed the plans for a while, boasting in her usual manner about the horses and carriage, the reception at a marquee in the gardens of a castle, and the honeymoon in the Caribbean, not to mention what it had cost to do everything so quickly. Then, as she was about to leave, she said casually, 'Sorry you and he have broken up, dear, I thought he was quite fond of you and that you'd always at least be friends.'

Ancret realized in disbelief that she wasn't going to mention Natalie at all. Probably because Helena and Angela were there. Well, she wasn't going to get away with treating Natalie as that unimportant.

'It was finding out about the baby,' she said as she held the door open for Caroline to leave. 'I don't think he'll ever forgive me for not telling him he has a daughter.' Ancret stared across at Helena, who was talking on the telephone. She didn't look at Caroline, who had stepped back from the door and collapsed into a chair, her face ashen. 'I have some photographs of Natalie if you want to see them,' Ancret went on. She went to a drawer and pulled out a couple of albums, oblivious of Caroline's distress.

With shaking hands, Caroline took the small album from Ancret and began to look through it. It contained snaps showing the child's development from a tiny, newly born infant to a child six months old. The second album followed on, depicting today's child, ten months old and already struggling to walk. She went through them both several times without a word, then her hands dropped into her lap and the books fell to the floor.

'She's my granddaughter and you didn't tell me?'

For the first time Ancret looked at her visitor and saw how shocked she was. 'Are you all right, Caroline?' She motioned to Angela to fetch a drink of water, and knelt beside Caroline while she sipped it. 'I'm sorry if the photographs upset you. She's very beautiful, isn't she?'

'Why wasn't I told?'

206

'Surely Jonathan has explained?'

'Lottie saw you with a baby, and I talked to Jonathan about her. But we thought it couldn't possibly be his. Surely this is a trick? A cruel joke? If the child belongs to Jonathan, why didn't you tell me?' she repeated.

This was the question Ancret no longer felt able to answer. 'Jonathan is the one to explain that,' she said evasively.

'He knew and I didn't?'

'No, not until— He hasn't told you?' Ancret gasped. 'The man is obsessed with secrets!'

'So are you!' Caroline sobbed.

Ancret led her upstairs to the flat, poured coffee from the machine and said, 'Jonathan didn't know until a few weeks ago. Why he didn't tell you then, is for him to answer.'

'Is that why you went away? To deceive us so cruelly? You're a wicked, evil woman, Ancret. Haven't I always known it? Haven't I warned Jonathan to beware of you and your mother?'

'Blame me if you must,' Ancret said calmly. 'I'll accept accusations of deceit, but you must know why I did it. Jonathan told me he never wanted a child, he was adamant in that. He also admitted persuading his ex-girlfriend, Babs, to abort a child. Twice. I wouldn't put myself into that situation. When I realized I was pregnant, I tried to tell him. But he said categorically that he would never have one. He told me unequivocally that if I was pregnant then I'd have to have an abortion.' Her voice broke with emotion at the memory.

She looked at her visitor's sad face, the make-up no longer disguising her age as swollen eyes and smeared lips, the result of hot tears, distorted it. Deep sympathy for her softened Ancret's voice. 'What would you have done, Caroline?' She coaxed Jonathan's mother to sip her coffee. 'Would you have agreed to such a terrible thing? I knew I'd lose him, but I wouldn't lose my child. So I walked away.'

'I lost a child after I had Jonathan,' Caroline whispered. 'It would have been seriously handicapped. I was so afraid, I never had another child. I considered myself lucky to have Jonathan. He was perfect. I refused to sleep with my husband after that. I couldn't have coped with having a handicapped child.'

'And this is the root of Jonathan's fears? You convinced him he couldn't have a child without it being less than perfect in your eyes? I don't believe it!'

'I – I've often told Jonathan of my fear.' More defiantly she said, 'Yes, I warned him. Babs loved and adored Jonathan and she agreed.'

'But that's far worse than my keeping Natalie a secret! He could have made her abort a perfectly healthy child!'

'We couldn't take that chance, dear.'

'*We* couldn't? Then you knew about it and supported him?'

Caroline lowered her head. 'I've always needed beauty around me. I couldn't bear the thought of a child who wasn't per . . .' She hesitated over the word and instead said, '. . . who wasn't like other children.'

'I could never have done what Babs was forced to do – in the name of love!' Ancret snatched the cup and saucer from Caroline's hands. 'I think you'd better leave. Go back to your beautiful son and pretend he's perfect. A man who can destroy an unborn child? Force someone he purports to love to end the life of her baby? How's that for perfection, eh?'

Caroline was crying when she went down the stairs and for a moment Ancret felt pity. She had been very harsh. Then she imagined a tiny helpless child, unwanted, left to die, and she cried too.

Later that day, Ancret was walking to the post box when she saw Lottie. In spite of her anger towards Jonathan and his foolish mother she still felt a stab of jealousy towards the girl he was about to marry. 'Congratulations,' she said as they came face to face. 'I wish you luck.' Her slightly twisted smile gave the word an innuendo confirmed by the tone of her voice.

'I'm sorry to learn that you're a single mother,' Lottie said. 'It must have been so disappointing for you when Jonathan denied responsibility.'

'I don't think you have the facts right, Lottie. I didn't offer him the chance of accepting responsibility. The plan was to tell everyone I was adopting Natalie. I could never trust a man who forced a woman to abort his child on a whim of

208

his mother.' Before Lottie could prepare a retort, Ancret went on, 'Be careful not to get pregnant, or you'll be out on your ear or at the clinic faster than you can say the word!'

Briefly heartened by her spiteful remarks, Ancret went back to the shop.

Because of the cold silence of the empty premises, Ancret sometimes went out in the evening to walk around the streets until she felt tired enough to sleep. She liked the feeling of being a part of the crowd, even though she was alone. The city was lively during the hours of darkness. Even as the time approached midnight, there were crowds everywhere. Lights spilled out of doorways, music filled the air, changing from one sound to another as she moved away from one club towards another. Most of the pavement cafés were closed, but everywhere people walked along still with places to go. Friends walked in groups, their voices high as they chattered. Couples strolled arm in arm, stopping occasionally to kiss and hug each other, men in T-shirts, the women scantily dressed, vanity more important than warmth. Giggling girls, strutting men and teenagers – many still at school, by the look of them – trying to sound sophisticated as they flirted and showed off. Ancret loved it all.

As she wandered, taking in the enjoyment of others, she thought about her situation. She would keep to her plan of leaving Natalie with Marguerite and Simon until February, when she had made arrangements for a nursery to take her for five days each week. The other matter had to be pursued or she would never have any rest.

After the distressing visit on the occasion of Marguerite's father's surprise party, she hadn't seen Jason, and when Sunday came she doubted whether he would be there.

She arrived at her usual time in the afternoon, and it was Simon who opened the door to her. She spent an hour playing with Natalie and giving the chocolates and small gifts she had brought for the boys. While Marguerite started to prepare tea, Ancret asked if she could go to see her father.

'You can try,' Marguerite said. 'Though he's been in a bad mood these past weeks. Very antisocial – even for him,' she added with a wry smile.

'I have this hope he might know something that will guide me to my mother's family. I know it's unlikely but I have to try. All my life I've wanted to know who I am and where I come from, and my mother died without telling me.'

'I understand, but why d'you think my father can help?'

'Only from the way he reacted to the name Connie, and Sullivan.'

'That's easily explained. My mother was a Sullivan. But it's hardly likely there's a connection. According to my father, her family came from Ireland, there's no one related to her around here.'

'Do you have any birth certificates, marriage certificates, anything relating to his life and family that I might be allowed to see?'

'You'll have to ask him. He keeps all that sort of thing up in his loft.'

Jason was already there when she reached the house and he smiled a welcome, touched her cheek lightly with his lips and invited her inside. 'John is watching a repeat of one of the soaps,' he explained, gesturing towards the door from which came the sound of the television. 'He pretends not to be, but he's an addict.'

Marguerite's father turned at the sound of their voices and nodded, before turning back to the screen.

'John, I think Ancret needs your help.'

'None to give,' Marguerite's father replied without turning his head. 'Now hush, if you're staying here, I want to see this.'

'He's already seen it once,' Jason sighed.

'Can I call again, when you aren't so busy?' Ancret asked without sarcasm. 'I really would like to talk to you.'

'Maybe, sometime,' Marguerite's father said, waving a hand vaguely. Ancret looked at Jason and shrugged.

'Have you seen Jonathan since the party?' Jason asked as he led her to another room. 'He seemed very upset and I can understand why, not being told about a child.'

'He wouldn't have wanted me to have her.'

'It's true then? That he really believes any child of his would be disabled?'

'It's true.'

210

'But why? What is it based on?'

'His mother has encouraged him to believe it's inevitable because she had a child suffering a serious handicap, a child who died. Perhaps I'm being unkind, but I don't think she really wanted him to marry. She's using it as an excuse. She did little to encourage me, and before I came on the scene there was Babs and she left him. Apart from her son, Caroline's alone. And having Jonathan to look after her for the rest of her life would be so convenient, wouldn't it?'

'What will happen if he marries Lottie and she becomes pregnant? She's taking a risk, isn't she?'

'She thinks she's prepared for it. She's young enough to believe she can change him. Yet he's afraid to even look at Natalie, utterly convinced that there will be some imperfection.'

'If there had been, what would you have done?'

'Give her what every child is entitled to. Love her, care for her and make sure every day is as perfect as I can make it. Why?'

'We use the word perfect often. Yet it doesn't mean without blemish, does it? Just something we want at the time.'

'A perfect darn in an old sock? A perfect operation to remove a leg? You can't talk about a child in those terms, can you? Every child is beautiful.'

They heard footsteps. Marguerite's father came to the door and leaned in. 'It's them up on the hill you want to talk to about Connie Sullivan,' he said, and shuffled off up the stairs. Although Jason called to him, he didn't reappear.

'Does he mean the gypsies?' Ancret asked, going to the window and staring up to the hill now lost in the darkness. 'Surely not. What would they know about us?'

'You once said you'd like to visit them. If you're still of the same mind, come earlier next week and we'll go up there. They might help, although it's unlikely,' Jason said. 'They stay there every winter. Only for a few weeks now, a sentimental gesture I think. When Simon and I were young they'd be there from October till the spring. They worked for the farmer and earned a little making things, repairing things.'

'My mother made a beautiful gypsy doll,' she told him. 'Perhaps I'll bring it to show them.'

'They'd like that.' He was smiling as memories flooded back. 'Simon and I used to walk through the fields with them, amazed at their knowledge. There'd be many more than today. We'd toboggan with them too, when we had snow. They're very friendly, up to a point. Very private about some things, and they were very proud too.' He laughed as she began putting on her coat. 'Perhaps John meant one of them is a fortune teller, with a way of disclosing secrets from the past.'

She shivered as though someone had touched her with cold fingers. When the past finally unfolded, if it ever did, would the secrets it revealed help her, or make her life worse? Would knowing who she was make her regret searching for the truth? Perhaps her mother had good reason for taking the truth with her to the grave.

# Twelve

Ancret stood in her mother's room staring at the willow basket, now brittle and almost falling apart. Beside it was the gypsy doll Loraine had made. Was there some connection between her mother and the family of gypsies who had once spent every winter up on the hill? Yet how could there be, unless they had become confidants of some disaster that had happened to her mother years before, something that had driven her and her child from home? And if that were the case, why hadn't Marguerite's father explained? Whatever it was, it was surely too long ago for anyone to be hurt by its telling.

She adjusted the flowers in the jam jars that stood in the basket. She had kept the basket filled ever since her mother had died; a memorial, or maybe just a pretence that her mother wasn't dead but would return one day. It was hard to accept that she was gone for ever.

She would have to visit the gypsies and hear what they had to say. It was likely that they would be as reticent as the rest, but she had to try. There were no other leads and, fragile as it might be, this was the most hopeful yet. As soon as work permitted she would go to see Marguerite, taking the beautifully made doll, and perhaps persuade Jason to go up on the hill with her.

Lottie's parents were frustrated. Their daughter was soon to be married, yet every arrangement they made was either cancelled or changed by Caroline. The hall Dolly Talbot had booked was no use at all, they were informed. Caroline had decided to have the reception at her brother Richard's house where she now lived.

'The grounds are needed for the marquee,' she explained

patiently, as though to children. 'We'd never cater for two hundred guests in a tiny hall. The caterers need a modern, well-equipped kitchen like mine. The house has rooms for coats, there are two bathrooms and an extra toilet, and space for cars to park.' She tapped her hands as she went through the advantages of using her home.

'We were thinking more like forty guests,' Lottie's mother said hesitantly, showing Caroline a handwritten list.

'Forty, that's plenty,' her father agreed. 'We don't want dozens of people we don't know. Do we, Dolly?'

Caroline ignored them. Asking to use their telephone, she rang the caterers to add six more to the list of expected guests. She could easily have done it at home, but these people had to be made to realize that she was in charge. 'These acceptances arrived this morning,' she explained happily.

Neither Dolly nor Henry Talbot were content with the way it was all going, and Jonathan was equally frustrated. He was still thinking of Ancret. Working with Lottie and her plans for their future, then listening to his mother going on about what she had arranged, was slowly driving him crazy. If Lottie so much as mentioned a serviette, he snapped at her. Was this his mother's idea, that they would swiftly end up hating each other and cancel the wedding? In the core of his being he knew he wouldn't be desperately sorry if they did. He wasn't sure that he loved Lottie – at least, not enough.

If he had married Ancret there wouldn't have been any of this fuss. His mother wouldn't have been so involved. Ancret had a gentle way of dealing with things. She'd have quietly got her own way, while his mother would be doing every-thing to break it up. Again, he wondered if that was what she was doing now.

Caroline had never actually stated that she didn't expect him to marry, but when she talked about the future, it was the two of them and no one else that her thoughts encom-passed.

He had to see Ancret. The child had to be discussed, no matter how difficult it would be. He needed to know what she intended to do, whether she would demand his involve-ment and expect financial support. Several times he went as far as the shop, but at the last moment his nerve failed and he drove away again.

One lunchtime he sat in the car, not far from Moments, and allowed misery to fill his head. He felt trapped. In the office there was Lottie, and at the flat there was his mother. Caroline had become a frequent overnight visitor as she dealt with the arrangements for his wedding. By telephone Lottie's irate parents complained about his mother's actions and begged him to intervene. Then there was Ancret, who had despised him so much she had kept from him the fact that she was expecting his child. And whom he still loved. Somehow it must all be resolved.

Leaving the car, he walked purposefully to the shop. He arrived as Angela was leaving for lunch.

'Do you fancy a quick snack?' he asked Ancret abruptly, avoiding her eyes. 'When Angela comes back will do. I don't have an appointment until three.'

Ancret shook her head. 'If you want to talk about Natalie then I'd rather not do it here. If you go to a solicitor and request access I won't protest. She's yours and I understand that you'll want to see her.'

'I don't want to talk about it.'

'It? Don't you mean "she"? You don't want to talk about her? Natalie?'

'Is she, you know, all right?'

'Natalie's fine. I'll be bringing her home in February. You and Lottie can discuss when you want to see her then. Although I'm sure Marguerite and Simon won't object to a visit before that. You know their address, don't you.'

'I don't want to see her.' What does 'fine' mean, he asked himself. You'd say that and be referring to her health. He wanted to ask if there was any handicap but he dare not. 'Second thoughts,' he announced, opening the shop door to leave. 'There's a client I need to see. Some other time, eh?'

'Whenever,' she said, closing the door firmly behind him.

There was no one needing her attention. Annie was finishing the stitching on a hat she had made for a new client and would be free if a customer came into the shop, so she explained her brief absence, went up to the flat and phoned Edmund.

'So you think he came to be told that Natalie is perfect and then went away because he didn't really want to know? Or daren't ask?'

'It appears so. I can't plead for him to see her, accept her. The truth is I don't want to encourage him to be involved. Is that wicked? I think with Lottie as his wife he'll forget about any plans he might make, and Caroline certainly won't want to be known as a grandmother!' She was half joking, but Edmund sensed her near-tearful mood.

'Look, I don't want to interfere in what's a tricky problem, but don't you think you'd be better dealing with one thing at a time? Natalie is safe and happy with the Flowers for the moment, so why don't you go and see the gypsy family who might help you search for your family? When you've succeeded either in contacting them or finding the strength to put it from your mind, then will be the time to deal with Jonathan. He'll be busy for the next couple of months anyway, with his wedding. Then, when he's married to Lottie, everything will change, so put it aside and let time pass.'

It was good advice and she thanked him. 'I'll go on Sunday, and ask Jason to go up on the hill with me.'

'Good, brave girl,' he said, and she smiled.

'I'll let you know if there's anything to report.'

'Please. I'll be waiting.' The words were a comfort. Having upset Marguerite's father and alienated both Jonathan and his mother, she needed a friend.

Jonathan walked past the Millennium Stadium, crossed into Sophia Gardens and strolled aimlessly along the River Taff. It began to rain, cloying drizzle at first, little more than a heavy mist shutting him away from the rest of the world, then pattering through the trees and on to the path. He walked on unaware. Droplets decorated his hair, growing to become rivulets that trickled down his neck and under his collar, and still he ignored the steadily increasing downpour.

It was only when he reached the road near the bowling club, and saw people running for the shelter of the pub on the corner, that he became aware of his discomfort and began to increase his pace. In the toilets he dried his hair and wiped

216

his face and neck before ordering a meal. He felt like running away.

He thought about Babs, his first love, as he waited. Where was she? What had happened to her since they parted? She had married, and had three children. She had moved on, but he had not. He tried to create an image of Lottie's pretty young face in his tortured mind but failed. He saw instead the serious little boy who had attended his uncle's funeral. *Hello, I'm Donald. Who are you?*

The law of averages was way out of sync when it came to me, he thought. How could it have happened twice? Babs and then Ancret leaving him because of a child? He had to find Babs. He was unable to talk to Ancret with the very real Natalie hovering in the shadows, but he could at least find out how well Babs had coped after he had so cruelly made her choose either himself or her child. In his melancholic mood he knew there had been no option for her. Given such a choice, who would choose him?

Ancret arrived at the Flowers's on Sunday afternoon as usual. After spending a hour with Natalie, she put on a nylon mac, lent to her by Marguerite, and went along the lane with Jason and up on to the hill to visit the gypsies.

She had her own and her mother's birth certificates stating her mother's real name of Connie Sullivan, and a rare photograph she had found in her mother's drawer of a little girl being held by a smiling Loraine – or Connie – on a garden swing.

The vardo was wooden, in the style called a barrel top, and had the shafts for a horse, although they were empty, resting on boxes. The brightly painted wheels were held in place by other boxes, and all was newly painted with scrolls and flowers. Jason held her hand as they climbed the steps to the entrance. He knocked, and they heard a gruff invitation to come inside.

The interior was a strong contrast to the muddy field, the over-moist air and the glowering skies outside. Every space had been beautifully decorated with painted designs, mostly of flowers and scrolls. The wooden cupboard doors, the edges of shelves, were all delicately carved, and everything shone with constant polishing. The mirrors and windows were etched in similar designs. The lightness and neatness of it all surprised Ancret.

There were just two people there: Frederick Sullivan, who she guessed was in his eighties, and his tiny wife, Daisie. Jason introduced Ancret simply as the mother of little Natalie. It was when Ancret gave her name and that of her mother that she knew she was about to have at least some of her questions answered.

'Ancret, you say? Unusual name, that. Eh, Daisie?'

'My mother was called Sullivan and I wondered if you could help me find some of her relations.' Ancret opened her shoulder bag and handed the certificates to Frederick.

'You're Connie's daughter? But I don't understand.' He turned to his wife, and they excused themselves and stepped outside. Ancret was excited as she heard them speaking quietly and, it seemed, in a language of their own.

'They're talking in their own tongue,' Jason whispered. 'I recognized the word *chavvy* meaning child, and *chored*, which I think means stolen.'

'A stolen child? I'm hardly that!' Ancret frowned. 'Will they be able to help me?'

The couple came back inside. Daisie put a kettle on the shining black stove and began to set out cups and saucers. 'You talk to her, Father,' she said.

'Mother's right. It's my place to set you right, if I can.'

Anxious now, Ancret reached for Jason's hand.

'My daughter was called Connie Sullivan.'

With shaking hands, Ancret took out the photograph of the country gentleman, which she'd had professionally enlarged and improved. She held her breath as the old man stared at it, holding it close to his face as though his sight was poor. Then he offered it to Daisie, who looked at him and nodded. 'That's her husband.'

Ancret was shaking. Were they telling her that she was half gypsy? At once the memory of her mother's treasured willow basket came to mind, and the gypsy doll she had made with such accuracy. She wasn't sure how she felt. Excitement and sheer panic were alternately making her heart race. Frederick tapped the photograph with a gnarled finger.

'Connie went with this gorgio, had two childer.' Jason interrupted briefly to tell her that *gorgios* were non-gypsies. 'She was a wilful young woman and when the girls were small she left her man for another, him belonging to one of the families staying here working on the scrubbies.'

'Potatoes.' Jason whispered in explanation.

'They were Sullivans too. Some cousins, I seem to recall. We used to come here regular then, and work for the farmer. Besides the seasonal work on the crops, there was casual work, depending on what was needed. Connie came, leaving her family to work alongside us day after day, with that man of hers complaining and getting nowhere. Then there was some talk of a child, then rumours of her man throwing her out and the child being stolen.'

Daisie handed them their tea and offered a plate of thinly cut bread and butter. 'We heard nothing more, not then or since,' she said. 'She never come back, nor sent word, not once.'

'So, if your Connie was my mother, I'm half gypsy?' She turned to Jason. 'It would explain so much, if it's true. But who was my father?' Both Frederick and Daisie looked away and Ancret had the feeling that she had learned all they intended to tell her.

'Please, may I come again?' she asked, after they had drunk their tea in silence.

'Daughter, you may come and be sure of a welcome,' Daisie said, and Frederick nodded agreement. 'For two nights more you'll find us here, then we go back to the house.'

Ancret looked at Daisie for explanation, but it was Jason who said, 'A pair of sentimental old lovelies, these two. Although they all live in houses now and have done for years, they keep the vardo here and come for a couple of weeks every now and then, to relive old memories.'

'And good memories they are,' Frederick said. 'Listen up tonight and you'll hear a most beautiful sound. Some of the other families will be coming and we'll celebrate all the old times in song.'

'So I'm half gypsy,' Ancret said as they walked back through the gradually easing rain back to the house.

'How d'you feel about it?'

'Excited, I think. Regret too, that I've lived twenty-five years without learning all they have to teach. But it isn't finished yet, is it? I still have to find out who my father is.'

'And it's my sister-in-law's father who has the answer to that question. But will he tell? I doubt it, but we can hope.'

Ancret stayed with Marguerite that night. When she went to bed, she opened her window and faintly, on the breeze, she could hear singing. A fire glowed up on the hill and she imagined the gathering of gypsy families, she listened to the soulful songs, the lament of a violin and accordion. Some were clearly dance melodies, but most seemed to be sad or sentimental, reminiscent of cowboy songs she seemed to half remember.

Unable to resist, she left the house and went back to the hill alone. There were others there, people she hadn't seen before, some cleaning and polishing instruments. A couple of rangy dogs approached when she came in sight of the encampment. A man in his sixties called and walked over to her. 'I'm George. Are you our Ancret, come back to us after all these years?'

'I'm Ancret. But as for the rest, well, I'm hoping to find out.'

'I doubt my father'll tell owt. Old Frederick be proud. He can't talk easy about his failures.'

'Is that what I am, a failure?' She smiled, but her heart was heavy. Whether she belonged with them or not, she wasn't going to be made more welcome than any other stranger who visited them.

'He didn't want Connie to leave us and go to that man, and when she came back to us it wasn't for long. Off she went again and we've heard nothing since. Look, meet me in the pub tomorrow night and I'll show you the man who's your father.'

Old Frederick came and offered his hand, and George walked away to stand by the fire, looking back at her curiously. Frederick led her back to where several families were sitting around the vardo. A fire was burning and from it came tempting smells. 'A stew to feed us all,' Daisie said, waving a huge wooden ladle. 'Will you stay and eat with us?'

'Thank you, I'd love that.'

Beside being introduced to a dozen or more members of

220

the extended family, there was so much talk about others, past and present, that her head reeled. They told tales, they sang songs and recited poetry. Daisie smoked a pipe which she filled with some herbs mixed with tobacco. The men drank beer and the women drank tea without milk. 'Milk was a luxury in past days,' one explained. 'Unless we could take some from the cows in the fields,' said another. This brought laughter, and Ancret joined in. Knowing she might once have been a part of this strange life made her want to remember every single word that was spoken.

She went back through the dark fields, to Marguerite and Simon and her daughter, singing one of the songs they had taught her. George, the man she was to meet the following evening, had sung it, accompanied expertly by old Frederick on the fiddle. She desperately wanted to commit the song to memory so she might one day teach it to Natalie.

Marguerite invited her to stay a second night instead of going home late. After telephoning to make sure Annie and Angela would cope, she agreed. She was too close to finding her family to risk leaving.

Jason and Simon went with her to the pub when the time came to meet George. The four of them sat at a corner table and George talked about many things, but he seemed unwilling to bring up the subject of her father. He watched the door constantly, and soon Ancret was doing the same, convinced that through it her father would appear. As time passed, she began to feel the familiar sickness she always suffered when she was excited or worried.

They had been there an hour. The door had opened many times, but each time George would return to his stories after a brief upward glance. Then, to Ancret's dismay, Marguerite's father came in. She held her breath, expecting him to walk over and talk to Jason and Simon, make it clear that she was unwelcome. But it was then that George nudged her. 'That's him. That's your father. May weasels cross his path,' he cursed in a low whisper.

She felt rather than saw the shock that shot through Jason and Simon. 'Marguerite's father is— That can't be so,' Jason gasped. 'There were only two girls. My wife Sophie, and Marguerite.'

'Truth won't change to suit what you're wanting,' George said. 'Now I have to be off. Most of us are gone already. Sorry if you're upset, but it's always better to know what you have to deal with. When you're given only half the facts, imagination can be a curse.'

Ancret watched the man turn to go as his announcement sank in. Then she jumped from her seat and went across to speak to Mr Howells. 'Is it true? Are you my father?'

'Go away! I've never wanted to see you or your mother from the day she walked out. You learning the truth doesn't change that.' He banged his pint glass down on the bar and almost ran out.

'But you paid for me, for eighteen years you paid for my keep. You must have felt something?'

'I felt cheated by a woman who I thought loved me.' His long legs took him away from her in angry strides and she made no further attempt to keep up. She rubbed nervously on the scar on her hand and went back to the bar. Simon and Jason were waiting outside. They both looked shocked, drained of colour in the light over the doorway. They each took an arm and guided her back inside.

'Now what?' Jason asked.

'We tell Marguerite and ask her advice.'

It was only then, as she began to circle around the revelation, that Ancret realized Marguerite might be her sister. Whatever might happen with Mr Howells, the struggle to find a family had not been in vain. But she cried anyway.

Jason and Simon walked Ancret back to the house. After whispered explanations to Marguerite, she was settled in the spare room and allowed to sleep.

'Tomorrow we talk,' Marguerite said, although her head was bursting with questions. 'A good rest and time for us both to think about the consequences, and tomorrow we'll . . . celebrate?' She asked the question hesitantly.

'Thank you,' Ancret said. 'I'm thrilled, but I wasn't sure how you would feel about suddenly having me as a sister.'

'I'm thrilled too, but rest now and we'll start being sisters tomorrow.'

\* \* \*

222

It was when Jonathan remembered the little cards which the mourners had been asked to fill in at his uncle's funeral that the breakthrough came in his search for Babs. His mother had kept them in a box with all the cards and letters of sympathy. At least he would have her married name. To his surprise, though, she had signed in her maiden name, adding the names Donald, Harry and Tracy. He tried the phone book and found her. It was as simple as that.

He didn't want to go to the house. It might be a very short-lived meeting. Perhaps she would close the door and that would be that. Instead he made a guess at which nursery school Harry would attend and waited there as the mothers gathered to collect their children. She didn't appear, and he spent the next two days trying other places before returning to the first, wondering if she had just been absent on that particular day.

He still didn't see Babs, but he recognized Donald holding the hand of Babs's mother.

'Coral? How are you? I was hoping to see Babs. How is she?' He was so nervous that a twitch developed in his cheek.

Babs's mother looked shocked. Then she recovered and said angrily, 'Babs is fine. And it's none of your business anyway. You did enough damage, keep away.'

'I just wanted to talk to her. I don't wish her any harm.' He forced himself to look at the blue-eyed Donald who was staring at him in his serious way. He touched the little boy's head and said, 'Hello, Donald. Remember me? I'm Jonathan.'

'Jonathan,' Donald repeated solemnly, offering his hand for him to shake.

Jonathan did so. 'Are you waiting for your brother?'

'I've got a brother and a sister,' Donald said proudly, tapping his own chest.

'Lucky you.'

'Lucky,' Donald said, with repeated nods.

'Please go,' Coral said as the entrance doors were opened, a member of staff standing there to make sure the children didn't leave without a parent or guardian. She led Donald away and headed towards the doors, Donald turning back to wave.

On the following morning Jonathan sat in his car until

223

mothers and children began to arrive. Then, getting out of the car, he stood and waited. Babs arrived with the baby in a buggy, Donald on one side and the three-year-old on the other. She saw him and stopped.

'Mum told me you were here yesterday,' she said. 'What d'you want?'

A man ran up before he could answer and hugged Donald and the little girl, before saying something about meeting them that afternoon. He took the hand of the little boy he called Harry, and went into the school.

'Your husband?' he asked.

'It's no business of yours, Jonathan. Now, what d'you want? I'm in a hurry to get to work.'

'Can you meet me at lunchtime? Somewhere we can talk.'

'I have nothing to say to you.' She frowned. 'What can there be to talk about after all this time?'

'Donald?'

'Donald is adopted, like the others.'

'How old is he?'

'He's six. Why are you so interested?'

'He's the right age to be mine, born after you left me. You didn't have an abortion, did you?'

'You are pathetic!' A bus was approaching. She ran from him and struggled on to it with the buggy, not looking back.

He couldn't let it go. Once he had the idea that Donald might be his, that Babs had lied and not attended the clinic, it became more and more real. Staying out of the office with Lottie and her excited chatter was no difficulty, more a relief. The following morning and evening he was at the school waiting for Babs and her children to appear. Each time she refused to speak to him and hurried her little family away.

After the second day, she sought the help of the school and arranged to avoid him. He waited until the school emptied and was locked up, but she didn't appear. It was only on the third day, when he'd had to park the car in a different street, that he realized she had left by a different entrance, going through the main building and walking a different way home.

He caught up with them after school one day in the park. Donald was kicking a ball ineffectively across the damp grass and he went forward and began pushing it towards him. During the fifteen minutes he played with the boy, helping him to achieve his aim of getting the ball through the improvised goalposts, he became aware that Donald was a child with a personality much like other children. Loving, curious, slow to learn some things.

Pretending to be out of breath, he sat beside Babs on the wooden seat and handed the ball back to Donald.

'He's a happy little boy,' he said.

'Most of the time,' Babs said, smiling as she watched Donald struggle to kick the muddy ball out of a depression in the grass. 'He can be very stubborn sometimes.'

'Does he have serious health problems?'

'Chest infections mostly, but they're dealt with more easily than in the past.'

'And is he mine?' He asked the question conversationally, as he had the earlier ones. They might have been two strangers meeting for the first time.

'Time to go, Donald. Beefburgers for tea if you come without arguing.'

Her three-year-old was playing on a slide and Babs went to fetch him. Jonathan walked over to Donald and went to pick up the ball.

'I carry this,' Donald said firmly.

'Of course.'

'Mustn't drop it near the road.'

'Good boy.'

Babs gathered the children and walked from the park. Although he pleaded, she refused to meet him again. He walked angrily back to his car. What did she want? He had tried to show an interest in Donald, had even enjoyed playing with him for a while, although he didn't think he could take Babs and her family on permanently. And he knew that neither Lottie nor his mother would want to be involved. So what was he doing trying to see her, talk to her? What did he hope to achieve?

Had she left him because she knew how feeble he was? How slavishly he followed his mother's lead? He had to know what she thought of him, why her love for him had faded. It was not knowing. That was what was killing him.

# Thirteen

Ancret didn't sleep that night. She lay awake, listening to the sounds in the house, aware of her daughter sleeping in the next room. Her thoughts were a kaleidoscope of excitements and anxieties regarding her father's attitude towards her – and that of her sisters, one of whom she was yet to meet.

She was fairly confident of Marguerite's continuing friendship. Although, once she had discussed Ancret and her mother with her father, that might change. Of Sophie she knew little, apart from the fact she had married Jason then divorced him when his business failed. So she was a sister to Jason's exwife. How strange that, when she was looking only for foster care, fate had brought her to this family.

Then she frowned as a memory returned. She remembered that it had been her mother who had found the paper in which the Flowers's details appeared. And Loraine – as she still thought of her – had never come with her to the Flowers's home. There had always been some reason for her cancelling any planned visit. Had this reunion been her mother's plan? Her way of telling Ancret about her childhood? She still wondered why her mother had been unable to talk to her about it. There must have been some shame in leaving her husband and her two daughters . . . But why couldn't she talk to me, she wondered sorrowfully. There must have been a reason. Her mother had always been loving and supportive; they had talked openly about everything. So why couldn't she explain what had happened to make her do such a thing, persuade her daughter to understand?

Light was growing around the curtains. She slipped out of bed and peered into the early dawn, to the garden hidden by shadows and up on to the hazy hill. What would today

226

hold? Would she be reunited with a loving father, once the shock had worn off? He had shown so little regard the day before, so could she expect continued anger, instead of the affection she craved from him? To have found him after twenty-five years and be turned away would be heartbreaking.

She heard someone moving about. Reaching for the borrowed dressing gown, she looked in on her sleeping child, then went downstairs. Marguerite was in the kitchen filling the kettle and she nodded to a chair, gesturing for Ancret to sit.

'I was hoping you'd be awake before the others so we can talk privately,' Marguerite whispered, closing the kitchen door. 'There's so much to say, to ask, and now you're here I don't know where to begin.'

'Did you know anything about me?' Ancret asked. 'Your father could hardly pretend I didn't exist.'

'Oh yes, he could. Sophie and I were told that we'd had a baby sister but she had been taken from us, and that was why Mummy had left us, she was so distressed. When we assumed he meant you'd died, he didn't put us right. So for all these years that's what we thought.'

'That your mother was dead? That I was dead? How could a father hate a child so much?'

'He's a very angry man. Not only about your mother leaving him, but that seemed to colour everything else in his life. Perhaps I mean bitter rather than angry,' she added with a frown. 'Bitter because of your mother's treatment of him, maybe, although you'd imagine that would have eased in all the years that have passed since.'

'D'you think he'll accept me?'

Pouring the tea into mugs and pushing one towards Ancret, Marguerite hesitated before replying, then shook her head. 'He's very stubborn. His own worst enemy, some would say. He'd lose out rather than be seen to change his mind once he'd spoken his opinion.'

'And you and Simon? Will you avoid me now you know who I am?'

'Ancret! Of course I can't let you go, and neither will Simon or Jason! I'm thrilled to have found a sister at my age. And discovering that darling Natalie is my niece. It's wonderful! Sophie will think so too when she's told.'

'Thank you.' Ancret was tearful. 'When will you tell Sophie she has a sister?'

'I thought I'd wait until we've all spoken to Dad, then telephone her. If I know my sister – my other sister,' she added with a smile, 'she'll be over here in less than an hour.'

'Thank you,' Ancret said again.

Simon, the next to rise, came into the kitchen carelessly dressed in jeans and T-shirt, carrying Natalie. Ancret hesitated to take her from him. At present, Marguerite would be the person she wanted. But to her delight, the little girl looked towards her and held out both her arms for her, and she took her daughter joyfully.

'See, she already knows you and loves you best,' Simon said. 'Clever little girl. Have you two been trying to catch up on twenty-five years?' he asked. 'There'll be a few sore throats in this family of ours in the next few days!'

This family of ours, Ancret thought, emotion filling her eyes once more with tears. That includes Natalie and me.

'I can't stay longer than today,' she said when she felt calm enough to speak. 'I'm needed at the shop. But if you agree, I'll come back next Sunday.'

'The room is yours whenever you need it,' Marguerite said, hugging her.

'Is there a chance that your father will talk to me before I leave?'

Simon nodded. 'I've already telephoned Jason and he's going to bring him here at ten o'clock, even if he has to drag him.'

There was a knock on the door at five minutes to ten. Ancret's heart began to beat rapidly, and she looked towards the door expecting to see the man whom she now believed was her father. Nervously she stroked the scar on her little finger and took a few deep breaths. Beside her, Marguerite touched her shoulder and smiled encouragingly.

But it wasn't Mr Howells. It was Bernard, one of the men from the hill who had taught her their songs. He was dressed in a suit; less than a perfect fit, and not exactly well pressed, it nevertheless probably represented his best clothes for a special occasion, with an open-necked shirt under the suit

228

and a loosely fastened tie. Around his neck, tucked under long, black hair, he wore a red paisley scarf. With his dark skin and amazingly clear blue eyes, there was no doubt about his ancestry, and this was clearly how he wanted it. Pride in being of gypsy stock, rather than the pretence that he was not.

'I'm Bernard Sullivan,' he said to the room at large. 'Remember me?'

'Of course.' Ancret introduced him, although Simon and Marguerite knew him well.

'We've known each other most of our lives, haven't we, Bernie?' Marguerite said. 'Although Father discouraged us from remaining friends after Mummy left.'

'We had a long talk,' Bernard told Ancret, 'and we want you to have an address or two where we can be reached, so as you can ask questions and get honest answers about your mother and all the rest of us.' He gave her a piece of paper bearing several names and addresses. 'There's also this.' He handed her a crumpled and much handled and folded envelope.

'What is it?'

'A letter. We've kept it for years in the hope of one day being able to give it to you.'

'But who is it from?'

'Wait till you're alone, then open it and find out.'

She took the letter from him. He took hold of her hand and smiled, touching the scar with his forefinger. There was a quizzical expression on his face as he stared at her and whispered, 'God bless you, our little Ancret.'

She stared at the grubby envelope and put it into the pocket of her long skirt. Now wasn't the time to open it, whatever it contained. Anyway, there was no time for more questions. A peremptory knocking was followed by Mr Howells's voice demanding that Simon should 'Move and let me pass, I haven't got all day,' and the man whom she believed to be her father strode into the room.

His reaction when he saw Bernard was typical, Ancret was beginning to realize.

'What's he doing here? Get him out! Out of my sight!'

Bernard smiled. Lifting Ancret's hand again, he pointed to

229

the scar, then looked at the angry man. 'A very good day to you, Mister. God bless, Ancret. Thank you all.' With surprising dignity, considering the way he'd been spoken to, he left.

To her alarm, Mr Howells strode up to her and grabbed her left hand. He stared at the scar and threw the hand away from him in disgust.

'You aren't my daughter,' he shouted. 'You've got the mark of your father, one of the gypsy people.'

'What d'you mean?' Ancret was shivering with fear. Reaching behind her, she grabbed the table for support. She had never seen such anger directed at herself before. 'This mark is nothing. It's where a slight deformity was removed when I was a baby. What has it got to do with you being my father?'

'None of my family has such a mark, but some of the gypsies do. Including Jack Sullivan. He had a small finger removed. It's him you've inherited that from, not me. Gypsy through and through you are, and I paid for eighteen years, and more besides, Connie wheedling money out of me for you to buy your shop. Always believing what Connie told me, that you were mine.'

Ancret listened to the outburst, waited until her heart had slowed from its racing fear. Then, speaking calmly, she said, 'So although you believed I was your child, you sent my mother away? Forced her to leave you and her daughters? I can't feel sorry that I'm no child of yours.'

Mr Howells sat down heavily, his head in his hands. Ancret and the others waited in silence for him to speak. Marguerite set breakfast in front of Natalie and began feeding her. Eventually Mr Howells lifted his head.

'I didn't send her away,' he said gruffly. 'She left me repeatedly and took the girls to spend time with her family throughout the summer, each time staying longer than before. Up in the fields they'd be, helping to lift potatoes, and gathering wood, and gleaning in the fields after the corn was cut. Selling holly and firewood around the roads. She and the girls took a tent and lived up there for days at a time. She seemed unable to settle while they were near. After they moved on she came back to us. Then she told me she wanted to take my girls away from me permanently.

'When she told me she was expecting another child, Marguerite was fifteen, Sophie eleven. It was a shock, but I was pleased. This would persuade her to stay. But it didn't. Heavily pregnant and still going up to stay in one of the caravans.'

Ancret was afraid to interrupt with a question. She didn't want to distract him from his story, as it might be the only time he would talk about her mother. Learning about her family's history at long last kept her enthralled. Nothing else was important. The fact that she was no relation to this man, that she was a full gypsy and illegitimate with it, had yet to penetrate. There was another silence and she held her breath. She was aware of Marguerite beside her, equally tense, her irregular gasps making her distress clear.

'Why did she leave, Dad?' Marguerite asked eventually. Her father turned his head to look at her as though suddenly aware of her presence. But he didn't answer her question, saying instead, 'She wanted to take you and Sophie. And I couldn't let her do that.'

Another silence.

'So you told her to go?'

'The child was born and she refused to come back. She wanted to go away.' He looked at Ancret, his eyes filled with sorrow. 'I locked the door and wouldn't let her in. I thought she'd come to her senses and settle down, but after shouting and begging me to let the girls go with her, she went away and I never saw her again.'

Ancret saw the scene clearly. Her mother nursing herself as a baby, crying and begging for her other daughters. It was a devastating situation relived so many times in Loraine's – Connie's – dreams.

'Was it at night?' she asked.

'She sat on the doorstep all day and half the night, nursing you and calling for me to let the girls go with her. It was three o'clock when I called a taxi and watched it take her away.'

Ancret felt a shock like the stabbing of a knife when he mentioned the time. Three in the morning – the time Loraine had suffered her terrible nightmares. She stood up, wanting to go to the man and offer sympathy. Whatever he had done, it sounded as though her mother was a victim by her own hand. She took out the photograph of the man in country clothes. 'Is this you?' she asked. 'Mummy kept it near her always.' As he took it, did she imagine a softening of his expression? A hint of comforting pleasure in his cold, hard eyes?

She still didn't understand what had made her mother leave. If she wasn't going back to her family, why couldn't she stay with her daughters? There was still the mystery of why she had left them.

She began preparing a question, but there were to be no further revelations. Mr Howells stood, and after looking at her with an expression she was unable to fathom, he left. Ancret stood and stared at the door, rubbing the scar on her finger, hating it for the disappointment she had suffered. She had no resentment about being told she was a full gypsy, but that scar, that evidence of her true parentage, had lost her a father, two sisters and two nephews.

'Don't worry,' Jason said, as if he read her thoughts. 'You're still a half-sister to Marguerite and Sophie.'

'If they still want me,' she replied sorrowfully.


Although unable to understand why, Ancret went to see Jonathan. He would be the first person she would tell. Lottie was in the office, and she shook her head when Ancret asked to speak to him.

'Sorry, but my fiancé is too busy at present. He's with an important client and can't be disturbed.'

'Tell him I'm here,' Ancret demanded. She knew that if she didn't tell someone she would burst into tears.

'I'm sorry, but—'

'What is it, Lottie?' Lucinda asked, coming out of the back room.

'I'm explaining to Ancret that Jonathan is unable to spare time to see her.'

'Come through,' Lucinda said, ignoring the angry outburst from Lottie that continued as they closed the inner office door.

'Ancret? What is it? You look awful,' Jonathan said, offering her a chair. 'Will you bring some coffee, please, Lucinda?'

Ancret waited until the coffee had been placed before them. Then, as the door closed behind Lucinda, she told him quietly what she had learned.

'What? You're a gypsy?' He jerked away from her as though she was tainted.

'I knew my mother wasn't what she appeared. I found out her family were gypsies. Yesterday I learned that my father was also a gypsy.'

Jonathan stood up and stared at her as though she had been suddenly transformed into an alien. 'I don't understand. How can you be? You're educated, and—'

He couldn't go on. When she looked at him, saw the horror in his eyes which were widened by shock and abhorrence, she gasped as though in pain, and ran from the office.

Lottie, standing very close to the door, slid back against the wall. She waited a moment, then went in to ask Jonathan what she had wanted.

'Nothing,' he snapped. 'Now go and take your lunch break. I have an appointment to keep.'

She was about to protest, ask why they weren't lunching together as they'd planned, but his expression took the words from her. She went silently out and closed the door. She drove to his flat and telephoned his mother. This was something she couldn't possibly keep to herself.

Jonathan went to find Ancret. He couldn't leave it like this.

Caroline listened in silence as Lottie told her everything she had learned.

'What good fortune that you came along and Jonathan left her.'

'I'm surprised she had the honesty to tell him. Imagine being told such a secret. If she expected sympathy she was sorely disappointed. Jonathan's face was a mask of horror,' Lottie went on, exaggerating as though she had actually been there.

'I never wanted him to marry her, there was something about the girl I couldn't fathom. You're different. You, Jonathan and I will get along just fine, dear, won't we? You'll be a far more suitable daughter-in-law. Living together in

Uncle Richard's house, you'll have the garden to plan just the way you want it. We can have wonderful holidays together, just like Jonathan and I have always done. It will be perfect.'

Warning bells began to ring loudly and Lottie pulled the phone away from her ear while Caroline prattled on. This was not what she had in mind for the future.

Distressed and confused by all she had learned, it wasn't until later in the day that Ancret remembered the scruffy envelope she had been given by Bernard. She took it out of her pocket and placed it on the table beside her, curious yet afraid to open it. She'd had sufficient shocks for the moment and couldn't face any more. If only there was someone to share them, help her through . . . But Jonathan's reaction made it clear he was not the one. And Jason . . . she didn't feel able to talk to him. The revelations about her mother were too raw. Putting aside the hat she was working on, she telephoned Edmund.

'I'll be there in twenty minutes,' he said. 'Just as soon as I finish serving coffee to seventeen retired teachers.'

He was there in fifteen. 'What is it?' he asked as he came through the shop door, nodding a greeting to Annie and Angela. 'I could tell from your voice that you're upset about something.'

'Coffee?' she offered, but he shook his head.

'Tell me.'

'I'm a gypsy,' she replied. 'And as I wasn't given my father's name I suppose I'm illegitimate too.'

'Yes? And?'

'Isn't that enough?'

'You're you. Ancret. Talented and so very, very beautiful. What does it matter where you come from? It's where you're going that should concern you, you silly, darling girl.'

'Why didn't Mummy tell me? It wouldn't have been so distressing if I'd learned it gradually, from her.'

'Start at the beginning.'

'My mother was married to John Howells. She had two daughters and much later, when Marguerite and Sophie were eleven and fifteen, I was born. She wanted to leave and take the three of us away from him, but I don't know why. Neither do I know why my mother changed her name and why I wasn't given the name of Howells.'

She went on with the story. Edmund listened intently, only speaking when he needed to clarify something.

'So I found my family and lost them again,' she said finally.

'Why lose them? They'd be crazy to let you go. I can't. Losing you is something I hope I never have to face. Please, tell me I'll never have to say goodbye, I couldn't bear it, my beautiful, adorable girl.'

She stared at him as though seeing him for the first time. 'Please mean that,' she said, and he wrapped his arms around her and kissed her slowly, gently, before releasing her a little and saying, 'I've never meant anything more in all my life. I'm only half alive when you're out of my sight. I've been waiting for you to get Jonathan out of your heart. I think perhaps he's still there, but hopefully no more than a shadow of what once might have been. I wanted to make sure there was room for me and my love. I have so much love to give you.'

'I haven't thought about you in that way,' she said, aware of a lightening of her spirits. 'There's been too much going on in my life.' She stared at him, seeing the open, honest face, the undisguised love in his eyes, and felt a lightening of her misery, a sense of peace after a long struggle. This was where she belonged.

Yet something made her hesitate. Her life was in turmoil. How could she make a decision about something as important as this? She didn't want to give him false hope then let him down. She was tearful as she said, 'Edmund, I don't know how I feel at present.'

'Patience I possess, in bucketfuls.'


Jonathan went into the shop below and, in a similar scene to the one Ancret had played out in his office, ignored Angela's refusal and insisted on seeing Ancret. She came down the stairs and into the salon with Edmund close behind her.

'Get rid of him. I have to talk to you.'

'Will you excuse me, Edmund? I'll phone you in a while.'

'No need. I'll wait outside in the car. I'll be back when Jonathan leaves.'

'Thank you.'

Jonathan pushed her roughly into the workroom and began telling her what he had come to say.

'I loved you, Ancret. It could have been so good between us, but the lies and deceit, from both your mother and you, ruined everything. I can never forgive you for Natalie. Your mother taught you well,' he ended bitterly.

'I know I was wrong. To keep the existence of your child from you was a terrible thing to do. But you were the reason for that dishonesty. When I tried – not very hard, I admit – to tell you I was pregnant, you made it absolutely clear that you didn't want a child, ever. Even if I'd persisted and told you the truth, admitted that I was expecting your child, persuaded you it was wrong to destroy a child on your mother's whim, her vanity, I couldn't have allowed the baby to decide our future. We didn't love each other enough.'

'I loved *you* enough. But now, what I thought I knew, what I see, is all lies.'

Ancret stood up and held her arms wide. 'This is who I am. You either love someone for what they are, or any declaration of love is a pretence. You were in love with a fantasy and what's fantasy if it isn't lies? You were deluding yourself, pretending to be in love with me as a way of escaping from your mother. Self-delusion is the worst, the most dangerous form of deceit.' She paused and stared at him until he looked away from her. 'I wonder whether you've ever truly loved anyone in your whole life. Babs loved you, but she left. And that was over your rejection of a child too, wasn't it?'

'Mother said it was risky to have a child, and—'

'Marry Lottie. She could be your last chance. The alternative is living the rest of your life as your mother's lapdog.' Mimicking his mother's voice, she went on, 'Come here, Jonathan. Go there, Jonathan. Sit. Do what I say and don't you dare think for yourself.' Then, aware of how cruel she was being, she burst into tears and ran up the stairs to her bedroom.

Jonathan stood for a long time before he turned and left the building.

Lottie knew that this was an important moment and had to be handled with great care. Besides coping with the revelations over Ancret, she had to state her conditions for their future now or never. She was determined to marry Jonathan, but the news about Ancret had upset him and it might not be she whom he would turn to. She went back to the office, told Lucinda she had a headache and went home.

Wandering aimlessly, Jonathan went back to the office. On being told of Lottie's absence, he went to find her. He parked the car near her parents' house but didn't get out. Instead he sat there trying to imagine marrying Lottie while he was still half in love with Ancret. A bruised love, but love just the same.

Inside the house, Lottie was noting the wedding presents which had already arrived, making sure the names and addresses of senders were filed ready for the thankyou letters she would have to write. But her mind was not on the task; she kept putting the list down and staring into space, unaware that Jonathan was doing the same only a short distance away.

Jonathan must be dissuaded from living with his mother. If they were to stand any chance of a successful marriage, she had to be allowed to make her own decisions, not follow Caroline's strong, albeit polite, demands. Caroline, so sweet but with the determination of a warrior.

Ancret found it impossible to work. Her head ached with such agonizing thoughts that when Edmund returned after having seen Jonathan leave, she phoned Helena and asked her to come in, then made her excuses to Angela and Annie and went up to the sitting room. It was then that she showed Edmund the crumpled letter.

'Open it,' he said. 'The sooner you learn all the facts the sooner you'll deal with them.'

She took her time breaking the seal on the envelope, not from patience but out of reluctance to see the contents. There were two sheets of writing paper and as she began to read, she gave a gasp, 'Edmund, please sit here and read it with me.'

'No, darling, read it aloud.'
'It's titled "Ancret, your story".'

Your mother, Connie Sullivan, was one of ten children, and she was born in a bender tent at the side of the road in 1934. The family suffered frequent hunger, fathers and the older ones hunting the fields and hedgerows for food and begging the use of a tap for water and a bottle for the babies. People were kinder then, but many times we were refused. Water was always scarce and sometimes had to be carried a long way. We washed in streams and lakes whenever we could, but often we'd do no more than wipe our faces with a cloth dipped in water, and a good wash was a luxury, especially in winter, when the streams were too cold for us to bathe.

Her brothers and sisters were sent away to work as soon as they were old enough, but one sister, closest in age to Connie, died of TB as did two brothers. Another brother was killed on the road late at night by a driver too drunk to stand. His victim being a gypsy, nothing was done about him. Connie was sent to live with a family for her own safety as her mother couldn't cope with them all.

There wasn't such a difference between the little we had, and the possessions of house people then, when your mother was small. No machines like now, to do the hard work for them. Floors and doorsteps were scrubbed. Down on their knees they'd be, sweating, hands red and cut from some of the work they did, just like ours. Carrying water was the lot of many, an outside tap was often all a house-dweller had. So we helped one another more, both being similarly placed. There were many houses where we'd call and be sure of a welcome and some good hot food. Farmers saved seasonal work for us and paid us with food and shelter as well as money.

But lest you think our lives were all sadness, I must tell you of the gatherings we had, where families would come together to celebrate something or other, we never needed much of an excuse. We'd sing and dance and eat

238

our fill. We all had something to offer, sword dancing was Connie's grandfather's pleasure, and he were a fine yodeller. Others played fiddle or mouth organ or tin whistle, and we'd sing cowboy songs and others that had been handed down since further back than memories go. Your mother's wedding was such a celebration. It went on for three days and two nights and was attended by near two hundred kindred folk. A real Gypsy wedding it was, even though her man was a gorgio.

'It's signed. Sidney, brother of Jack,' Ancret said as she put the letter down.

'There's something written on the back.' Edmund turned it over and read, 'Be proud of your mother as she's ever proud of you.'

'If Jack was my father, Old Frederick is my grandfather, and Daisie my grandmother.'

'How do you feel about that?' he asked quietly.

'Disappointed.'

He tilted his head and frowned questioningly.

'Disappointed for all the years I should have known them and learned what they have to teach.'

Edmund held her then, saying nothing, allowing her thoughts to take in the new discoveries.

Jonathan stepped out of the car and went to Lottie's front door. Before he could knock, she opened it and reached up to hug him.

'Jonathan, darling. What's wrong? You look upset.'

'Ancret, in a word,' he said, as they went into the living room.

'As ever! What has she done now?' she asked innocently.

He blurted out the story about Ancret's gypsy origins in a flood of words, as if they'd been held in check with great difficulty. She listened patiently, then told him he'd had a lucky escape.

'Mother mustn't be told,' he said, as the angry words slowed.

She hesitated too long then, so she couldn't tell him Caroline already knew.

'Look, I can understand your being upset, darling, but

239

really, it has nothing to do with you now. You're marrying me and Ancret is history.'

'But how can I deal with Natalie? She's mine and I have to acknowledge her.'

'Are you sure she's yours?'

'Of course she's mine.'

'In that case, why weren't you told? Doesn't it make better sense that she'd had an affair, found someone else? Why would Ancret plan to conceal her from you, deprive you of her, not for a while, but for always? She had no intention of telling you, had she? The plan was for her to pretend the child was adopted. It seems to me that she kept it from you because the child wasn't yours.'

'She wouldn't do that.'

'It's a better explanation than insisting you'd have wanted an abortion.'

'But I would. I can't have a child. Any child of mine would be handicapped.'

'What d'you mean?'

'My mother had a child after I was born and he was – I don't know – he had serious problems. He died soon after birth. Mother had a brother who was also born with some disability, suffered some problems she won't talk about. He was a sickly child, and he died too. When Babs lost a baby the doctors said it was "nature's way". That means there was something wrong, doesn't it?'

'And Natalie?'

'I was afraid to look at her.'

'Have you spoken to any doctors? This might not be true.' She wondered whether it was one of Caroline's tricks to make sure her son stayed single, so he'd be with her through her old age, when she'd need him.

'Of course it's true. Why would Mother warn me if she didn't know for certain?'

Afraid to say more, Lottie put her arms around him and pressed her cheek against his. 'She wants the best for you, darling, as every mother should. I'm so glad she's a friend of mine. I couldn't have a better mother-in-law, could I? I'm so lucky, engaged to marry the man I adore and with a perfect mother-in-law.'

'I'm glad you feel that way.'

She removed his jacket and led him up the stairs.

A while later, when they were both in the shower, she said, 'Jonathan, when we're married, I hope you don't expect us to live with your mother. I'd prefer to stay in the flat. I'm not a country girl, even though I loved helping Uncle Richard in his garden. No, it's the city for me. The flat is big enough for the two of us, although there wouldn't be room for your mother to stay. But she loves her home and we'll be going to see her rather than the other way round, won't we? Sunday lunches, evenings out.'

'You won't mind? Not having children, I mean?'

'I'm young. I don't want to be tied down for a long time yet.'

'I don't want a child. Not ever.'

'What about Natalie? She must be perfect or you'd have been told.'

'But if she isn't mine—'

'Of course Natalie's yours, Jonathan. Whatever Ancret is, she isn't the kind of woman to cheat. Not on someone as desirable as you. Natalie's perfect and she's yours.'

When he woke the next morning, Jonathan made an appointment to see the doctor. Lottie had raised doubts in his mind. What if his mother had got it wrong and there was no certainty about his having problem children? Natalie must be all right or he would have been told. Ancret would have been distressed and certain to tell him, blame him for being right.

When he asked the doctor about the chances that he might have a disabled child, the doctor, having opened his file, smiled and said, 'So she's told you, has she? I'm so pleased. You should have been told you had a brother years ago. I can never understand why people keep such secrets.'

'A brother?' Jonathan gasped. 'I had a brother, but he died.'

'Oh.' The doctor's face froze for a moment. 'Look, forget what I just said. I was mixing you up with another patient. Power, it's not that uncommon a name. Talk to your mother, she's the one to ask about this. But,' he added, speaking quickly, not wanting Jonathan to ask any questions he wasn't

241

at liberty to answer, 'if you're worrying about having a child, then don't. The chances are minimal. Forget it and enjoy building a family with . . . er, Lottie Talbot, isn't it? Congratulations. I wish you both every happiness.'

'Where is he?'

'Sorry?'

'Where's my brother?'

It took a while to grind the doctor down, but Jonathan finally learned about the brother of whose existence he had known nothing. Roland, aged twenty-nine, was in a care home thirty miles away.

He drove dangerously fast to his mother's house and demanded she come with him.

'Where are we going, somewhere nice for lunch?' she asked.

'Wait and see.'

She could tell he was upset. She wanted to ask whether he and Lottie had been arguing, or whether he'd had a confrontation with Ancret, but the look on his face stopped him. Her mind was buzzing with the news about Ancret's gypsy background, but instinct told her not to admit to knowing. She settled down to enjoy the journey, speaking only to beg him to drive more slowly, comments he ignored.

He didn't look at his mother's face when they reached the gates of the large house not far from Newport, yet he felt her turn and stare at him.

'Yes, Mother,' he said in a tight voice. 'We're going to see my brother.'

'Please, Jonathan, don't do this. Let me explain. You don't understand what it was like. I had my career, and—'

'Shut up and get out of the car,' he said as he parked carelessly and jumped out. For the first time ever, he did not open the door for her and help her alight. Stiff with anxiety, she climbed out and stood beside him, then followed as they went towards reception.

Roland was smaller than he expected, a good six inches shorter than himself. He was casually dressed in trousers and a woollen sweater at which he pulled. There were ragged areas where it was obvious he had plucked at it continuously. He had a full, pleasant face, and showed no appear-

242

ance of any illness. He smiled, wide mouthed, at one of the attendants walking past and she smiled back, touching him affectionately on the shoulder.

'Hi, Roland. I'll bring you and your visitors a cup of tea, shall I?'

The mumbling acknowledgement sounded wordless, but the attendant replied, 'All right, some biscuits too. There's a face you've got for biscuits, Roland. Never full, are you? Always hungry.' Roland smiled his extra-wide smile, then stared at Caroline and Jonathan.

Jonathan stood back and watched as his mother spoke to the man. He saw no recognition, nor even any sign Roland had heard. He sat silently, his eyes roaming around the room, glancing often towards the door, obviously waiting for his tea and biscuits.

His eyes were blue with a gentle expression, similar to Uncle Richard's, but his figure was rounded, like Caroline's. Jonathan guessed that he and Roland looked enough alike for people to know they were brothers, although Roland's face was relaxed and he looked out at the world with an untroubled gaze.

They didn't stay long, and Jonathan's thoughts were confused as they drove back. As she was getting out of the car outside the flat, Caroline said, 'Your father didn't want to send him away. I did it for you.'

Jonathan got back in the car and drove off without a word. Her defensive remark had filled him with horror. He was responsible for locking up a human being? Guilty of what amounted to the imprisonment of a man like himself, depriving his brother of a normal loving home? Guilt descended on him like a storm. Responsible for forcing Babs into the abortion clinic? And for giving Ancret so much distress that she was forced to deny him his daughter? Now learning he was guilty of committing his own brother to a life deprived of his rightful place in the family home? So much agony, lying and deceit. Was all that down to him? His mother said it was, and she was always right.

What a monster he was. And for what? So he could marry a girl like Lottie and deny her children and drive her away too?

He drove west, past the towns of Penarth, Barry, Cowbridge, Bridgend, Port Talbot and Swansea. He kept his foot down, relying on others to react when he came too close, not caring what he was doing. He wasn't seeing the road. Instead he saw a cavalcade of people hurt because of himself. How could his mother have believed he wouldn't want to know his brother? What justification could she have found for hiding Roland away, and blaming him for his abandonment? Then there was Babs; he had broken her heart by telling her he didn't want her baby. Ancret too had been turned away, left to cope with the birth of her child alone.

He drove on, unaware of where he was going, not caring whether he would ever come back. When he reached Mumbles, impatient with the traffic, he overtook dangerously. Ignoring the angry horns, he drove up through the rocks towards Limeslade, then past the café where a queue was waiting for teas and ice cream, foot down as hard as it would go. He turned the wheel sharply and the car went straight over the cliffs. He didn't see the rocks or the angry waves rushing to meet him. His last vision before pain, shock and unconsciousness, was the hurt, questioning face of Babs.

On the following day, Ancret went again to visit her daughter and took Natalie for a walk in her pushchair. She went to John Howells's house and knocked on the door. She hoped this time, without Jason there, the privacy to talk would persuade the man to explain why her mother had left him.

It was a long time before he opened the door, but when he did he stood back for her to enter, helping bring the pushchair into the hall, waiting while Ancret lifted the baby out. Then he reached out for Natalie, and took her, legs waving and kicking in excitement, into his arms.

'I've just made some coffee,' he said, and led the way into the kitchen. 'You've come with more questions, I suppose.' He set out mugs, biscuits and a drink for Natalie. He left the pouring to her while he sat at the table with Natalie, crowing with contentment, on his knee.

'Why did my mother leave you?' she asked.

'Because she couldn't settle while those on the hill were

244

there. She was all right while they were away on their summer travels, but the minute they came back she was gone, taking Marguerite and Sophie. It was as though I didn't exist during the months they were there.'

Ancret waited. This wasn't an explanation of why Loraine had taken her baby and left without her other daughters.

'I used to get so angry with her,' he said, coaxing Natalie with a rusk biscuit. 'I'm not a violent man and I've never been so angry before or since. It was only Connie who made me lose my temper.'

'You lost your temper?' Ancret coaxed.

His voice was low as he admitted, 'All right, I hit her. Not once but several times. Once she fell back and hit her head on the door. I thought for a moment that I'd killed her. It was after that she left.' His voice became more defensive. 'You can't imagine the frustration. She'd spend night after night up there with them, taking Marguerite and Sophie, treating them like farm labourers, sleeping in a filthy old tent.'

'They talk about those times as their holidays.'

'Hm! No holiday for me!'

Ancret looked at him, cuddling her child, with his head bowed, shoulders curled in misery, and she felt a warm feeling of sympathy sweep over her. He had tried to keep his family together, and although hitting his wife was inexcusable, she was beginning to understand his frustration. She could see that the guilt of his violence had remained with him every moment since. Deep down, he was a decent man who had been badly treated.

'You acted honourably, sending money to help us. It was so generous to help us buy the business.'

'I thought you were mine. All these years I thought you were mine.'

'And now?' she asked, touching the small scar. 'Now you know I'm not? Do you want me to go away again?'

'You're still half-sister to Marguerite and Sophie. I think they'd want you to stay.'

'And you? How do you feel?' she persisted. 'Would my staying cause you continued unhappiness? Me and Natalie?'

'I can cope,' he said gruffly.

For the moment, Ancret decided that was the best she'd get. 'I'm staying for lunch. Simon and Jason will be back by half twelve. Will you come? Marguerite told me you're invited. We can walk back together. Please?'

'Very well.'

'Mr Howells, can I ask one more question?'

'If you must.'

'Mummy changed her name from Sullivan. Why wasn't I called Howells?'

He started out of his chair glaring at her and she shrank away from him. What new Pandora's box had she opened for herself?

'We had a gypsy wedding,' he said as he turned to stare out of the window up on to the hill. It was visible from a different angle from Marguerite's home, and the top with its vardo could be clearly seen.

'They told me that,' she whispered.

'That was *all* we had.' Still looking out on to the hill, his voice softened as he seemed to see the memories so clearly. 'It was so romantic. I loved her so much, you see. She was so exciting and very beautiful. We planned to arrange the legal ceremony in secret but we never did. I told the girls when they were old enough and they didn't seem to mind. I painted a picture for them of the love and happiness of the occasion and they understood.'

He kissed Natalie and put her back in her pushchair, and it was he who pushed her, talking to her, pointing out things they could see, all the way to his daughter's house.

Ancret heard of Jonathan's accident later the following day, when Edmund brought the news. She rang Caroline to ask for details.

'In Morriston Hospital in Swansea, he is,' Caroline sobbed. 'So distressed about what you told him, he had an accident,' she lied. 'My son could die and it's because of you!' She couldn't say what the police suspected, that he had driven like a maniac after meeting his brother and tried to kill himself. She couldn't take the blame for this. Her son might die, and how could she live with that? Admit that her secrets had been the cause of his accident? Better to accuse Ancret. She was young. She'd have time to recover.

Ancret's hand was shaking when she put the phone down. Her face was ashen. 'She's blaming me,' she said.

Edmund took her in his arms and held her close. He could feel her heart beating against his own. 'That's hardly likely, is it? He's about to marry Lottie, so why should anything you say cause him to hurt himself? He isn't dead, so we'll learn the truth. I promise you we'll be told the truth.'

With bruises and a broken collar bone, a fractured sternum, plus slight concussion and cuts on his face, Jonathan's injuries were remarkably light. Lottie went to the hospital, taking Caroline with her, but he refused to see either of them. Ancret sent cards and messages, but only Babs was allowed to speak to him.

She had learned of his accident from the local paper and had driven down to see him. After the politenesses, she said, 'What happened?'

'I went to the doctor, asked if what Mother had told me was true about the likelihood of having a handicapped child. And—'

'Was it finding out about your brother?'

'You knew?'

'I knew, although Caroline denied it at first. She begged me not to tell you and convinced me it was best, after so many years had passed, that you remained in ignorance.' She waited a moment, then asked, 'Was it an accident, Jonathan? Or did you want to kill yourself?'

'Look at the harm I've caused. I nearly made you abort Donald . . .'

'Donald's adopted, Jonathan,' Babs said gently. 'He isn't yours. Everything else is in the past now.'

'It's all gone so wrong. You losing the babies, my losing you. Then Ancret lying rather than tell me she was carrying my child. Worst of all, my mother said she kept my brother away from us, locked away, because it was best for me. I couldn't cope with all that.'

'Your brother might be in a kind of prison, but so are you, Jonathan. Don't you see that what your mother is doing to you is the reason for all that's happened? She wants to run your life to fit in with her own. She didn't want you to marry me, have a family and leave her alone. She didn't want you to marry Ancret either.'

'She likes Lottie, and she's encouraging us to marry.'

'Perhaps she sees in Lottie someone more malleable, a young girl who she can persuade to do as she wants.'

'This is nonsense, Babs. You make her sound like a manipulative control freak. She isn't like that at all.'

'Isn't she? I loved you. Ask yourself why I didn't marry you. Ask yourself a few more questions, Jonathan. Take the time while you're in here, while you're alone, to work out what you want, without considering what your mother demands of you. I think you'll be surprised. She isn't evil. Just afraid of a lonely old age.' He still looked doubtful, and she added softly, 'Being an only child can be a terrible burden to bear, Jonathan. Your shoulders alone carry all your parents' hopes and dreams.'

The first thing Jonathan did when he came out of hospital was ask Babs and her children to visit him. The second was to write to Lottie to tell her that he wouldn't hold her to her promise to marry him after recent revelations. He didn't know what the future held, but he wasn't certain he could be trusted with her happiness. The third was to phone Ancret and ask if he could go with her the next time she visited Natalie.

He met Babs and her three adopted children a few days later and took them to a café. Tracy flattered him by insisting on sitting on his lap. He was self-conscious, unused to the straight stare that children give and how to deal with it. But as soon as he began talking to her, the curiosity took a different form and she listened with interest, although as yet unable to communicate her understanding. Harry concentrated on the food placed before him, and Donald, like Tracy, stared.

Once Tracy was involved with being fed he turned his attention to Donald. It wasn't hard to talk to the little boy. He was curious, interested, and although sometimes slow to understand, he was anxious to please, considerate and polite. He had clearly taken on the role of big brother, and watched the younger children with doting care. Unexpectedly, the meeting Jonathan had feared went on for longer than planned, and he was sorry when it ended.

'Can we do this again? Just as friends?' he asked when they had been seated in Babs's car and safely strapped in.

'If you're sure,' she said doubtfully. 'But making friends isn't a game. They'll soon trust you and be saddened if you get tired of this.'

'I'm tired of games, especially when I'm stupid enough to allow others to make the rules.'

'Then I think we should meet without the children, you, Lottie and me, to talk about what you want to do.'

Lottie was waiting for him when he returned to the flat. She greeted him with a loving kiss, then tore up his letter. 'I love you, and I want to be with you for ever,' she said, holding him close.

'I'm in such a mess. Chaos all around me. Babs and her children, Ancret and our child. And you, Lottie. My darling girl, how I can ask you to share my life?'

'Let's make a fresh beginning. There's you and me,' she counted on her fingers. 'There's your mother, and your brother Roland. They're important and we'll care for them, they'll be our family. Then there are the children and Babs. No surprise relationships there, but being friends won't be difficult. Last but most important, Ancret and Natalie. However much time you want to spend with your daughter will be fine with me, as long as you can promise that it's me you love, and that any remnants of your feelings for Ancret are gone.'

He held her tightly. 'Put like that, there's nothing we can't cope with. Lottie, I'll do everything I can to make you happy, and yes, there's no one I love more than I love you. Will you still marry me?'

'I'll even smile and allow your mother to plan it all. Except the honeymoon. I would object to her involvement there. That's strictly for you and me.'

'Darling, don't you want to spend it at Uncle Richard's house with her?'

His laughter was the encouragement Lottie needed to believe that, whatever demons had haunted him, they were now going to leave him in peace.

\*　　\*　　\*

Ancret replied to his request to visit Natalie in the affirmative, but pointed out that Edmund would be with her.

'That's fine. Lottie will be with me. I just want to meet her properly, and see how we all feel about my keeping contact with her.'

They went on Sunday afternoon, and Ancret realized that there would be few more Sunday visits before she took her daughter home. Edmund came in the eight-seater he used at the hotel and they called for Lottie and Jonathan before setting off. Jonathan wore a sling and his bruises were still very apparent, but otherwise he seemed unaffected by his dangerous escapade.

Simon met her at the door and hesitated before inviting them in.

'Prepare yourself, Ancret, your other sister is here.'

'Sophie?' She walked slowly into the living room where Marguerite stood holding Natalie. Beside her stood a smartly dressed, elegant woman a few years younger. She wore her black hair down around her shoulders, and in her smart suit, black, formal, and with golden chains and chunky bracelets that glinted as she moved, Ancret felt the joy seep away. There was disapproval in the stranger's dark eyes and a hardness around her mouth that reminded her of John Howells. She had inherited her lovely hair and her elegance from Loraine, but her expression told Ancret that her temperament was her father's.

She held out her hand and smiled a nervous smile. 'I'm Ancret. I believe we're half-sisters,' she said foolishly. Sophie was certain to know that.

Jason stepped forward, stood beside his ex-wife and said brightly, 'What if we leave these two to talk.' He held out his arms for Natalie and led the others out of the room. Jonathan, Lottie and Edmund followed, Edmund pausing to touch her cheek and give her an encouraging smile.

'When did you learn about us?' Sophie asked, her voice cold, tinged with anger.

'Not until after my mother – our mother – died. I so desperately wanted to know who I was and where I came from, but Mummy had always refused to tell me. My only clue was the terrible recurring dream she had.'

'What was in the dream?' Sophie remained standing, making it impossible for Ancret to sit, and her expression was still without warmth.

'She would hold the bedding tangled up into a bundle as though it was a baby and cry and plead for help. It used to break my heart. Doubly so when she refused to explain.'

'My father never got over the shock of losing her and, because he was upset, I hated her.'

'If you'd known her you'd have forgiven her.'

'I did know her, for eleven years. And she left us without telling us why.'

In a flash of knowledge, Ancret guessed she and Marguerite knew nothing about their father hitting their mother. She decided it was better they didn't find out. 'We'll never know why,' she said.

'Whatever happened between them, it's all a long time ago. And none of it was your doing.' Sophie relaxed and offered her hand to Ancret, who gratefully took it with both of hers.

'It'll be fun getting to know each other, won't it?' Ancret said, and was rewarded with a glimmer of a smile.

Marguerite came in to announce lunch. The small crack in Sophie's resistance opened, they all talked easily. Questions and answers flew. When John Howells joined them for coffee, Ancret turned to Edmund and said, 'My family, at last. I don't think I'll want another thing.'

Jonathan leaned across and kissed her lightly on the cheek. 'I'm happy for you, Ancret. It's the best of all possible endings.'

Jason was talking intently to Sophie when they left. Ancret said nothing. But from the way they were laughing together, she couldn't help but hope for another happy ending.

After taking Lottie and Jonathan back to the flat, Edmund drove her to Toad Hall.

'Marry me, Ancret, and I'll do everything I can to make you happy. You, me and Natalie and my family and yours, we'll have such a wonderful life together.' She didn't reply, and he went on, 'If you like the idea, there's a conversion under way on one of the barns in the grounds. We could live there, but only if you like the idea. I'll live wherever you want us to live. All I ask of life is that we're together. You, me and Natalie.'

'A barn?' She smiled. 'For my gypsy ancestors that would have been considered a luxury.'

Together, arms around each other, they walked into Toad Hall to meet the rest of her remarkably extended family.

NEWPORT COMMUINTY
LEARNING 252 IBRARIES

Central Library and
Information Service

6·1·06  NPC
        6|3|08

**Z490774**